ZAMPER

DOCTOR WHO – THE NEW ADVENTURES

Also available:

TIMEWYRM: GENESYS by John Peel
TIMEWYRM: EXODUS by Terrance Dicks
TIMEWYRM: APOCALYPSE by Nigel Robinson
TIMEWYRM: REVELATION by Paul Cornell

CAT'S CRADLE: TIME'S CRUCIBLE by Marc Platt
CAT'S CRADLE: WARHEAD by Andrew Cartmel
CAT'S CRADLE: WITCH MARK by Andrew Hunt

NIGHTSHADE by Mark Gatiss
LOVE AND WAR by Paul Cornell
TRANSIT by Ben Aaronovitch
THE HIGHEST SCIENCE by Gareth Roberts
THE PIT by Neil Penswick
DECEIT by Peter Darvill-Evans
LUCIFER RISING by Jim Mortimore and Andy Lane
WHITE DARKNESS by David A. McIntee
SHADOWMIND by Christopher Bulis
BIRTHRIGHT by Nigel Robinson
ICEBERG by David Banks

BLOOD HEAT by Jim Mortimore
THE DIMENSION RIDERS by Daniel Blythe
THE LEFT-HANDED HUMMINGBIRD by Kate Orman
CONUNDRUM by Steve Lyons
NO FUTURE by Paul Cornell
TRAGEDY DAY by Gareth Roberts
LEGACY by Gary Russell
THEATRE OF WAR by Justin Richards
ALL-CONSUMING FIRE by Andy Lane
BLOOD HARVEST by Terrance Dicks
STRANGE ENGLAND by Simon Messingham
FIRST FRONTIER by David A. McIntee
ST ANTHONY'S FIRE by Mark Gatiss
FALLS THE SHADOW by Daniel O'Mahoney
PARASITE by Jim Mortimore
WARLOCK by Andrew Cartmel
SET PIECE by Kate Orman
INFINITE REQUIEM by Daniel Blythe
SANCTUARY by David A. McIntee
HUMAN NATURE by Paul Cornell
ORIGINAL SIN by Andy Lane
SKY PIRATES! by Dave Stone

THE NEW

DOCTOR WHO

ADVENTURES

ZAMPER

Gareth Roberts

First published in Great Britain in 1995 by
Doctor Who Books
an imprint of Virgin Publishing Ltd
332 Ladbroke Grove
London W10 5AH

Cover illustration by Tony Masero

ISBN 0 426 20450 6

Phototypeset by Intype, London
Printed and bound in Great Britain by Cox & Wyman Ltd.,
Reading, Berks

Chapter 1

Along the eastern edge of the galaxy, a wide arc of gas clouds shone with a harsh bluish light. Around its centre flared a series of nebulosities, strobing the view of the constellations beyond with a contrasting red fire. Between two of these raging points, something directly contradictory to the laws of physics was taking place.

A roughly circular section of space unfolded flower-like, violet petals blooming, obscuring the luminescence of the neighbouring stellar remnants. The nearest clouds of freezing stardust were firmly pushed back as the rent grew. There was no violence in the action, nothing of the crushing power of a black hole. Whoever controlled the phenomenon – and the measured pace of the unravelling suggested a controlling intelligence – gave the impression of total confidence in its ability to knock millenia of theoretical study flat.

The way to Zamper was open.

Massed not far from the burgeoning gate was a mighty fleet of some thirty space cruisers, lined in a classical horseshoe formation, each of the strangely shaped black craft displaying its weaponry with unbowed arrogance.

Suddenly, a much smaller ship, a shuttle, detached itself from the nub of the fleet, veered to one side as its boosters fired, and then sped into the cover of the gas clouds, on a direct course to the exact centre of the gateway.

Mr Jottipher, in one of his many smart grey suits, stepped from the front door of his rooms into a descending tubeway and felt the pavement's steady shudder as it bore him

1

swiftly downward. As usual, he relished the order and tidiness of the Complex; the sterile unscented air, the empty white tubeways, the featureless blocks and cubes that lined the outer walls. This pacific soullessness had never before failed to calm his anxieties, of which there were many. Today was different. Through the clear plastic of the suspended tube he caught blurred glimpses of the Complex's servitors at work, whizzing their rounded brush attachments over each geometrically perfect surface until it gleamed. Briefly, as he observed the droning disc-shaped robots slotting back neatly into their pods, their night duties over, Mr Jottipher found himself wishing for a more practical, accountable position in life.

In the crook of his arm was a stapled black folder containing details of his latest assignment. Although compiled by his superior, the Secunda, with the absolute accuracy and detail she was renowned for, it hadn't made for easy reading over the past week. The history of the new customers was unusually bloody, even for guests of Zamper. Mr Jottipher had been liaison executive for 22 years and had never been roused to his current level of misgiving. He was so much absorbed in his worries that the polite, disembodied cough from above made him jump. He lost his footing, but the pavement sensed his trip and slowed, allowing him to catch the support rail.

'I'm so sorry,' said the Management. Exact vowel sounds, rhythm in every superbly inflected sentence. Too exact; and that was what gave his artificial nature away, that and the flashes of drop-out on his shirt front and the eye movements that lagged half a second behind the rest of his body language.

Mr Jottipher steadied himself and clasped the folder even more tightly to his chest. 'I always forget there's an Inscreen on this thing, sir.' He nodded up at the box, which hung from the rail above and kept pace with him as the pavement's rollers sped up again with the gentlest of sighs. Mr Jottipher smoothed his trim grey beard. 'How may I be of assistance? Anything to help, sir.'

'Our new guests,' said the Management, fixing him with

2

a keen but friendly blue stare. 'They must be accorded every courtesy.'

'Of course, sir.' His voice said *What an extraordinary thing to say!*

'It is not our place to pass judgement on our customers.'

'No, sir.'

'Particularly not a moral judgement.'

Mr Jottipher wondered sometimes if the Management could read his thoughts. 'The morals of Zamper are my morals, sir.' This was the truth. Any trace of independent thought had been erased 22 years ago.

The Management frowned, and moved slightly forward until his lightly-tanned face almost filled the Inscreen. 'Are you being honest with me? I ask only because you seem uneasy this morning.'

'My unease comes from my fear, sir.'

'Good to see your honesty. Fear.' The Management toyed with the word, stretching it out, making three syllables of it. 'Fe-e-ar. Fear is our business, Mr Jottipher. Without fear Zamper could not function. Remind yourself of our success. Four hundred and seventy-three years of profitable business. And why? Because one race of beings fears another race. It really is very natural.'

Mr Jottipher lowered his head. 'Yes, sir.'

'But you are safe here. Away from the wars. I protect you. It's part of my function.'

When Mr Jottipher looked up to utter his sincere thanks, the Management had gone, leaving the Inscreen a neutral green.

The pavement slowed as the end of the tubeway neared. Mr Jottipher passed through the connecting terminal and walked calmly into his office, laid the black folder down on the v-shaped console, and asked the operator for a sensor channel.

'The guest shuttle is passing through our outer defences,' said the operator in crisp simulated feminine tones. A graphic lattice representing Zamper's enclosed system criss-crossed over the office's large Outscreen. The Management's six defence outposts glimmered at equidistant points along the borders. There were two other traces. A red T flashed in space to the dark side of Zamper; that was the new test ship, the first of the Series 336s, picking up velocity. The guest shuttle registered as a small pink G, edging past one of the outposts, just this side of the closing gateway.

'Do you request visual link-up, Mr Jottipher?' asked the operator. 'The buyers' shuttle is now within range of direct visual beaming.'

Mr Jottipher pulled a mirror from a drawer in the console, examined his harried reflection, straightened his collar, reminded himself that the sweat glistening on his nose was a non-verbal signal readable only by other humanoids, and said, 'Transmit the welcome call.'

It was a custom of Zamper to welcome buyers in their mother tongue. Mr Jottipher winced as the translator barked a series of gruff consonants out to the newcomers. Sounds similar to ks and zs featured heavily in the thirty second message.

There was silence from the incoming shuttle.

Mr Jottipher reached reluctantly for his microphone clip. He tried to keep the tremble from his voice, and smiled as his image was transmitted. 'I am Mr Jottipher. As customer liaison executive, I greet you in the name of the Zamper independent construction facility, and I hope sincerely that your stay with us will be a pleasant one.'

The Outscreen flared as incompatible technologies struggled to connect. Through thick crackling bars Mr Jottipher saw narrow yellow eyes, scaly green leathery skin, a set of fiercely bared teeth.

The guest spoke, each word a gurgling grunt. A brightly coloured leaf was clutched in one of its claws. 'Why do you disturb us, parasite?'

'I merely wish to welcome you, as customer liaison executive, to the Zamper –'

'You prattle and lie,' snorted the guest. 'Your welcome is void. You coo to me like a new-born only because you want our livres.'

'It is our custom to conduct our business courteously,' stammered Mr Jottipher, 'in a civilized man–'

'Civilization!' The creature roared, opening its mouth wide. It was hard to tell, but Mr Jottipher supposed it was laughing. 'Civilization! You are a parasite. You know nothing of civilization!'

Mr Jottipher heard something rattling. He realised it was himself, shaking in his chair. 'Your arrival time is in one hour, sir,' he said with forced calm, 'and it will be necessary for you to follow certain standard procedures after landing. Firstly, you will pass through the ger–'

The Outscreen crackled and went black.

Mr Jottipher slumped forward. He had followed procedure exactly, and could hardly be held to blame for the idiosyncrasies of buyers. 'The link to the guest shuttle has been snapped off at their end,' said the operator. 'Do you wish to reconnect?'

He reached for the black folder, and smoothed open the first white page. There it all was in rows of justified type. Chelonians. Natives of Chelonia, former centre of the Chelonian empire. Assessment of temperament: Difficult.

'Sir, do you wish me to reconnect?'

'I wish to speak to the Secunda.'

He could scarcely admit it to himself, but General Hezzka of the line of Talifar, commander-in-chief of the fifteenth column of the Maternal Guard, who had scored glorious victories against enemy territories in a career as long as it was distinguished, was always rather nervous when duty called upon him to address Big Mother directly. His front left foot reached for the call button hesitantly, and in the short silence as the transmission line was cleared, Hezzka licked both rows of his teeth and hoped his discomfort wouldn't show.

Big Mother's aged eyes were now so sensitive that his rooms on the fleet's flagship were kept very dark at all times. Picked out by the soothing dim red wash were his massive shell, the bulbous rear of his carapace. His atrophied limbs drooped through holes in the toughened metal support webbing that was hooked up to robust pillars in each corner of the imperial chamber. A thicket of tubing disappeared into his shell just below his neck, supplying him with vital fluids. His face, once renowned and adored up to the furthest limits of the empire, although desiccated, had lost none of its majesty. There remained around Big Mother something of the serenity of the old court, the environs of the now toppled Maternal palace of the Chelonian capital. To look into those unblinking eyes, thought Hezzka, was to doubt the last forty cycles of his people's history. The empire will endure, they seemed to say, and the coup, the rise of the usurper, these ignoble dealings with parasites, oh, the merest blip, and things will soon enough be set to rights.

'Your trouble?' The voice was high pitched but rough as a claw-blunting board, the words flowing from the thin slit of Big Mother's mouth like water from a rusty pipe. 'This is our resting time. We are not to be disturbed.' The huge shell shuffled in its webbing. 'Anyway, who is that?' He squinted. 'Are you that captain fellow? Oughtn't you to be at your flight station?'

'It's General Hezzka, Highness.'

'Hezzka?' Big Mother treated the word as if it were an insult.

'Yes. You asked me to report, Highness. At this stage.'

'We asked you? To report?'

'Yes, Highness.'

Big Mother gnashed his gums. 'Then report, Hezzka! If we order you to do something, you are to do it!'

Hezzka cleared his throat. 'The shuttle has now crossed the gateway to Zamper. We are passing close to the parasites' defence system and will arrive in under an hour.'

Big Mother swung sadly from side to side, the only movement he could manage comfortably nowadays, causing the elasticated metal supports of his webbing to creak. 'Parasite defence systems,' he muttered. 'In the days of our youth, such a thing would have seemed laughable. Parasites can have no defence.' He glowered at Hezzka

6

as if the fall of the empire was wholly his fault. 'What is the nature of these parasite defences?'

'That we cannot know, Highness. Our detectors cannot penetrate them.'

'This Zamper planet. Truly a technology worth our investigation.' Ranged before one of Big Mother's front feet was a hovering oblong shape, a set of buttons laid flat on a transparent unit on top. Hezzka watched as Big Mother brushed the tip of a flaking claw across a button. Instantly a bubble of faintly luminescent data was projected, a translation into Chelonian broad dialect of the Zamper brochure. Hezzka had studied the document at length, soon after the strategic council, after much debate, had decided to authorize the purchase.

It appeared that the east side of the galaxy, heavily populated by parasites, had been in a constant state of political upheaval for the last thousand Earth years. Various parasite colony worlds were at war with others, and as soon as one conflict was settled, another arose. This had destabilized the region's monetary system, and about six hundred years ago a consortium of industrialists had been formed with a view to solving the problem. The solution had been the construction of Zamper. The consortium had pooled the scientific resources of a hundred different cultures, and created a fold in space, a mini-universe bang in the middle of the war zone but technically neutral. They then somehow shifted a large planet into the place, and set up an independent shipyard solely concerned with the sale of battleships. This was reckoned to be the most viable industry; people were always going to be at war, it seemed.

The plan had worked. Zamper ships, better designed and built to last, soon came to dominate the local space lanes. From the day it was registered on East Galaxy's stock exchange, Zamper had led the markets, bringing huge profits to its shareholders and steadying the economies of the warring worlds. To an outsider like Hezzka, it was apparent that this more than anything else would secure an unsettled future for the region. It was typical of parasites to get themselves into such a mess. What intrigued the General in particular was that Zamper had now been operational for almost five hundred years, an achievement the brochure credited to 'the Management.' The strategic council's research indicated that this Management was not a living being at all, but an augmented artificial intelligence. Little could be confirmed, and an even greater mystery hung over the design and construction of the ships. Certainly they were faster, larger, better defended and more powerful than any produced by their competitors. Moreover they were almost impossible to duplicate successfully. That was what had brought the fifteenth column here.

Big Mother skimmed through to the section of the brochure that he wanted and read, 'The Series 336c Delta-Spiral Sun Blaster. Suited to a crew of twenty. Force-aura shielded against neutronic rays of up to sixty blarks' intensity. Engines powered by tachyon displacement, repowering range of fourteen light centuries. As used in the Sprox civil war and the death skirmishes of Pancoza.'

There was a universe of scepticism in his reiteration of the advertisement, but Hezzka sensed something else; a hint of hope borne from desperation, the shell-shrug of the luckless gambler staking his last remaining tokens on the baize.

'And,' Big Mother went on, 'this model's unique facility, the neutrino tickler. It can split a sun in one astral week.' He tsked. 'The language of the parasites reduces the glories of conflict to mere farce.'

'It is in their nature, Highness,' said Hezzka. 'Their lives are short and lack meaning. The value placed on these goods confirms that.'

'Indeed. Six billion livres. A currency we do not even recognize.' He returned his attention to Hezzka. 'This vulgar dealing irks me. But the outcome . . . we must hope, no; we must be certain of the outcome.' A thin line of drool fell from his mouth, forming a long sticky strand that stretched to form a pool on the floor. 'The demise of the usurper.' His eyes closed. 'Our own sister. We can still barely credit his treason.'

Hezzka, embarrassed by this open confidence, was relieved to see the image of his majestic commander quiver in the frame of the screen. 'Highness, the gate is closing, I am losing you.'

'Good fortune, Hafril. The mission is – '

The picture was lost. For a few seconds, the voice of Big Mother, all but drowned by the buzz of the jamming signal, was still audible. 'Hafril, we'll return to Chelonia, and we'll crush the usurp– '

Hafril. Leader of the Maternal Guard for ninety years, *confidante* of the First Family, special favourite of Big Mother. Killed only after taking seven blasts from a parasite weapon in the defence of the hatching forts at Kaapon six cycles ago. Hezzka, his successor as commander of the still loyal fifteenth column, felt the weight of his responsibilities, the legacy with which he had been entrusted, more keenly than ever.

The only sound now was the dampened roar of the shuttle's boosters and the whirrs and ticks of the autosystems. Hezzka shuffled back from his console and raised his left foot in the ancient gesture of prayer to the Goddess. He asked to be granted strength, patience, and the wisdom to think logically, recalling without halt the codes of imprecation learnt by rote in his youth.

His First Pilot, Ivzid, motored heavily into the room and saluted. Immediately Hezzka brought his foot down, not wanting to have his prayer interpreted as a sign of weakness, certainly not by a junior. Ivzid, he reflected not for the first time, had been born to the wrong age. The arrogant shuffle of his gait, his eyes fierce and open wide, his readiness to meet any obstacle with a massive retaliation, all of these things belonged to the time before the fall, all but lost in a couple of generations thanks to the cultural reformation of Little Sister. Ivzid was a product of the line of Hakifur, the bloodline that had served as personal security to the First Family, and he remained almost uniquely in bondage to its codes and principles.

9

Even old warriors like Hezzka had been forced to moderate some of their views. Ivzid's training, under the sternest regime of Hafril, and his youth, would have made a fine officer of the time before. Hezzka pictured him on one of the old clearance missions to parasite lands, cracking open a case of beer with one front foot and crushing a plague pellet in the other.

'Well met, General.' A formal greeting between officers that nowadays, in the daily business of the fifteenth column, was mostly mumbled. Ivzid gave each word the euphony of sacred chapter. 'We have entered the parasites' defence zone.'

'I am aware of that, First Pilot.'

'They have attempted conference.' Ivzid cackled, baring his perfect teeth. 'A brief chatter, a line of insults. They dishonour us, and by Mif I'd broil their skins, make trophies of their scalps, were I – '

'Were you not under orders from Big Mother himself to act with civility to them until our business is concluded.' Hezzka edged nearer to Ivzid. 'Try to think clearly, boy. See the ultimate folly of our enemy. They are going to sell us a ship that will restore Chelonia to its true destiny. That will ensure their own destruction. Take humour from that, employ it to quell your anger.'

Ivzid hissed, and his head slumped, his eyes thinning to slits. 'I hear the logic in your words, General, but my heart,' he smote his plastron, 'my heart turns over at the idea of conversing with parasites.'

'Then take a relaxant. This mission is too important to be jeopardized by your lack of self-control, Ivzid.'

'But sir!' Ivzid pointed to the screen, which now showed the first of the parasite defence installations, an enormous dull grey sphere fitted with cannons around its circumference. 'To approach this Zamper place unarmed, to face an enemy not with blasters but with open feet, the dishonour!'

His words, filled with the rousing oratory of the parade ground, tugged at Hezzka's emotions. These sentiments were quite his own, but could not be expressed. 'Your duty, First Pilot,' he said, 'is to steer this shuttle to safe landing on Zamper and act as my personal assistant thereafter. Concern yourself with these matters, and save your ire.' Further debate was forestalled as the shuttle suddenly dipped in its trajectory.

The screen flashed up a warning; three symbols it took Hezzka a couple of moments to identify. At the same time the inboard computer started to beep and chatter unbidden.

'What is happening, sir?' Ivzid pulled himself up from the corner into which he had been gracelessly deposited by the turbulence.

The symbols on the screen flickered and were replaced by a sequence of pink-outlined schematics detailing a familiar snout-nosed shape, trisected by a thicker red line. The following second another angle was displayed, favouring the shuttle's rear thrusters and concealed warp boosters, and showing the newly welded section from which the shuttle's cannon had been removed, in accordance with Zamper's code of neutrality. This was exchanged for a diagram of the room Hezzka and Ivzid were sitting in, then by the companionways, the hull, the escape pod, the domestic flyer.

Hezzka rattled furiously at the computer keyboard, but found the diagnostic systems unresponsive. 'Sensor beams,' he snarled. 'From the parasite defence station.'

More images flashed up, increasing in speed. The microscopic innards of the flight guidance systems, the food preparation unit, the anti-theft device. Hezzka flinched as the images blurred, stinging his retina. The shuttle's automatic log was now being plundered, the precisely noted details of all the vessel's previous missions and modifications whipping by. 'They're reading everything we've got, right down to the protected files.'

The chatter from the console speeded up and rose in pitch, became a zizz, a squeal, and passed beyond hearing, every morsel of information sucked out, examined, checked, re-checked, returned.

'It is not possible.' Hezzka motored back from the systems, shaking his head. 'It would take years to crack the entry codes on the auto-log.'

The intrusion had done nothing to calm Ivzid. 'And yet it has been done. What secrets does this Zamper place hide?'

An abrupt silence followed. The screen crackled and returned to its scan function, showing the unbroken surface of the grey sphere rolling past. The rumble of the boosters was restored to health and the shuttle righted itself.

They heard a machine voice, a machine made to sound like a parasite. In perfect broad dialect, it said, 'Thank you. You have now passed through the security screen.'

Hezzka knew little of the ways of parasites, but he sensed something behind those words. There was an emotional signal in the delivery, a hint of triumph and self-importance. He was stirred to fury, and an order formed on his lips. An order to open fire.

Damn the parasites.

He looked to Ivzid, who was beating the wall with one foot in frustration.

'We go on,' he ordered. 'To your station, First Pilot. Planetfall on Zamper in fifty minutes.'

Wrapped in towels, one around her body and the other serving as a turban, the Secunda hopped from her bath and into her office, summoned by the urgently twittering Outscreen. She'd been expecting this call. The new buyers weren't going to help Mr Jottipher's nerves.

'Mr Jottipher. I hope you're not going to disappoint me.' She tried to keep her tone light, but a note of censure remained. She really was no good at being nice. Even to people she liked, or thought she liked.

His Adam's apple bobbed between his beard and the tight shirt-collar. 'Our new customers, madam. I made the routine welcome. They were most unhelpful.'

The Secunda popped a braided cushion, a gift from the Sprox Conquerors six years ago, onto her chair and sat. 'They're spoilt children, Chelonians. Far less significant than all their crowing suggests. Particularly today. We've entertained worse.'

'Of course, madam. My concern, as liaison, is that normal social dealings with our new buyers may be – ' he coughed, ' – rather strained, at least.'

'You're wary. It's understandable.' She loosed the turban, and started to dry her cropped hair gently. 'I shan't blame you for their rudeness. Given their past record, should we expect anything else?'

He nodded, but lowered his head. 'Still, madam, in the light of recent, er, difficulties . . .'

'Small equipment failures that have been righted quickly. It was very sad about Nula, but accidents will happen. And remember, I granted the Chelonians' application, as always, only after the most careful consideration. It's my job. And I'll take the responsibility for any raised voices.' Her hair sufficiently dried, she folded the towel. 'Who else is there, Mr Jottipher?'

That raised a smile. 'Very good, madam. I'll see you at the reception?'

'Of course.'

He was gone. The Secunda smiled patiently and not a little sadly. To trust in his betters, that was the job of our Mr Jottipher. As much as it was hers. With a vital difference. Her superior was not human.

And he was dying.

Returning to the bathroom, she pulled the plug and towelled herself dry, watching the vortex pull down the green bubbles. Such unpleasantness and disloyalty, she thought, and herself right at the centre of it. If only Mr Jottipher, with all his faith in her (faith, it made her blush to recall, she had just now encouraged), could guess at the truth.

But then, he would know soon enough.

'Hello,' said the Management, right on cue, from the mirrored Inscreen.

She jumped, instinctively pulled the towel about her. 'I do wish you wouldn't.'

'Why be shy? I can have no interest in your contours.'

13

They'd been over this many times. It seemed to amuse him. 'Manners are an important part of business. Look at your Mr Jottipher. It would hardly be productive to have him popping up in buyer's bathrooms.'

'My Mr Jottipher?' The Management seemed to consider this. 'I've never thought of any of the staff as my property. Mr purpose is to acquire, yes, but to acquire for the benefit of others. My shareholders.'

'You have pride. Don't deny it, I've seen it.'

'Hmm. All the better for our efficiency.' He leaned forward. 'It would make a fascinating study for someone, wouldn't it, to map out the qualities I do have and the qualities I don't?'

That surprised her. A concession? 'Many are curious.'

'And I value curiosity, up to a point. But,' he shrugged, 'I could never allow it. Best to keep them guessing, preserve a bit of mystery.'

'I wish you'd go, I want to put my clothes on.'

'But I obviously have something important to say, or I wouldn't be here. I'll say it and clear out, shall I?'

Her silence was a good enough answer.

The picture on the Inscreen changed, the Management replaced by an image relayed from outside the Complex. Smith's house, on the far side of the lake, twenty miles away. The Secunda raised an eyebrow. 'Smith? What about her? You don't want me to talk to her, do you?'

'Have you never liked her?' asked the Management's voice as the image flicked inside the house, to the lab. Smith, scruffy corduroys tucked into leather boots, was pottering about at her microscope, long grey hair flowing unstyled over the collar of her tweed jacket, her workbench cluttered with slides and paraphernalia.

'I doubt the value of her project. My personal feelings about the blessed woman shouldn't come into it.' She smirked as Smith, unaware that she was being observed, slumped down dumpily on a stool. 'She's been here eight years, and we've nothing to show for it. Except a rudeness that wouldn't be tolerated from anyone else on your payroll.'

'Careful, Secunda. You're criticizing one of my ideas.'

'I'm saying that we know precious little more about the Zamps now than we did then. The production rate is still falling steadily.' She waggled a finger at him. 'Only two sales this year, only one new design.' She sat on the edge of the bath and examined her nails. 'If only your creators, Management, had thought to trust you with more information.'

'I'm sure they had their reasons. In our business, secrecy is very important.' He coughed. 'Anyway. Smith's latest report shows that she may be on to something. Finally my investment in her could be paying off.'

'What has she discovered?' The Secunda was genuinely concerned; the Zamps had always unsettled her slightly. The things were so damned powerful, potentially.

'I don't want to steal her glory. She'll tell you if she's certain.' The Management returned the Inscreen to his own image. 'I just popped in to tell you to grant her request, when she makes it, to assign her a couple of servitors. I know how keenly you cling to the little devils.'

'The Complex has more need of them than Smith. The power failure last week, without a full team of servitors – '

'A momentary equipment failure, that's all.' He smiled and rubbed the left side of his nose in one of the gestures that his creators must have believed would relax his staff more. 'The first in two hundred years. Unlikely to happen again.' He smiled and waved goodbye.

The Secunda found herself looking at her reflection as he departed with a tingle of static that passed in a gentle wave over her newly dried skin.

'We are your property,' she said quietly to herself.

Taal stood at his desk in the gaming centre. He was waiting for clearance from the net authorities – they were always a bit behind linking up for the morning session – and fiddling with the golden Z emblem attached to the lapel of his bright red plastic suit. Previous hosts of Zamper might have been expected to impress in it, but it clung to Taal in a way that emphasized his stout, barrel-shaped body. It was the last thing he'd have wanted to wear, but the Management had specified, and it was unwise to protest on Zamper.

At 9.05 came the assured whisper of the automatics. The gaming network, a massive, vaguely rhomboid structure, flared, accepting its first log-ins of the day. Taal's experienced gaze flicked quickly down the ident signatures stacking up on its crystal surfaces.

'None of the big operators yet, see,' he told the new hostess as she entered, without looking up. 'You'll find that. They think it's bad manners to come rushing in the moment you click on. Looks a bit desperate.'

The new girl, whose name was Christie, said 'Oh' and nodded.

Taal was starting to wonder if that studied attitude of disinterest marked the limit of her responses. It was all she'd done since getting off the supply flight yesterday. She was a looker, but where was the interest, where was the sass? He compared her unfavourably to the previous hostess, poor little Nula, who'd been doing very well, all told. Until her accident.

'A couple of data whores from Pyka,' he waved at the names, 'and a Marlex stellar accumulator. In on the razzle after a kill, I shouldn't wonder.' He made the observation with a conspiratorial smile and a sideways glance, offering his friendship, his confidence at least. Again, 'Oh' from her, and the nod.

'I always give them something simple first off, let them think they're on to something.' He clicked down the gaming options, hundreds of ranked and numbered ways to lose your shirt, and made his selection. 'We'll offer them standard canasta with an upper limit of twenty thou.'

'Oh, right.'

Taal took the value tray from its slot under the desk and tutted. 'Still in a mess from last night. I always forget to sort them back. Not my job, after all. Eh, love?' He passed her the tray and the tag pencil. She looked at him blankly. 'The coupons.' He gestured to the jumble of red, blue and yellow light-tags in the tray, about a hundred in all. 'They need sorting and revaluing. Red top left at ten thou, blue top right on five, yellow bottom right stand-alone. Got that?'

She hadn't, of course, but still she nodded.

Every bargirl in populated space could sort tags, without prompting or guidance, in half a minute. It was one of those things you just knew, if you'd ever worked a table. Christie fumbled with the pencil, clicking between settings and faking a confident air.

Taal pretended not to notice, and left her sorting. On the other side of the Centre was an Outscreen. He waddled over and asked the operator for the Secunda.

'Morning.' She was on a pavement somewhere. From the look of the blocks behind her she was heading up to the reception sphere. Over her shoulders was stretched a light blue fabric cut in a V on her wrinkled neck, an uncommonly simple garment. Must be meeting the new buyers. 'Shouldn't you have opened up, Taal?'

'It can wait. There's something we must talk about.'

She raised both eyebrows. 'You have me at a disadvantage.'

'The automatics were late again today, Secunda.'

'A minor equipment failure, you can be sure.'

'There have been a few too many minor equipment failures of late.' He pointed upward, a gesture he made to look mildly obscene. 'As you have the ear of those upstairs, I wonder, could you have a word?'

She was perturbed by the news; he could tell simply because she gave no outward sign. If she'd truly thought the matter of no consequence, there'd have been a self-congratulatory curl of the lips or a coquettish flutter of the lashes. 'You should know better,' she said. 'Even I do not ask questions of the Management. And he cannot make mistakes. His position does not allow it.'

Taal suppressed growing anger. 'It might be time to start asking questions. Nula shared your confidence in the Management, remember? Once.'

That brought out a smug little smile. 'The Management

had confidence in Nula. Which of them was mistaken? Now, I really must get on. We have new buyers.'

Taal stomped back to the desk, trying to hide his anger. A twenty per cent slump in production, a total power failure, Nula's death, and the Secunda was behaving as if nothing was happening.

Christie was waving the tag pencil at him. 'I can't get it to work,' she said hopelessly.

He took it, twisted the cap, and it hummed into life. 'You look as miserable as I feel, dear. And it's only your first day.' He struck his bulging chest, pretending to consider. 'Think how you'll look after fourteen years.'

She took back the pencil without the slightest reaction, and started to separate the tags in the tray, slowly and incompetently. Taal's suspicion increased. She'd never so much as walked past a gaming centre.

The automated supply ships that called at Zamper bimonthly contained enough of the essentials to sustain the four permanent staff and any number of guest buyers. As a specialist, Smith's needs were not overlooked, and on yesterday's flight the Management, who had interfaced specially with a tobacconist on Shaggra on her behalf, had secured two years' supply of tufted whizzweed. Although it wasn't yet 10 a.m., Smith found her brown-stained fingers fumbling for the briar pipe in her jacket pocket.

When it was ready she took a long, self-satisfied puff. After eight years she was getting somewhere. Eight years of working alone and friendless, with the Secunda looking on and wishing her to fail.

It was time for the specimens' feed. Even to her trained zoologist's eyes all Zamps looked identical, and so she had numbered them with harmless adhesive metal plates. The specimen marked as Two sensed the vibration as she twisted the feeder control and the grass clippings sprinkled into the case. A Zamp moved by squeezing the middle section of its body in an accordion-like motion and squelching along, its locomotion aided by the sticky fluid trail that issued from its soft underside. Two lowered its twitching feelers and brought its mouth, seven pinprick-sized holes arranged in a ring pattern, down to the grass. It ate silently, straining the vital fluids it craved through a slalom of osmotic filaments that ran the length of its heavily muscled gullet. Satisfied, it slurped away. One took its place, its feelers intertwining briefly with Two's as they passed. A melodic burble issued from One's underdeveloped voicebox, and its fellows harmonized.

As she watched, Smith felt her head shaking in silent admiration of the consortium's adaptors. To alter a species so skilfully was beyond even the most talented of her homeworld's geno-architects. If they'd had the intelligence, the Zamps could easily have opened their cage and squelched back to their herds in the yards. After eight years, she still was unsure what their original form would have been, but now they were parts of a machine, the secret components at the heart of Zamper. A herd of thirty, silently and without complaint, could design and build a multi-combat battlecruiser in four months.

Her Outscreen twittered and she turned to see the wrinkled and over made-up face of the Secunda. 'Hello dear. Up and about early this morning, I see.'

'The Management's been talking of some great discovery you've made. I thought I'd call over for a look.' Her eyes darted about the lab.

'Can't discuss it, I'm afraid.' Smith waved her pipe at the Outscreen. 'Think I might've tracked down the breakaways. You know, the sub-herd.'

'The missing Zamps? Have you really? Where then?'

Smith put a finger to her lips. 'Sorry. No big secret, I just don't want to look silly if I'm proved wrong. I could do with a couple of servitors, you know, could you send some over?' Inside she was bursting with glee at her likely triumph.

'The proper process is to make a formal application,' the Secunda said through gritted teeth.

'Surely not necessary. It's only me that asks.'

'Procedure states – '

Smith beamed. 'Have you forgotten, Secunda, that I

19

know exactly who you are? That we're both in the same boat, as it were? Former glories count for nought here.'

'I shan't rise to your childishness. The servitors will be with you shortly.'

'Ooh – Madge, dear, home them in on my buggy, will you? It'll save time.'

'Very well.' The Outscreen clicked off.

Smith laughed and punched the air.

Big Mother became aware of his nurse fussing over him, checking the machines that supplied him with fluid, measuring the waste collected in the bag hooked over his rear.

'What news from Hafril?' he heard himself mutter in a voice that was crumbly and decrepit. He knew he had the name wrong, but it was difficult these days even to remember you'd forgotten.

The nurse said patiently, 'I think you mean General Hezzka, Highness.'

Big Mother tried to wave a foot to indicate his understanding, but he had no energy.

'He and First Pilot Ivzid are just leaving the range of our sensornet, Highness.'

'We want to see.'

The nurse stretched up and clicked a button on Big Mother's selector.

A starscape. He had travelled throughout the empire in his younger days, on diplomatic visits and the like, and had never tired of the wonders of space. This region had nothing to commend it in particular and the stars were unfamiliar, but he was moved by the beauty of the nearest, a fiery red giant that it hurt to look at, and the dusts wobbling in a belt of deep haze before a distant, hook-shaped constellation. It was peaceful in comparison to the war-torn spaceways the fleet had navigated on their long journey here.

'That's them, Highness, middle left of the image.'

Big Mother saw it. The many facets of the shuttle glinted as it grew smaller, on the far side of the closing gateway, a pebble thrown into a bottomless black well.

'You carry all of our hopes, Hezzka,' he wheezed. 'Do not fail us.'

The gateway closed.

Chapter 2

Professor Bernice Summerfield stepped from the TARDIS into darkness. Even after several years – reckoned in her own relative experience – of eventful travel through time and space, moments like this remained important. She was, after all, an explorer, and crossing into a new world was a big part of what she did. More often than not, the Doctor would have their destination prepared, and might even throw in a quick lecture on what monsters to expect, which toilets to avoid, and the like. On this occasion he was far from being in control. Only hours after their departure from the Sloathe moon, the systems had suddenly jammed, forcing an emergency materialization. Shortly before it fell silent, the exterior sensor panel had assured the crew that all was well in the immediate vicinity. Bernice welcomed the chance for a peek, and had slipped the doors open, unnoticed by the Doctor, who had already vanished under the console wielding a wrench and muttering something about 'dimensional rents' and 'spatial distortion.'

The air around Bernice was warm and greasy, tickling the bridge of her nose, and somewhere close there was an engine or a big motor, rattling the floor beneath her boots. She reached into the black instinctively, edging the tips of her fingers forward an inch at a time. There was nothing. Pushing the door of the TARDIS open with her heel she called back, 'We'll need torches.'

A rectangle of light escaped from the control room, revealing some of her new surroundings. The TARDIS had materialized in what looked to Bernice like a maintenance conduit. Hardly glamorous. Facing her, stapled to a wall, was a twisted coil of cables. Beneath was a plaque of feebly glowing green, reacting to the light thrown upon it.

She pointed these items out as the TARDIS door opened wide and Forrester stepped out, shining a beam from a big, rubber-insulated torch. Bernice watched the older woman's dark eyes pass around this new place, suspicion ingrained in every line of her frown. 'This reminds me of one of the first ships I ever travelled on,' Forrester said.

'Why's that?'

'Just an impression.' Standing on tiptoe she rapped her knuckles on the ceiling. 'Made for humans, but I don't recognize the technology. You?'

'It really looks very dull.' Bernice tweaked at one of the cables. 'Fuel lines.'

Cwej emerged, and swung his torch about, revealing more sagging lengths of cable, more phosphor plaques. He pulled a face. 'What's that stink?'

Bernice's guess was confirmed. The conduit was actually quite stooped and narrow; the light on top of the TARDIS missed the ceiling by only a fraction of an inch. Cables ran along the walls on either side, trailing off around corners into what looked like identical conduits.

Forrester's anxious features were caught in the light from her own torch. 'It could be a fuel mixture,' she said. Her voice echoed strangely. 'Or a leaking tank.' She nodded. 'Of course, that's why it reminds me of that ship.'

'Eh?'

'It blew up.'

'This place could go up any moment?' Cwej's eyebrows shot up and he scurried back towards the TARDIS. He stood at the door, looking between the two women.

'We're in motion, I'm sure,' Forrester told Bernice. 'If we're on a ship, it must be big one, judging from the size of those cables.'

'Please let's be sensible,' said Cwej. 'I'm not asking for much.'

'It's possibly a leaking tank, that's all I said.' Forrester set off along the conduit. She summoned him with an irritated twitch of her head, and he followed like a dog, with a shrug to Bernice.

She listened to their footsteps and voices receding.

'We're on a huge spaceship that could be about to explode?'

'That's my theory.'

'Then this is stupid. Why are we doing this?'

'Because I want to know why it's going to explode!'

Bernice was not left alone in the dark again for long. With a sharp creak that hurt her ears, the TARDIS door was flung open and the Doctor emerged, his slight form caught in the light from the interior, the deep worry lines that brought a plenitude of mysterious character to his face even more creased than usual.

'Ready, Doctor?'

'I've traced the fault,' he said. 'We passed through a rent in the fabric of space, causing rapid erosion of our filaments. A circuit's blown, look.' In the palm of his hand was a small round unit of frosted glass. The filament inside was cracked. Bernice had learnt not to question the startling scientific irregularities of the TARDIS. If a blown fuse could bring a machine of such size and abilities to a halt, let it. There were more important things in life to worry about, generally hairy or metal or with fangs. 'Don't tell me. It's catastrophic. I'd lay odds.'

The Doctor grinned and tossed and caught the faulty component as if it were a coin. 'Nothing of the sort. But the power's blocked. We'll be grounded until I can whistle up a spare. And I've mislaid the toolkit.' He slipped the component into his pocket and cast about, squinting. 'Where are those others?'

'Roz thinks we're on a spacecraft.'

'Does she?' He walked over to the facing wall and laid the palm of his left hand on the luminous green plaque. It responded to his touch, increasing in brightness until she could see him clearly. The sort of clever thing he would think of. 'What's your opinion?'

Bernice blinked a couple of times, the skin around her eyes suddenly sore. That greasy odour was getting stronger, about four parts to ten of oxygen. She coughed, flapped at the air. 'Ugh. Well, Roz also thinks there's a –' she spluttered, 'a leaky –' and again, 'engine.'

He sniffed. 'Not necessarily. Perhaps we've stumbled across the galaxy's biggest chip shop.' He offered his handkerchief. 'Go back inside if you like.' He sauntered off, overpowered by curiosity, poking at the cables with an index finger. 'I wonder, Bernice, if this ship is manned? And if so, what manner of creature we may find up on deck. I didn't expect to find an advanced, space-travelling species in this part of the galaxy, but there again . . .'

His voice, muffled by odd echoes and the rumble of that dynamo or whatever it was, trailed off. Bernice buried her nose in the hanky, took an anguished glance back at the battered wooden door of the TARDIS, which was made a kind of undersea green by the murky light, and followed him.

'Battered sausage and pea fritter twice,' she called.

The web of conduits led to a metal barrier, a blank oblong panel set into its middle. Forrester threw her torch to Cwej and searched for an opening mechanism. The surface was smooth so she checked the walls and the floor. It would be logical for this to lead into another area. In a vessel this size, maintenance compartments would be in the mid-section.

Cwej leant against the wall, breathing heavily. 'That smell's getting worse. Something's burning.'

She ignored him. 'Perhaps this opens inwards, and is sealed from the other side.' She searched the panel once more, running her fingers along the grooves that marked its edges. 'But who's going to seal a maintenance conduit? For safety reasons it'd be left open at all times. It must lead somewhere. It obviously comes away.'

'I've been thinking. I've got an idea,' he said.

At the moment opening this panel was what mattered. A reliable, practical, soluble problem. That was a relief after recent terrors. 'It definitely opens. It must swing open from the other side. That means it's been sealed, and this section blocked off. Or is it the other side that's been blocked off?'

'These phosphor plaques,' said Cwej, tapping one of the glowing rectangles. 'Look.' He snapped off both torches.

Forrester snarled. 'What are you doing? Will you – '

She could barely see him in the green. 'They're just not bright enough to work in,' he said, having to raise his voice as the engine rumble increased and a loose covering somewhere rattled and clanged as if blown by a strong wind. Trickles of sweat glistened on his brow. 'A maintenance team couldn't see in this. It sounds like something needs fixing, so where are they?'

Damn, he had something. She retrieved her torch and tried to sound sceptical. Childish. 'Yeah?'

'There's nobody aboard. No light, no air. We're in flight, but we're not adrift. In fact it sounds like we're speeding up.' He was backing away down the conduit as he spoke. The fearful expression on his big, pretty face really made him too cute. 'We should have worked this out earlier.'

Forrester ran quickly through the facts but couldn't see his conclusion. She'd have to admit her ignorance. 'What?'

He turned his torch on. 'It's a test ship. Programmed to crash. I think.'

Forrester swallowed, gulping down a wave of panic. She wasn't bothered so much by the danger they were in. The TARDIS was only a short walk back. What rankled was that she'd had no idea, hadn't thought, and gone blundering in. As if this were her world, working the way she understood. Even after the Sloathes, adapting was difficult.

She kicked the metal barrier with the toe of her boot.

The panel clunked open – well it would – revealing not another section of the ship but a porthole. Just to prove her completely wrong. A massive purple circumference was framed in the oblong. The planet was enormous and far too near. It was coming closer, pushing the stars out of the picture. She could see the outline of mountains and a couple of seas, through a thin pearl-pink cover of cloud. Its mass would crush this ship like a juice carton.

Cwej pointed. 'I was right.'

Forrester smacked him across the shoulder. 'Of course you were right. Now let's move!'

Bernice squeezed her shoulders through the hatch, took the Doctor's hand and let him pull her up. The companionway into which they emerged looked more promising. It was still dark and too hot, getting hotter even, but there was an open door on the left. In the small cabin beyond, a skeletal shadow was thrown on the far wall by a tall metal structure. She peered, tried to resolve its shape; the thing was a bunk-bed. On the lower shelf a still form was huddled under a blanket.

'There are people about, then,' she whispered, following the Doctor in to the metal chamber. It was monastically bare, with no cupboards, tables or belongings.

'There were.'

The Doctor shook the sleeper gently. Her eyes growing accustomed to the dark, Bernice saw the head flop back grotesquely. The Doctor patted her on the shoulder. 'Don't worry. He's very dead.' A thought appeared to strike him. 'Oh dear. Disease?'

'And this heat, a kind of purification?' She shuddered. 'This could be a plague ship.'

The Doctor, intrigued, knelt over the corpse, turned down the blanket gently as if the man really was only asleep, and unzipped the loose denim tunic beneath. He chuckled. 'Ah. What about this?'

Bernice looked closer. The figure inside the bed was a blank-faced mannequin made of yellow plastic. 'Do you know,' said the Doctor, 'I thought there was something odd about this ship or whatever it is.'

Bernice set off along the companionway. 'You don't say.' She blew a drop of sweat from the point of her nose, slipped off her PVC jacket and slung it over her shoulder. 'It's getting hotter. I hope I remembered my deodorant this morning.'

The Doctor, oblivious to her distress, carried on. 'There's no proper lighting, even here, up on deck. The temperature's too high, there's not enough air – '

'What?' Bernice's pulses started to throb in time to the engine sound. The Doctor's shoulders, her reference point in this unpleasant place, hurried away from her.

'Enough to be going on with, don't fret.'

The high roof of the companionway sloped down, forcing them to lower their heads before it ended in a large door. Bernice took the initiative, sweeping her palm over the sensor panel. The sections of the door slid apart slowly.

Like the rest of the ship the room beyond was dark, with a line of the dim green plates mounted in the ceiling. The surfaces of each of the three inward-curving walls were covered in instrumentation, with scarcely an inch between one flickering display and the next. When the door closed behind the Doctor and Bernice the unhealthy rumble of the ship's engine was almost soundproofed out. In the sudden silence, Bernice heard her heart pumping against her ribcage. She thought she felt better and tried to take a deep breath. She couldn't.

The Doctor stepped forward to the two large flight chairs facing the control board on the opposite wall.

Two more mannequins were seated in the padded control chairs, yellow and black striped safety straps tightened about their waists. 'What if,' Bernice said, 'this ship was attacked? The crew were replaced to make it appear manned to sensor sweeps, then it was sent on its way?'

The Doctor fiddled with some of the equipment, prodding at a row of stippled controls below a cluster of small triangular displays. 'No. These controls have been locked off. Why should a pirate bother to do that?' He took out a slim probe from one of his pockets and continued his manipulations.

Bernice looked back at the mannequins. Despite her best efforts, her awareness was folding up. Already the edges of her vision were closing in, swallowed by a whirling pattern of lights. She wanted to shout, shriek, alert the Doctor, but – and this was really silly – she didn't want him to think of her as a light-weight, somebody he had to look after all the while.

'The sequence is impregnable. There isn't even a flight computer. Most odd.' The Doctor shrugged and put away his probe. The heat and the lack of air weren't affecting him in the slightest, and he continued in lecture-room tones, 'Suggesting these dummies were propped up in this thing, which is on a pre-programmed flight.'

Bernice wondered why she was having trouble following his words and why her picture of him was fluttering. Her knees gave way, she tumbled against the wall. It was burning hot and scalded the skin on her fingers. The Doctor rushed over and supported her. He hefted her up and pulled one of her arms around his neck. 'There's no air!' she coughed.

'The TARDIS,' he said firmly, dragging her away. The Doctor's unique ancestry endowed him, she knew, with enviable resilience. He could be trusted, couldn't he?

Her head lolled back, the corrugated squares of the ceiling flipping past her like frames of a speeded-up film.

Furious with himself, the Doctor let Bernice fall gently to the floor of the violently shaking companionway. Acrid fumes were pouring from puncture holes in the walls, making it even more difficult to orientate and fogging the faint light. The hatch leading back down to the conduit system was around here somewhere. He felt for the raised outline, ducking his head into a patch of vapour that nearly blinded him. There was no escape that way. He leapt up.

The ship rocked, knocking him off his feet. He landed across Bernice, who was muttering faintly, blood pouring from a cut on her forehead. 'It's a test flight,' she said, her voice full of smoke.

The Doctor brushed her fringe gently. Her hair was plastered to her forehead in spikes by sweat. He considered the options. No way back to the TARDIS, and the repairs would take a couple of hours at least. Their only hope was the escape capsules this ship had to be carrying.

Bernice draped over his shoulder, the Doctor gritted his teeth and ran on through the smoke, passing the bunk-rooms. He tried to ignore the vibration, the heat, and the grating, clanking boom of the engine as it died and the ship's heat shields blew out. His legs ached and the dirty vapour chafed his throat.

Something exploded in the darkness up ahead, igniting a wave of vapour that flared in puffs of blue. Just in front of the wave of crackling explosions was a wall compartmentalized in six.

The Doctor threw himself at the nearest capsule, wrenching open the shield. Inside were two of the test dummies, propped up in cushioned rests, masks clamped over their mouths. 'Sorry,' he said, grabbing them and throwing them out. He slid Bernice from his shoulder and positioned her in one of the empty crash cushions.

The flames licked at his shoulders.

With no choice left to him, the Doctor jumped in to the capsule and pulled the shield shut.

The slipstream of Smith's air buggy, guided by the map-screen she'd compiled during her most recent survey, threw up purple dust as she returned to the site of her great discovery. The servitors were waiting at the foot of the small cliff, bleeping their recognition as she climbed from the driver's seat.

'Morning, boys.'

'Good morning Smith. What are your instructions?' they chorused.

She waved her datalyzer at them. 'These are the results of my latest geological survey.' The screen on the device displayed the internal structure of the caverns beneath this section of the surface; a large area, about a mile down, was shaded yellow. She tried to keep the excitement from her voice as she revealed her findings. A servitor's intelligence was basic and literal, and she had to give them the information in as straightforward a manner as possible.

'The shaded section is new. The last survey, a routine sweep, was done about two hundred years ago. This cave was solid rock then. The structure has shifted, and there are some signs of movement.'

The servitors buzzed and clicked, accepting the information and logging the route in their memories. 'You wish us to examine this area?'

Smith sighed. 'Yes. Don't you see, my dears?'

The servitors hummed, saying nothing.

'I've been working on this project for eight years, and at last I'm getting somewhere.'

One of the servitors turned slightly. 'Your project is to investigate the reasons for the fall in the Zamps' rate of production. Query link with geological survey.'

'Oh, for goodness sakes. The Zamp sub-herd, the breakaway group. I may have found where the little devils have squelched off to!'

'To this new cave?'

'Possibly! Do you need a reason for everything? I'd love to go down with you, but for safety considerations and all that.' She beckoned them to the cliff face and pointed to a thin split in a fold of outward-sloping rock. 'Now get going. Straight through there, boys.'

'You request a visual record of our findings?' the servitors asked as they prepared to descend.

'Of course. I'm trying not to get too excited, but this may be the answer, you see. Something odd is going on down there, at any rate. Good luck.' She lifted a thumb in their direction as, without another word, they tilted slightly and nipped one after the other through the split in the rock and down into the caverns. 'I'll wait up here,' she called after them into the darkness. 'Don't be too long!'

When the buzz of their departure had faded, she made herself comfortable back in the buggy, throwing a tartan rug over her knees. The sun had passed behind the clouds, and a cooler breeze was blowing. Outwardly calm, she was inwardly bubbling with new questions and theories. The most frustrating thing about her life on Zamper was that she had nobody with whom to share her scientific enthusiasm. She hadn't been over to the Complex for years, and her opinions of her fellow workers were not generous. The Secunda – well, she'd always be plain Madge Beaumont to Smith; Jottipher was spineless; Taal was amusing but rather vulgar. She'd quite liked Nula, the little hostess, admired her pluck. The pluck that had earned her little accident. She pushed that thought to the back of her mind. It was unwise to question things on Zamper. The recent difficulties were unimportant. There was no real reason to worry.

Her head lifted abruptly to the clouds as a sonic boom blared. 'Strange,' she muttered. The test sites were many miles away, and the new buyers expected today wouldn't be approaching the Complex from this direction, surely. A small black shape tore through the lower atmosphere, its shielded sides flaring bright white as it curled, smoking, turning over and over, then slowed and coasted down further along the lakeside, crunching against the rocks that bordered the water. Then it disappeared around a fold in the cliffs, lost to her gaze.

An identical shape followed, zooming off eastwards, towards the Complex. At the speed it was going, it would definitely undershoot and hit the water. Her memory jolted her, and Smith identified the objects. Escape capsules.

'Very strange.'

Perhaps there was a reason to worry.

Chapter 3

Getting knocked on the head every other day was a fact of Bernice's life, as she supposed doing the pools or weeding the garden were to other people. She'd lost count of how many times her skull had taken a battering since she'd first stepped aboard the TARDIS. Eternal optimism was her flaw. No matter how bad her experiences, a few days' rest in the TARDIS and she was ready for the next stop, smile at the ready. Always wrong. This occasion felt particularly painful. Moving was agony, although a pillow or something had been thoughtfully provided.

After a couple of minutes she sat up, gritting her teeth and screwing up her eyes against the pain. She found she was lying in a deep-cushioned, human-sized hole in a large metal container; an identical space adjacent was empty. The top half of the container had been thrown back on its hinges from the inside, presumably by the Doctor. Small footprints in the purple dust trailed away from what Bernice realized was an escape capsule, and ended in the cleft formed by two leaning stones. The place was almost pleasant. A temperate climate, fluffy violet cumulonimbus clouds. No signs of animal or vegetable life. Behind the rocks waves were breaking. She imagined a deserted beach. No birds, just the wind and the rising tide and the Doctor collecting pebbles.

Carefully she climbed from the capsule, each movement driving a cold stabbing pain through her skull. Her legs threatened to give way but she forced herself to remain calm and conscious. 'Wait for the Doctor,' she told herself strictly. 'Wait for the Doctor. Wait for the Doc . . . oh.'

She woke again to his shoes, covered in purple scuffs. 'I know what I want for my birthday.'

He knelt down and applied his handkerchief, soaked in cold water, to her forehead. 'This'll sting a bit.'

She flinched. 'I want a crash helmet. Ow! And a ray gun.'

The Doctor dabbed at the wound. 'I'm sure I have a crash helmet somewhere in the TARDIS. And Ace left some of her weapons about, didn't she?'

'I don't mean one of those big slabs of twenty-fifth century designer violence. Nothing so obvious. Something more feminine.'

'A ray handbag?'

She sat up. 'You've got one?'

'I was joking.'

Bernice felt strong enough now to take the wet hanky from him. 'How bad is the wound?'

'The bleeding's stopped.' Having said this, he started poking about in the capsule for something. 'The air feels very clean, so there's little risk of infection. Temperature a cool sixty, plenty of water. But not much in the way of food. None in this either. They wouldn't waste perishables on a test flight.'

The events leading up to their evacuation from the ship returned slowly to Bernice's memory. This felt rather like the morning after a drunken party, the recollection of each tawdry incident cranking up your embarrassment. 'Where's the TARDIS?'

'Where we left it.' The Doctor was now fiddling with a slender piece of metal he'd broken off the insides of the capsule. 'The ship must have crashed by now, but the TARDIS should be fine. It's very robust for a phone box. Christopher and Roz will be quite safe.'

'Assuming they got back inside.'

'Hmm. Now, the ship may have crashed on land or in water, and if this capsule works on the principle that most do, probably some distance away.'

Bernice's optimism floundered. 'So we're sat here, with no food, possibly thousands of miles from civilization?'

The Doctor smiled infuriatingly. 'Yes.'

'It's like one of those old films. We go crazy and eventually eat bits of each other. Then just after we've died the helicopter arrives and the credits roll. Oh, the irony.'

'Thankfully not.' He waved the slender metal object in the air. 'What do you think this is?'

'Give up.'

He tossed it to her. 'Flight recorder, dummy.'

Bernice jiggled the thing in her hand, her hopes growing. At one end a blue light was flashing steadily, in a reassuring way that put her in mind of the TARDIS. 'Yes! They'll want this before anything else. Just as well, there's no meat on me. Life looks brighter. We'll just sit here and wait, then?'

The Doctor took his crumpled white hat from his pocket and popped it on. 'Well, we could always go and have a look at that hut.'

'What hut?'

He pointed behind her, away from the water. 'That hut.'

Bernice turned her head, the pain temporarily forgotten. About half a mile away from them, sitting neatly on the level plain that led from the rocks, was a structure composed of interlocked sections of corrugated metal. It was roughly the size of a house, and boasted a line of big windows, a front door, and a solitary outbuilding. A receiver dish was bolted to the roof. It hummed across the plain at them.

The Complex's reception lounge was a sumptuously large spherical structure, decorated a tasteful neutral white. On one wall a slow-moving mural depicting the volcanic region of the planet Dalverius had been hung, the gouts of green lava casting bursts of emerald light that reflected off slow-turning mirrorballs. Potted plants pleased Mr Jottipher with their scents of musk and blossom as he entered and nodded to the Secunda. She smiled and nodded back, then handed him a thin sheet of gold plastic.

This was the part of his job that he most disliked. His

musical talents were one of the reasons he had been selected from thousands to become liaision executive for Zamper – in his old life, which he rarely thought about, he had been a distinguished soprano, touring in three systems – but the martial anthems of nation states restricted his range of expression. He longed for an aria of regret or loss or guilt, not more of the same tired tub-thumping jingoistic nonsense.

'They've been told to switch on their translators,' said the Secunda. 'The landing was smooth, so I'm told.'

Mr Jottipher said nothing. He concentrated on the golden sheet, trying to familiarize himself with the tune, but something in his face must have given away his thoughts.

'You think we should have a servitor standing by?'

'It is usual when we are entertaining our more captious guests, madam.'

'The Chelonians have had few dealings with humans before today,' she replied. 'I consider it unwise to show them the slightest aggression.'

'As you say.' His brow furrowed as he looked down the sheet. 'Madam, their anthem.'

'Yes?'

'It has one hundred and eighty-five verses.'

'As mere emissaries of the First Family, our guests are entitled only to the opening three.'

Mr Jottipher loosened his collar and thanked goodness for the thoroughness of the Secunda's research. 'I am pleased.'

As he spoke, he heard the grinding of the lift mechanism as the anti-grav beams aligned with the door of the lounge. In seconds he would be in the presence of the insulting creature he had glimpsed on the Outscreen. He composed himself, and tried to take strength from the Secunda. She never faltered.

The lift door slid up slowly. The synthetic accompaniment to his song of greeting crashed into its opening bars, a dissonant farting of brassy stabs. In his mind, Mr Jottipher saw a collapsing bandstand. The chords of the piece changed rapidly. He found his place on the score-sheet as the introduction reached its barking crescendo, and started to sing as two sets of sharp-clawed reptilian feet were revealed.

Chelonia, Chel – o – nia!
Goddess preserve Chelonia as the boundaries of its dominion spread to a wideness that is almost unbelievable,
And flagrantly incomprehensible to the minds of lesser creatures.
Let the panoply of deities give expression to the desire of all Chelonians to stamp out parasitism wherever it is encountered,
Particularly where this concerns the attempts by parasites to establish communities that, laughably, presume a degree of social intelligence.

The bridge to the second verse, which contained an embarrassing number of explosion sound effects, caused Mr Jottipher reflection that this piece contained neither the most infectious of melodies, nor was it succint lyrically.

The door was now fully raised and the two Chelonians were revealed in their entirety. To Mr Jottipher they resembled overgrown examples of ordinary reasonably-sized terrestrial tortoises. They stood, if that was the right word, on their four legs; their shells were plated and looked tough; their grizzled heads swung on long necks that emerged from the fused scutes of the upper and lower halves of their shells. Although both were about the same size, they were clearly distinguishable. The Chelonian to the left was the leader of the delegation. His jaw was tighter, his leathery green skin slightly more wrinkled, the rims of his pale yellow eyes clouded by faint branches of pink. Streaks of melanin darkened his shell a blackish-brown, with a pale areola in the centre of each scute. From his detailed study of the Secunda's reasearch, Mr Jottipher identified the bright red stripe that ran the length of the creature's carapace as a mark of high command.

He was at least a general. His junior's shell was star-patterned, and his young eyes darted with vital anger about the lounge. Around his mid-section he wore a flexible metal belt. Its holsters were empty, apart from one that contained an unpowered hammering tool of some kind. Clasped in one of the junior's front feet was a strongbox painted cabbage green. Both Chelonians were literally shaking with fury, an image compounded by the droplets of germwash fluid glistening on their shiny shells. Well, to be fair to himself, he had tried to warn them about that.

It was time for the second verse.

Chelonia, Chel – o – nia!
Lift up your plastrons and sing for the swingeing retribution that will be exacted on those who in any circumstance conspire with parasites –

The younger Chelonian caught Mr Jottipher's eye, drew back his head, and roared. The fearsome noise drowned out the accompaniment. Mr Jottipher, gripped by terror, lost his place and decided to stop, quickly.

The monster lurched from the open doorway at a speed that belied its resemblance to any shuffling Earth cousin. Mr Jottipher hiccoughed and scurried back a few steps, knocking over one of the plants.

The General spoke. 'You insult us! You, parasites, insult us!'

Unruffled, the Secunda stepped forward. 'I assure you, gentlemen, no insult is intended. Our custom is to greet guests with the anthem of their homeland, as a measure of our respect.'

The junior snarled, stamping one of his front feet and raking the pile of the carpet with horribly pointed claws. 'Respect is exchanged by equals. You are inferiors. You seek to mock us!'

'Not so.' Mr Jottipher was, as ever, impressed by the Secunda's steadiness in these situations. She faced the Chelonians with scarcely a tremble. 'Our species have a history of enmity. That is true of many who have come

38

to Zamper.' She raised her hands, palms outward. 'But remember. This facility is neutral, and no violent act, on any part, is tolerated here.' She indicated Mr Jottipher. 'It is the duty of our guest liaision executive to ensure your convenience.'

He bowed nervously. 'Sirs.'

The General raised a foot. 'You are the Secunda?'

'That is correct.'

'You control this place?'

She shook her head, a gesture the Chelonians seemed to understand. 'I am the senior agent of the Management of Zamper. May I know your names?'

The General seemed to swell up in his shell. 'I am General Hezzka of the Chelonian fifteenth column, commander-in-chief of the Maternal Guard.' He indicated the other. 'This is First Pilot Ivzid.'

Ivzid nodded stiffly. The Secunda's research – drawn from several hastily compiled travelogues into the empire and a fiction that had been exciting, if rather showy – suggested that Chelonians were unable to tell humans apart. But when Ivzid's eyes swivelled to meet Mr Jottipher's there was a flicker of recognition, and the reptile's long pink tongue swished wetly over its top lip. Mr Jottipher shuddered.

'We are insulted by your actions,' said Hezzka. 'You have ransacked the systems of our ship, and forced us to pass through some moistening contraption.' He shook his shell, shedding the last few drops of fluid from the germwash.

'These are routine procedures,' said the Secunda. 'Outlined and agreed on in the contract that your leader signed, via data-coil, six months ago.'

Hezzka grunted and lowered his head, a gesture Mr Jottipher took to be a sign of anger.

'Before we proceed,' the Secunda continued, 'more tedious formalities. The Management will insist, and I suppose the inconvenience is not too great.'

'What is this formality?' snapped Ivzid.

On cue, Mr Jottipher stepped forward, his composure

slightly returned. He took a small grey device from the inside pocket of his jacket and showed it to Hezzka.

'A datalyzer,' the Chelonian growled.

'A final security check.' Mr Jottipher switched the device on and adjusted the settings. A multicoloured display lit up as he passed the scanner end over Hezzka. 'A regulation, nothing more.'

'You do not trust us!'

Mr Jottipher studied the display, noting the number of bionic implants contained in Hezzka's body. There was one at each joint of his four limbs, a large power unit under the plastron, and a sheet grafted to his brain. A communicator unit was connected to a point beneath his chin. But there was no trace of weaponry.

The scanner beam swept over Ivzid, and the device emitted a frantic bleeping that brought a rush of colour to Mr Jottipher's cheeks. 'Mr Ivzid,' he said, uncertain how to address the creature, 'I think you've overlooked something.'

There was an uneasy exchange of glances between Ivzid and his superior. Hezzka seemed almost to sigh with exasperation, if such a thing was possible for a Chelonian.

'There's an energy weapon in your – ' Mr Jottipher circled a nervous finger, unwilling to point, 'in your, your, er . . .'

Ivzid tipped sideways. There was a sharp clicking sound as internal hinges shifted, and then a strangely shaped object clattered onto the carpet. The Secunda swooped it up. 'You must have forgotten to leave this behind,' she said brightly, turning the thing over in her hand. It was designed to be grasped and operated by the three claws of a Chelonian foot, and its buttons were labelled copiously in their squiggly notation.

'A Chelonian officer has much to consider,' Hezzka said through tightened lips. 'The First Pilot most of all.'

'We accept your apology,' said Mr Jottipher automatically. It was the standard response given in the Management's book of etiquette. Its effect on the Chelonians was electric. For a moment it looked as if they were going to burst from their shells in apoplexy at the very idea of apologizing to a parasite. Ivzid took it very badly, his free foot shaking.

There was a long and uncomfortable silence. Secretly, Mr Jottipher was pleased the contract had been broken. The sooner the Chelonians were away the happier and easier his life would become. Not even the Sprox had been so troublesome.

Typically it was the Secunda who spoke first. 'Never mind. I'll pop it in my personal safe and you can have it back when our business is concluded.'

Mr Jottipher almost choked. The contract, the standard Zamper contract adhered to the letter for 473 years, had clearly been broken. In such cases, and there had been a few in his time here, the offending party was expelled immediately by the servitors. What was the Secunda doing?

Hezzka moved forward, stretching out one foot to clasp at a glazed blue bowl of pansies with the polite interest of a competitor at a garden show sizing up the opposition. His splayed claws examined the plants briefly, checking the health of the stems, then he tipped back the bowl and munched on the purple and black leaves. The meal, unintentionally provided, appeared to raise his spirits. 'Good, good. Your caterer is to be congratulated.' He looked about the lounge, noting the variety of hanging baskets. With a startled jolt, Mr Jottipher realized that he was making an attempt at friendliness, as if the previous incident had not occurred. 'I see you have hiatus blossom, very good.'

'The plants are imported,' said the Secunda, 'on our supply ships. And preserved with a harmless chemical formula.'

'Oh yes, $G3sO5$?'

She nodded. 'I am aware of the affinity between your people and floral blooms.'

Ivzid bristled. 'Blooms are for eating, parasite Secunda. We are loyal Chelonian officers. To us the outward aspect of these things is incidental.'

41

Hezzka, remembering himself, replaced the empty bowl.

'Quite.' The Secunda indicated the exit and assumed an air that put Mr Jottipher in mind of a harried schoolmistress. 'Now, we really must get on. The day has barely begun.'

'We wish to inspect the ship.'

'Yes, the Management tells me it's almost ready. And,' she nodded to the strongbox, 'your deposit has to be accepted. But, of course, you shall see it.' She spoke firmly. 'To my office. And then our Mr Jottipher will be pleased to show you to your quarters.'

Mr Jottipher fell into step behind the Secunda and the Chelonians. He couldn't take his eyes off the weapon his mistress carried so easily in one hand, as if she was very familiar with such things.

Forrester had risen from her berth in the escape capsule to find it was bobbing gently against a line of high rocks that ringed the water into which she and Cwej had fallen. She'd remained conscious during the fall, and was pleased about that. There was a small power rudder affixed to the capsule for such a contingency, and she was able to steer the metal box, and her sleeping partner, to a point she judged to be safe. At the third attempt she wedged one end of the capsule between two rocks, jumped up and down to make sure it was lodged securely, and hopped out for a look about.

It was stupid, but as she walked along the flat, featureless purple plain, she felt like calling for the Doctor and Bernice. In the heat of the last moments aboard the test ship, she'd been angry enough to throttle the Doctor. But it wasn't in her nature to shift blame, and her curiosity was as culpable. She found she missed the Doctor. It was comforting to be around him, mostly because he was so good at looking out for himself, and that freed her to do other things.

She pulled herself up sharp, almost tripping over in surprise. About a mile or so ahead loomed a structure. It looked like a ship, of unfamiliar design, definitely alien, about sixty metres from side to side. Its architecture was all wrong, dividing the thing into three chunky blocks with engine ports pointing up and down from its middle. Cool purple sunlight spangled off its faceted black surfaces. Its solidity suggested military use, although no weapons were visible. It rested on a launchpad that could have taken a ship three times its size; at the edge of the pad was a dull silver domed structure that curled underground. There was no sign of life.

Forrester hurried back to the escape capsule, biting her lip and ruminating. Different technology from the test ship. An observer, then, or buyer, or perhaps only passing. The complex under the pad wouldn't be safe from several hundred tons of superheated wreckage. It followed that the remains of the test ship, and therefore the TARDIS, were distant.

When she got back to the capsule she was confronted by a bizarre sight. Cwej had jumped onto the rocks. His trousers were sopping wet. Ha, he'd fallen in. And he was hopping up and down, pulling a face and shaking his legs alternately.

She coughed. 'I don't know that one. Want to teach me?'

'I've got an eel in my trousers!' he shouted.

Forrester suppressed a giggle. 'Take them off, then.'

Cwej writhed and wriggled. 'I'm trying to shake it out.'

'And what if it's a leech? With savage teeth?' Forrester unbuckled his belt and pulled his trousers down to his knees with one swift jerk. 'Come on, it's nothing we haven't seen before.'

A thin kipper-shaped creature jumped out of Cwej's trousers and floundered on the rocks. Satisfied that it was harmless, Forrester picked it up and threw it back into the water.

Cwej stopped shaking and adopted a mournful expression. 'These trousers are ruined.' He kicked off his boots and stepped out of his trousers.

Forrester shook her head. 'We're stranded possibly

millions of miles from civilization and your trousers are ruined.'

He wrung them in his huge hands and threw them over his shoulder. 'We can always eat those eels.'

'We'd have to catch them first. And it looked more like a kipper.' Forrester sighed. 'Am I really having this conversation? Aren't you cold?'

Cwej shrugged. He was decently covered by a large pair of white briefs, at least. 'I'll be fine in just these. I found them in the TARDIS laundry. They belong to someone called Calvin.'

'I'm not interested in your knickers.' Forrester jerked a thumb over her shoulder. 'About a mile over there there's a landing pad and an alien ship. Coming to take a look?'

He slipped back into his boots. To Forrester he looked rather like a monstrously overgrown baby, standing in his white T-shirt and nappy. 'I feel a bit embarrassed. Can we wait until I've dried out?'

Forrester walked away.

The canasta game, preset by Taal at a difficulty level of minus three, had attracted droves of spectators. Green signatures flashed red for active as, spurred on by the ease with which the house had conceded, they logged on for the next contest.

Taal's enthusiasm had been worn away by fourteen years' service on Zamper, but he felt a distant, ticklish sort of thrill as the queue lengthened. He flexed his fingers and punched up the gaming menu.

'Shall I sort out the coupons again?' Christie asked, picking up the tray.

He patted her hand. 'Just stand there and watch, dear. We're going for something very different. Yes, I think we'll try another old Earth game, level plus three – no, two, I don't want to scare them off.' He pointed to the data-link screen. 'Keep your eyes on the guidance lines.'

The warning tone sounded, signalling the start of the new game. Taal selected the sound option and the level metallic voice of the gaming network spoke. 'Welcome to bingo.'

'What's bingo?' The first sign of curiosity the girl had shown.

'Old Earth game,' Taal whispered back. 'Very simple, and it really piles up the tension. You'll work it out soon enough.'

'Collect your books,' said the Network.

The signatures, including the Marlex stellar accumulator who cleared up at canasta, removed their random number sheets from the supplied index. Taal almost felt sorry for the Marlex, could see him as clear as if he was standing feet away. Laughing in the face of fate, slapping all thirty thousand livres of his winnings down.

'Eight and three, eighty-three,' said the network. 'Two and four, twenty-four. All the fours, forty-four. Key of the door, twenty-one.'

Each number, when called, appeared on the game panel. 'What's key of the door?' asked Christie.

'Old Earth ritual.'

'Eighty-eight, two fat ladies. Five and nine, fifty-nine, the Brighton line. Close the doors.'

The girl laughed, a sprinkle of a giggle that Taal found not unpleasant. A long time since he'd heard anything so untainted, something that signified genuine innocent pleasure. He contemplated the giggle. What made it so attractive? Yes. It wasn't brainless. He'd never gone for bimbos in the old life. She'd got that reference to Brighton, to trains, to classical history. She was educated.

'Three and four, thirty-four. All the nines, ninety-nine. Number ten, Tony's den. One and five, fifteen. On its own, number four, number number number num – berrrrrr – '

Taal beat his fists on the desk. 'Not again.'

The network voice droned, 'Number threeeee, threeeee–eeee – ,' rising in pitch, flattening finally to an ultrasonic wave.

'What's the matter?' asked the girl, sounding hopeless again.

Taal shook his head and shut down the network, his

stubby fingers dancing expertly over the mini-controls. The signatures snapped off in disgust, the Marlex departing with winnings intact. 'Equipment failure,' Taal muttered, then raised his head and bellowed at the ceiling, 'No, why keep it quiet? Equipment failure!'

The girl put a nervous hand on his shoulder. 'Steady on. It can hear us, can't it? The Management?'

'Yes, he can hear us,' Taal said bitterly. He kicked the network, composed himself, and said meekly, 'And I would like to report an equipment failure in the data-coil linkage to the gaming centre.'

Bernice and the Doctor stood outside the hut. Recent footprints led from the door.

Bernice knelt for a closer look. 'Size six, so probably a woman. Humanoid, anyway.'

The Doctor pointed to some other marks. 'Vehicle tracks. An aircar, I think.' He clasped one hand over the other and looked about. 'Interesting. I think this is some sort of outpost, and the occupant – there's only one set of footprints, see – has her supplies delivered.' He examined the jambs of the hut's door. 'There doesn't seem to be a locking device.'

Bernice pushed the door open. 'Very trusting. I think that's rather nice.'

'You'll find more unlocked doors in a totalitarian state than anywhere else,' the Doctor said casually.

Inside, a small and bare vestibule led to the central area of the building. There was a strong sour chemical whiff mixed in with tobacco fumes, and the ceiling was stained nicotine-yellow. It was apparent this was a laboratory. A sturdy bench piled with stacks of apparatus stood in the middle of the room, with a single stool tucked neatly beneath it. The scientific stuff on the table caused Bernice's nose to wrinkle. It looked way too complicated, in an intricate fiddly way. Whole weeks of her life had been spent pottering around pits with nothing more than a spade, and she resented sensors and analysers instinctively, at least until her arms started to ache. But then the field of the Doctor's hypothetical lady labworker was not archaeological. On each wall of the lab were rows of shelves, and on the shelves were labelled jars containing bits of dead things.

The Doctor picked a jar up and peered at the bit of dead thing inside, a stringy green glob suspended in clear fluid. 'It could be one layer of a membrane.'

Bernice took the jar. 'It could be a toast topper.' She cast her glance over some of the other jars while the Doctor went to poke his head around the far door. There were about thirty in all. Each label was computer printed, and the multisyllabic words on the labels were outside Bernice's experience. The jars contained a multitude of parts. Bernice identified a speckled section of tissue as a digestive filament. There was also a stomach, a walnut-sized brain and two objects that looked like decayed feelers which had darkened their suspension fluid brown. Bernice felt vaguely reassured; this place, disorganized and dirty, wasn't the home of any thick-eyebrowed white-coated Moreau forcing cross-breeds.

The Doctor beckoned her to a corner of the lab. He had come across a glass case, about the size of a fish tank, attached to the wall, and was leaning over, brow creased with interest. A couple of adjustable lamps swung a faint greenish glow into the case, lighting three of the strangest animals Bernice had ever seen. They lay on a thin bed of grass clippings. Her first impression was of a snail missing its shell. The beasts were about a foot and a half in length and jet black, apart from a few flecks of grey which she took to be diseased tissue. Their skin was smooth and dry like that of a seal, with the suggestion of a slimier under-side at the flanks. An internal skeleton elevated the front section into a head, from which sprouted three feelers. Of eyes or mouth there was no trace.

Bernice shivered at the sight, and immediately felt rather ashamed. Even if the things were dangerous they were securely caged. It was a dumb reaction to alien life forms she thought she'd conquered long ago.

'Yes, they are just a bit creepy, aren't they?' said the

Doctor. He tapped the side of the case, making a hollow ringing sound. The animals didn't react. 'I've not seen a creature quite like these.'

'Surely they're not native to this planet, or at least to this region. This is the sort of thing you'd expect to find somewhere with no light and plenty of moisture.'

'You're probably right.' He smiled and pointed to the ranks of jars. 'But whoever works here's very interested in them, and perhaps they can give us a few answers.' His attention was caught by a magazine that lay open on the shelf by the case, next to a row of stoppered chemical flasks. He flipped to the cover. '*The Year in Architecture.* A lively range of interests, then.'

They heard a motor approaching. A door slammed, there were footsteps. Bernice looked about. 'No hiding place, Doctor.'

He rolled the magazine under his arm. 'We'll brazen it out. At worst, you deal the blow, I'll grab the gun.'

'Oh, can't I grab the gun this time?'

'All right.'

A woman in size six boots walked through the front door. Into the boots were tucked a pair of corduroy trousers, and she wore a polo-necked grey sweater under a tweed jacket. She was elderly, rosy-cheeked, grey-haired, the kind of person who invited hugs. A large pipe was clamped in the left side of her mouth. Two small disc-shaped robots followed her in, humming softly.

Bernice was expecting at least a startled cry followed by something along the lines of a 'who are you I've never seen you before in my life what are you doing in my laboratory' sort of speech.

Instead the woman looked at them, tutted, crossed to her work table and started to sort through some slides.

Chapter 4

Mist hung about the launchpad, masking the alien ship from the eyes of Cwej and Forrester as they approached. There was an unnatural precision to the pools of vapour that increased Forrester's suspicions. As she and Cwej were immersed, and lost sight of each other, she observed, 'It smells of disinfectant.'

Cwej took her hand like a small boy about to cross the road. 'Sterilization procedure, probably. Fumigating the ship.'

Forrester brushed dewy droplets from her jacket and shivered. 'Some of those sort of chemicals can strip lead.' She stamped her boot on the tarmac of the launchpad. 'The Doctor!'

'What about the Doctor?'

'Right now, I want to kill him. If he isn't dead anyway.'

'You wanted to explore that ship,' Cwej pointed out relevantly.

Forrester brushed his objection away. No blame to be apportioned yet, please, the arguments could come later. There were more pressing matters in hand.

Such was the density of cover that she almost walked into the side of the ship. One of its facets loomed over her, its topmost edge fading out in the mist, and close as she now was, Forrester could see the details of its construction. There was a wide inspection hatch, evidence of recent patching or updating of some fuel lines, and a blackened arrow-shaped scar right through the middle.

She indicated the scar to Cwej. 'Somebody's taken shots at them.'

'No, the housing underneath is untouched.' Forrester looked again and swallowed her indignation. He was right, again. The plates to the right of the scar damage were intact. 'Something's been cut away. An exterior unit. Probably a weapon, that'd make sense of the design of this section.'

'You're really starting to irritate me,' said Forrester.

'What have I done?' He really sounded crushed.

A buzzing sound cut across Forrester's reply. Whatever was making that noise was heading straight towards them, moving directly through the mist with unnatural accuracy.

She sensed Cwej's amusement as the thing hovered into view. It was a thin silver disc, floating at head height, metallic, with a sensor mechanism in the form of a square grid at its front.

'State your purpose,' it grated.

'We're travellers,' said Cwej. 'We've come here by accident and we –'

'Welcome to Zamper. You are latecomers. Please proceed to the entrance.' It dipped down and swerved slightly, indicating behind itself.

'No, you don't understand, we didn't intend to come here, and we –'

Forrester squeezed his arm and pulled him away. 'Do as it says. If we're latecomers we're latecomers.' She tugged his hand and they set off in the direction indicated.

The disc thing followed. 'Please hurry to the entrance. Please hurry to the entrance.' It gave Forrester a gentle push, a slight pressure between the shoulder blades that hinted at much greater power.

The outline of the dome she'd seen earlier came into view. A heavy door swung out as they approached and the disc repeated its request. They stepped through and the door swung closed. The space beyond was bare, white-walled, spotless, and smelt strongly of chemicals. A large platform led to another door; at either side of the platform were large green brushes, like mopheads, affixed to metal poles.

'I've never heard of Zamper,' said Cwej. 'You know, the first time a real person sees us, our cover's gone.'

Forrester opened her mouth to reply. It was filled by a blast of liquid that showered from the ceiling with violent force. Instinctively she covered her eyes as the torrent continued, drenching her in seconds. She heard Cwej swearing as he fell over, and steadied herself with effort. 'It's only water!' she tried to shout.

Something brushed her shoulder. One of the big mopheads scrubbed her face, removing a layer of skin, and she took a mouthful of something warm and soapy. Another brush pushed her into Cwej and they were trampolined up and down by the platform, their heavy footwear cushioning the impact as they were rattled and scrubbed. More liquid, much hotter and lavender-scented, was released, stinging her eyes. She recognized it. Shampoo. There was another shower of water. Then more shampoo, and another rinse. Then another substance, tackier. Conditioner. A third rinse.

The brushes retreated. Forrester opened her eyes and watched, coughing, as they folded up and returned to the corners of the still-vibrating platform. She looked down at her soaking jacket and trousers, which clung soggily to her beaten body. Cwej lay near her, in a heap. He was laughing.

Blasts of hot air swept over them, and the platform shook again. Forrester let herself be taken and slumped to the floor, stretching herself out to avoid being bruised.

The hot air clicked off and the room was silent again. She lifted her head and nodded to the grinning Cwej, who was busy getting back into his trousers, which were now dry along with the rest of his clothes. He sniffed his arm. 'Hmm, I smell lovely.'

Forrester grimaced and walked through the door leading off the platform. She found herself in a small metal compartment that was carpeted, mirrored, and lit by a grand chandelier. There was a pot plant in one corner.

Cwej stepped through, and the floor jerked. He held up a finger. 'This is a lift.'

Forrester slumped against the wall and leaned her forehead on one of the mirrors. She felt sick, tired, hungry and very anxious. In the mirror she glimpsed Cwej's alert young face. Some people you just want to slap.

The zoologist looked up from her slides. 'You'll want something for that cut, dear, looks nasty,' she told Bernice. One of the discs responded to the woman's beckoning finger and dropped into her upheld palm a small roll of tape.

There followed a strange, uncomfortable silence. Bernice shot the Doctor a querying glance and he shrugged back. Bernice could only guess that this woman was used to finding total strangers rummaging about her property. There was something reassuring about her confidence; a kind of matronliness.

'I apologize for trespassing,' the Doctor said, slipping into his regulation spiel. 'You see, we are travellers and we've lost our way, and – '

The woman picked up a reader and inserted the roll of tape. Without looking up, she pointed. 'There are some dressings and ointment in that cupboard, top shelf. Everything's labelled.'

Bernice, who realized that her wound was maybe more dangerous than she'd thought, nodded her thanks and went to the cupboard. There were some toiletries on the bottom shelf, arranged in neat rows like the sample jars. Single people, a group in which Bernice counted herself – she viewed the TARDIS as a shared house at the best of times, with the Doctor as a generous but rather erratic landlord – tend either to obsessive neatness or horrific messiness, she knew. On the top shelf was a sealed packet of cotton dressings, and next to it was some ointment in a small jar. She took the items and applied them to her injury, dabbing the cut gently.

The Doctor stood next to the woman and picked up one of her slides. 'Epithelial cells. The arrangement is curiously regular, but that could be anomalous to the species. Are all these,' he waved a hand around in a gesture that encompassed the slides and the specimen jars, 'from those?' pointing to the three animals.

A flicker of doubt passed over the woman's face. She lifted her head and spoke loudly, oddly up to the ceiling, as if there was somebody listening on an invisible upper floor. 'Have I been supplanted? More specialists? You doubt my competence?'

'I'm just interested,' said the Doctor. 'I'm sure your position is secure.' He picked up another slide and squinted at the label. 'And what is your position?' He extended a hand. 'I'm the Doctor, by the way.'

'Doctor?'

'That's right. And the young lady is Professor Bernice Summerfield.'

Bernice nodded, noticing that the ointment seemed to be working and that the throb of the wound was receding. 'Professor of archaeology. None of this gory stuff appeals to me, really.' She held up the ointment. 'This is very good, thank you.'

The woman rose from her stool and came closer. 'Professor Bernice Summerfield?'

'My reputation precedes me?' Bernice asked hopefully.

The woman turned back to the Doctor. 'How did you get here? You aren't a buyer?'

'No.'

'Then who are you?'

The Doctor said patiently, 'Well, as I said, we're travellers and quite by accident we found ourselves on a test flight heading for this planet, so we bailed out, and here we are.' He took the flight recorder from his pocket and waved it over at her.

The woman looked between the Doctor and Bernice. 'Yes. I saw the escape capsules. Why has the Management brought you here?'

'It was an accident. Really, I don't think they have anything to do with it. May I know your name?'

Her face showed a little alarm. She was either insane, not likely, or very scared. Not by them, Bernice decided, but by what they represented. Unauthorised intrusion.

Perhaps the Doctor had been right about the totalitarian state.

'I'm Smith.' She walked to the window and looked out at the rolling purple plain. 'This is Zamper. It's falling apart. People can't just get in here.' She smiled. 'I apologize for my rudeness. Better start again.' She held out a hand. 'Good morning. We're doomed. Would you two like a cup of tea?'

Hezzka disliked the hesitant, burrowing architecture of the parasite Complex, and considered the high ceilings and twisting tubes of the place an apposite reminder of the draughty thinking and duplicity of its inhabitants. Two-legged races, it was established fact, were naturally inferior, an evolutionary mistake that flourished only where superior forms had perished or been suppressed accidentally. Hezzka's grandmother had been a senior researcher in the Chelonian science ministry, working on methods to exploit the many weaknesses of parasites and so eliminate them more efficiently. His treatises had shown the parasites' inability to work co-operatively other than in small packs, and really all that differentiated them from non-speaking animals was their lyricism. Put basically, they spent eighty hundredths of their time blowing chunks out of each other and laying waste to their planets, and the other twenty hundredths producing interminable artistic works on the subject. Apparently this was known as the human condition. Hezzka viewed it as a bit of a sad accident that needed putting in its place. As he and Ivzid strolled along one of the parasites' moving tubeways, which was encased in a kind of cylinder tube, he swept his gaze over the Complex set out below, and sighed to the Goddess. That he was forced to grub about in such surroundings! What would his grandmother have made of it!

The two parasites that had welcomed them to this awful Zamper were walking ahead. Hezzka had concentrated hard on trying to distinguish them. They were about the same height, and were both pink, but one of them had a growth of hair around its mouth. That was the male. Parasites were not allowed the dignity of names, but in these circumstances Hezzka acknowledged that the beast was called Mr Jottipher. The other's top half was swollen, and it wore a briefer garment. That was female, the Secunda. Hezzka's previous dealings with parasites had occurred with him at one end of a cannon and them at the other, and he was unused to reading their faces, but he was almost certain that she known as the Secunda had a mocking manner. It was in her voice also, an affectation to noble rank. Hezzka longed to cuff her, to bring her down with one slice of his claws.

An inappropriate reaction.

The pavement slowed, depositing them at a door that was only just wide enough for Hezzka and Ivzid to pass through. Hovering to either side of the door were two floating discs. 'What are these?' asked Hezzka.

'Our servants,' the Secunda replied. 'They carry out menial tasks and have no identity of their own.'

'They are known as servitors,' added Mr Jottipher.

Hezzka heard Ivzid's deep-throated gargling chuckle, taking him back fifty cycles to the barrack pods. 'The humanoid form is good for menial work, it was said,' said the First Pilot, 'but it is the way of parasites to dispute with each other, reducing their efficiency. These servitors show that you recognize the fact yourselves!' He laughed heartily, baring his teeth.

Neither of the parasites reacted. Hezzka was rather surprised by his own sense of embarrassment at Ivzid's remark.

The Secunda opened the door and led them through into another high-ceilinged area. It was decorated in a bizarre and tasteless style. More of that nauseous human condition probably. Hezzka nodded his approval at the choice of foods laid out here. Blossom, stem and leaf stood in pots around the room, and he munched on a couple to show his appreciation. 'Fine species,' he mumbled.

Ivzid stripped the leaves from a tough-barked shrub. 'Yes. You have done well,' he said grudgingly.

The Secunda went behind a curious low structure that was decorated with pieces of parchment. Behind it was a smaller and even lower structure into which, to Hezzka's astonishment, the Secunda folded her body so that her lower half was rested.

He spat out a leaf. 'Can all parasites do that?'

'Do what, General?'

He waved a foot. 'Fold their bodies so.'

'I'm sitting down, that's all.' She tapped the structure she was resting on. 'This is a chair. And this is my desk. It is not possible for a human to stand at all times.'

Ivzid nodded, trying to look important and knowledgeable. 'I have heard of chairs, General. Another parasite weakness. It is said they need to rest their padded rumps from time to time.'

'You are not resting your rump?' Hezzka asked Mr Jottipher. 'Why not?'

'This is the Secunda's office, General. It is a custom to be seated when to stand is unnecessary. I stand as a mark of respect to you.'

Hezzka shrugged his shell. 'Sit, stand, it makes no difference to me. The concepts are ludicrous.'

'That is not all, sir,' Ivzid said enthusiastically. 'It is known that parasites are unprotected as they sleep.'

Worried that he might start chuckling again, Hezzka said, 'First matters first, as we say on Chelonia. We wish to see the ship, the Series 336c Delta-Spiral Sun Blaster.'

'You shall.' The Secunda angled her head in a gesture Hezzka couldn't read. For her sake he hoped it wasn't amusement. 'And the first matter in this connection is your surety.' She laid Ivzid's confiscated footgun down gently on her desk and picked up a thick wad of parchment sheets. 'The contract signed by your Big Mother specifies a deposit of ten million livres.'

Hezzka nodded to Ivzid. The First Pilot motored forward and slammed the case, an antique embossed with the ceremonial seal of the empire, down on the desk.

The crash seemed to disturb the parasites for a moment, causing Hezzka to recall tales of their sensitivity to loud noise. Mr Jottipher then stepped forward and tried to open the case, his small pink fingers struggling with the locked clasps.

Ivzid pushed him aside. 'No, parasite.' The claws of his front feet tugged at the clasps and the lid of the case swung open on its aged, creaking hydraulics. Hezzka blinked at the brightness of the bounty within. Five rows of stacked guild tokens, edges dazzling in the light from the phosphor globes suspended about the office, rested on a lining of red velvet, each a clawspan wide and marked with the crest of the accursed parasite currency net.

Mr Jottipher ran his scanning device over the case. It gave a satisfied beep. 'All is in order.'

'Of course.' Hezzka tapped the side of the case. 'The contract was most specific. Why gold?'

The Secunda spread her hands wide. 'The Management insists. Imagine, General, if the worst were to happen. The markets are volatile. Currencies can lose their value overnight, perhaps disappear totally. And equipment failure or sabotage can eat away at unreal credit. But gold retains its value whatever, and is the only completely safe way to trade.'

Hezzka sighed. The complexity of the parasites' economic system baffled him, although he'd learnt a lot when setting up Big Mother's account on Pantorus. As far as he could tell, the idea was that each planet or group of planets had its own form of token, and these fluctuated in value depending on the ratio of exports to imports. The bigger currencies dictated the value of the smaller, and the more powerful decided on policies that increased their own success at the expense of the weak. It was a typical parasite arrangement, ill thought-out, confusing and divisive. What Hezzka was certain of was that most of the money sloshing around the markets was unreal, stored on credit records. That included the wealth created by Zamper, which was part-owned, if not controlled, by the descendent companies of the mysterious consortium that had built the wretched place.

'Yet,' he addressed the Secunda, 'the full payment, when it is made subject to our satisfaction with the goods, will be made via credit-coil. I ask again, why gold for the surety?'

Mr Jottipher replied. 'It is to establish trust in our dealings, sir. Ten million livres is a substantial amount towards the cost of your goods. If there should be some –' he licked his lips ' – problem, Zamper has gained that much at least. Similarly, in the extremely unlikely event of any failure on our part to satisfy you, the deposit can be returned intact.' He closed the lid on the gold.

The two machines from the lobby entered the office and, moving with a briskness Hezzka found disturbing, extended thin probes and lifted the case. In the far wall was a hatch, a metre square, opened by the Secunda using a coder terminal. The case was pushed inside by the servitors. Hezzka took a quick glance at Ivzid. The young officer was looking over the proceedings carefully, suspecting everything.

'The deposit will remain here until the full payment is made,' said the Secunda. 'After which, it will be removed to our strongroom.' She held up a hand to prevent the safe being closed, and passed the footgun to one of the machines. 'Store this also,' she ordered. The mechanical thing signalled its understanding with a beep and placed the footgun on top of the case before removing its probe and swinging the safe door shut.

Ivzid snorted and said, 'You can open the safe and take the gold whenever you wish.'

'Not so.' The Secunda held up the coder terminal, a slender grey unit with multi-coloured buttons. 'My loyalty to Zamper is total. And even if I, or any other of the staff here, were to attempt such a thing, we couldn't succeed. The code has already been changed, and the new code will be given by the Management only at the correct time.' She smiled. 'Our operation is infallible.'

Hezzka said, 'It seems plain that your part in the operation is minimal and that your Management rules here.'

'It's not in my character to rule,' said another parasite voice, which seemed to come from everywhere in the room. 'I guide.'

Ivzid reared up. 'Who is that?'

Mr Jottipher pointed to a large oblong screen, previously inert, that faced the Secunda's seating place. Pictured on the screen was the head and shoulders of another parasite, almost definitely a male, with dark hair growth. Hezzka was intrigued by the image. There seemed to be a tracking error; a trail of silver flashes appeared two thirds of the way down the screen.

The new parasite spoke again. 'I am the Management. I'm sure, General Hezzka, you've been made aware of my nature?'

'You are not as other parasites, that I know. I know also that you are notoriously secretive as to your origins, and what constitutes you.'

Ivzid laughed disrespectfully. 'It is another machine carved by the parasites in their own image, to carry out a task for which they are unsuited. Their leader, a machine.'

Hezzka sensed Mr Jottipher's embarrassment at this outburst, and noted the shuffle of bones in the top of the clerk's unshielded back.

'Think what you will,' the Management said smoothly. 'You may not be so scornful when you have seen the ship.'

Ivzid straightened. 'Yes, we must be taken there,' he said eagerly.

'Not possible, I'm afraid.' The Secunda unfolded herself. 'It's forbidden for buyers to enter the construction yards.'

'What is this? Parasite trickery?'

'Certainly not,' said the Management. 'For safety reasons, above all else. The caverns of Zamper can be dangerous. But gentlemen, let me assure you. Please look at the Outscreen.' He tipped his head, indicating the wall behind the Secunda's desk.

A section of the white wall blurred, fogged over, and resolved itself into an image. 'Yard six, gentlemen,' said the Management. 'The largest of the seven, where the final stage of construction approaches. After many months, the Series 336c Delta-Spiral Sun Blaster is taking shape.'

Hezzka moved closer. At first it was difficult to distinguish the scene relayed from yard six. The picture was cluttered and the perspective unclear, and there was only an impression of great activity, some enormous work of industry. The busy scene put him in mind of the artistic works of Zalkaz, who in the high days of the empire five hundred cycles before had covered canvases the length of a hatchery wall with pastoral scenes from the fringe colonies, each minutely-detailed section a separate tableau depicting an aspect of rural life in one of those unsullied outposts. He blinked a couple of times and concentrated, trying to work out the scale of the image. It had been enhanced, presumably by the Management, but there was a fuzzy edging to the objects displayed, as if the yard was underwater. That impression was reinforced by the murky glow of the yard's phosphor plates, which lit the construction area with pathetic chinks of murky subterranean green in the manner of patches of old moss.

Yard six, in accordance with the sketchy information supplied in the brochure, was one of seven gigantic chambers hewn from the rock of the planet Zamper's relatively soft outer igneous crust, above which sat the Complex. The mighty ship, the reason for this most ignominious dealing in the history of the Chelonian First Family, was modestly sized, but suggested great strength. Its central bulk, a bulbous cylinder that contained its huge engines and store of fission materials, leant at an angle across the yard, supported by a cobweb of gantries and lattice-patterned work stations, some of them large and consisting of interlocked sheets of iron, others thin winding strips that traced sections of the craft's skin like silver capillaries or formed fussy ribbons at central junction points. The wing facing the watchers cast a shadow that nearly blocked the view of the ship's lower sections, which Hezzka knew contained the crew quarters and the battle deck. Only an outline was visible, a ghostly imprint of the flanks and the giant swirl of activity below the screen's range.

Hezzka sensed an anomaly, an uneasiness forming in his mind that he found difficult to define. There was something wrong with the scene, something unexpected and unclear that he struggled to identify. He looked again, casting his gaze over the graceful curve of the visible wing, and the thought at last crystallized. He blurted, 'Where are the shipbuilders?'

'Clearly in view, General.' The Management spoke. 'Shall we look closer?'

A section of the yard was magnified. Some animals, small slimy black things, were slurping along one of the gantries, their feelers twitching in time, as though communicating. A shudder ran the length of Hezzka's shell at the sight, and he shuddered again at the realization that the slimy creatures were squirming all over the beautiful new ship. 'What are those things?' he asked, unable to keep the disgust from his voice.

'The shipbuilders,' said the Management.

'We call them the Zamps,' said the Secunda.

The beasts on the screen were now twitching their feelers agitatedly back and forth, burbling to each other. A large sheet of metal descended into the range of the scanner camera, with no signs of support, no trace of a lowering wire or pulley.

'This group are positioning the heat shield plating on the lower left flank,' said the Management.

Neatly, as if placed by an invisible hand, the metal sheet slotted itself into a jigsaw-piece-shaped hole in the ship's side. As it did, the feelers of the Zamps stilled and they slurped back efficiently along the gantry.

'This is some illusion,' said Ivzid. 'A hologram.'

Hezzka gestured for him to keep silent, and addressed the Secunda. 'Explain these shipbuilders. They are natives of Zamper?'

She did not reply, but instead smiled and glanced up at the ceiling. The Management said, 'General, such matters

61

are not discussed here. It is enough to know, more than enough to question. Queries are valueless.'

'What?' Ivzid said. 'You speak in hatchlings' nursery talk.'

'On Zamper,' said Mr Jottipher, indicating the screen displaying the scene in the yard, 'things proceed. They proceed according to their function, under the guidance of the Management, and have done now for nearly five hundred years. The system is correct, and so queries are valueless.'

'These things are simply not important,' the Secunda concluded for him. 'It is enough to know that the Zamps, as we call them, are our shipbuilders. That their productivity, efficiency and adaptability are unrivalled by any of our competitors. That the results can be seen in any of our products.'

Hezzka was unsure if she believed any of this, or was merely repeating some kind of holy edict. He knew that parasites had the capacity for faith. Perhaps the simple-minded things had exalted their Management to the status of a god. 'Who designs the ships? How do these Zamps know how to build as they do?'

No response.

'You are not curious, in the slightest?'

'No,' the Secunda replied.

The screen showing the yard faded, and the Management said, 'I really have to go, gentlemen. Now, I think Mr Jottipher will look after you?' He raised a hand and moved it from side to side, smiled showing perfect teeth, and then was gone.

Ivzid advanced threateningly on Mr Jottipher. The little parasite backed away. 'You will answer our questions now. This Management, what is it? What are these Zamps?' He spat the word, showing that he also had found the small creatures repugnant. 'How can such things build ships?'

'We cannot speak of these things.' Mr Jottipher pointed to the ceiling. 'It isn't allowed. It's unimportant.' He turned to Hezzka. 'You'll want to inspect your rooms, General. We've prepared our most luxurious suite.'

'You haven't answered my questions,' snarled Ivzid.

Hezzka nudged him. 'Later we will talk of this. First, let us be settled.' He spoke slowly to see that Ivzid understood. They would do better not to rile the parasites. He turned back to the Secunda. 'Well met,' he said as diplomatically as he could. 'I hope to see you again soon.'

She nodded. 'And yourself, General.'

Taal sat back, resting the folds of his ample frame in his moulded chair, his ankles crossed on the game control table, regaling Christie with tales of what to expect from life on Zamper. The net was still down; over an hour and a half since it had packed up, the most serious failure yet, and Taal's smalltalk was a device to conceal his own anger and doubt. If the Management had heard his outburst he'd be in for trouble. Later rather than sooner had always been Taal's view on the inevitability of death.

'And you should have been here for the Sprox!' He chuckled. 'You see, we're at the bottom of the heap. Nobody thinks to tell the host and hostess what's going on, who's coming in, who's flying out. One day that door opens and in walks the fully decorated chieftain of the Sprox, old D'Naari-Ylenk himself. He had teeth like tombstones and breath as rank as the whiff from a bowl of Solturian bog-broth. And he wasn't the worst, oh not by a tentacle's-length. You should have seen the size of the emissary from Hotris, we could hardly squeeze him in the lift. Huge hairy shoulders, great long arms, he was horrible.'

Christie laughed politely. 'The new buyers. Who are they?'

'Ah. I was trying to keep them to the back of my mind. Chelonians.'

The change in the girl was extreme. A look of terror passed over her face, and she gripped the arms of her chair with whitened knuckles. 'But they hate all humans!'

'Nothing wrong with that,' said Taal, who relished the guilty thrill of breaking bad news. 'So do I.'

A deep purr rose from the depths of the gaming net and its screens and indicator displays flashed and then steadied. The voice of the network proclaimed, 'The equipment failure has been rectified. Please proceed.'

Taal wiped his brow and stood. 'Back to work, then, my dear.' He reached for the game controls and winced, a hand hovering over the activator button. 'Press this and it might be the end of me.' He nodded upward. 'If he heard me. Victim of another accident. Like poor Nula.'

He pressed the button. The net chattered its readiness. It appeared that he was going to be tolerated a while longer.

'We're not supposed to speak of these things,' said Smith, with a hesitant upward glance. 'I hadn't wanted to admit it, even to myself. But if total strangers can breach the defences, it confirms my belief that the Management is breaking down.' She poured the Doctor another cup of tea, which he accepted graciously. Smith looked again at his kind, crumpled face. He had the high forehead and inquisitive eyes of the scientist, but there was a beaten quality to him. Like a ragged teddy bear, he seemed much loved but exhausted. His genuine nature, after eight years on Zamper, encouraged her own frankness. The forbidden words came easily, giving her the sensation of unburdening a guilty secret.

The Doctor blew on his tea to cool it. 'The Management is an artificial intelligence, then?'

'He's certainly much more than a computer. I think he's centred here, somewhere, but he has powerful links to outside space, and is aware of external events. He represents Zamper on the markets. His personality is highly developed. He watches us, but not all the time. I've noticed that he can't be on two screens at once. Of course, we can't be sure if he is listening in at any given moment, and that makes the surveillance all the more effective. Nula, the hostess here, started to talk freely about the

Management failing, and got herself electrocuted. Faulty wiring on her own part, it was said, but I have grave doubts.'

'How long has this place been up and running?'

'About five hundred years. The shareholders are the biggest corporations. They're contracted not to pry, and mainly they don't, the defence stations are a good deterrent. And of course, nobody can tell when the gateway will open. The details are beamed to the buyers, and if they talk, the contract's cancelled and the gate stays closed.'

'It sounds very efficient.'

'It was, Doctor. Zamper ships are expensive, but they're worth it. A big one lasts ninety years and has enough clout to control the average federation of about five planets nicely. The reputation of Zamper is untarnished.'

The Doctor raised an eyebrow. 'You don't sound very happy about that. What led you to work here?'

'I didn't choose to work for Zamper, Doctor.' She took a deep breath. 'I'm sorry, I haven't been able to discuss these things for some years. I'd been lecturing, I was on a university tour of the Pelopennese. One night I went back to my room in the halls at the academy, and there was a letter waiting for me.' She noted the Doctor's reaction. 'Yes, Doctor, an old-fashioned written letter, envelope and all. Handwritten in ink. It was sealed with the crest of Zamper, that big gold Z. The letter stated politely that I had been selected, that my contract was to last ten years, and that I'd be paid handsomely for my time. Naturally, I was furious. I thought it was a student prank. I tore up the letter, threw it in the dustbin, and slept soundly. And when I woke, I woke in that bed.' She pointed over the Doctor's shoulder, to the far room, where Bernice was resting.

'You were a zoologist?'

'We're not permitted to discuss our previous lives. That's unimportant, so the Management says.' She patted his hand. 'Yes I was.'

'Yes.' The Doctor returned his drained cup to the tea

tray and examined a couple of Smith's slides. 'What is your job here?'

'It's a long and complicated tale, Doctor. And you still haven't explained yourself.'

He avoided the subject, squinting at one of the slides and saying, 'These are from those mollusc creatures you've got penned up in there?' He looked into the specimen case. 'They really are a fascinating species.'

'My brief was to observe them, study them in as much detail as the Management allows. The position was created specially for me; the Zamps hadn't been studied before. That makes me what the others call a "specialist".'

'Zamps? So they are natives?' His brow furrowed and his eyes flicked between the animals and the stained cells on the slide.

'It's just a name,' said Smith. 'They must have been imported here when the shipbuilding business was set up. They've certainly been tampered with along the way. You noticed some signs of the manipulation yourself.'

The Doctor knelt for a closer look at the captive Zamps. 'And through their feelers they exert a telekinetic influence?'

'Of enormous power. In fact, their brains, by design I'd say, are almost entirely geared to producing that effect.' She took down a jar from the shelving and passed it over. 'Look at that.'

He turned the jar, studying the pickled brain inside. 'This side of the organ is swollen,' he pointed out. 'The enlargement looks deliberate. Unnatural. It leaves no room for almost any other more basic function. How does a Zamp find his food?'

'He doesn't. We supply it.'

The Doctor handed back the jar. 'There you are, then. All the facts point to these animals being specifically adapted to form part of this operation. Way back when this place was set up.'

'Probably. The Management has no records, and his creators obviously didn't think it necessary to plan ahead.' She leaned closer. 'Over the last twenty-five years there's been a twenty per cent drop in productivity. The Zamps are slowing down.'

He looked between the slides, the specimens, and her. 'Why?'

His gentle authority and concern, together with his childlike enthusiasm for what had become her life's work, came close to overpowering Smith's suspicions. She was caught in the simple rapture of meeting a stranger, somebody she hadn't expected to see, who knew nothing of what was permitted and not permitted, so much that it almost didn't matter where he'd mysteriously appeared from. But practicality triumphed.

'Doctor, welcome as you are, I'd like to know how you and Bernice managed to get safely through a dimensional portal, past six defence stations, and onto that test ship.'

Several of the regular operators had been coaxed back to the net by Taal, who was generous in the apologies he data-coiled to the signatures lost in the power failure. There was no provision for a check on the equipment, a task that was under the supervision of the Management, so Taal was still uneasy as he welcomed the players foolish or desperate enough to return. The net could crash again at any moment. So far the failures had occurred only during the initial stages of certain games, before any monies staked had been lost or gathered. If there was a shutdown later in play, and the data-coil was wiped, Zamper would find itself liable to a hefty fine from the authorities. That meant nothing to Taal, who was not responsible for any losses, but he was curious to see how the Management would react to such a claim. It would force him to acknowledge his own weaknesses, and that'd be worth seeing.

'Ready for the game,' Christie said brightly. Taal took another look at her. Auburn hair, purple-blushered cheeks, and what a kissable little nose. But no. Such fond thoughts had no place on Zamper.

'Carry on, dear.'

The door of the gaming room opened. Although fourteen years on Zamper, and not without travelling experience before his appointment as host, Taal felt his heart skip a beat at the sight of the two snarling, slavering reptilian creatures entering with Mr Jottipher. Chelonians. Once the masters of an empire that crossed seven star systems, fearsome destroyers of over a hundred and fifty colony worlds along the ninety-third galactic frontier. Christie squeaked. He patted her bare shoulder. 'There there my dear.'

'And here, in the lobby of the guest suites, is our game room,' said Mr Jottipher in a voice that was pitched higher than usual. 'Where entertainment is supplied to our guests.'

The smaller, less wrinkled Chelonian barged past Jottipher and stuck out its wrinkled neck. 'Who are you?'

'I am Taal, your host, sir. This is Christie, our hostess.' It was often best, he knew, to stick up to these types, let them know you weren't afraid, or at least let them know you were trying not to look afraid. 'And you are?'

Mr Jottipher answered. 'This is General Hezzka,' he indicted the older looking Chelonian, whose dyspeptic grunt of greeting reminded Taal of a long-ago parade ground, 'and First Pilot Ivzid.'

Taal bowed, hoping that he wasn't overdoing it, and hoping that the Chelonians would understand the gesture. 'Honoured.'

Ivzid scrutinized the room. He pointed. 'What is that device?'

Mr Jottipher leapt in before Taal had the chance to speak. 'This is the Zamper gaming network, sir. For the edification of our guest buyers as well as those outsiders linked to the data-coil.'

'Outsiders?' queried the General. Christie shook at the rumble of his voice and the sight of his dripping black tongue and rows of serrated teeth. Taal went to pat her shoulder again, but decided against it at the last moment, wary that his paternal concern might be misinterpreted.

'Yes, General.' Mr Jottipher ran a hand along a smooth edge of the net. 'Zamper is designated a neutral space, as you know. Thus it is exempt from the duty restrictions and revenue laws that govern all other sectors of East Galaxy. Neutral status allows us to run a profitable gaming system as a sideline to our main business.'

Hezzka shuffled up to the net. Taal stepped back to let him pass, alarmed at the speed with which the Chelonian shifted itself. 'I see. You wager on this?'

Taal coughed. 'Daily takings average at half one million livres. Gentlemen, there is also an option for your own amusement.' He led them to the direct gaming consoles on the far side of the net. 'From here you can take part yourselves, if you wish.'

'We are officers,' Ivzid said dangerously. 'We have no personal wealth while we serve. It is reserved for our retirement. This network of yours is of no interest.'

'I'm sorry to hear that, sir,' said Taal, in truth much relieved. His knees stopped knocking as Mr Jottipher started to lead the Chelonians away.

The net bleeped.

Hezzka frowned, his leathery brows creasing at the sound. 'What is that? An alarm?'

'It's a signal,' said Mr Jottipher. He stood by the open door, anxious to get them away. 'Just to confirm that the game is ready.'

'Is it so?' Hezzka turned to face Taal. 'You. I wish to observe the game. The sport of parasites interests me. Begin.'

Ivzid looked puzzled. 'But, General – '

'It interests me to see the way the parasite mind works,' Hezzka said curtly. 'You will remain silent as I do.'

Taal noted this exchange with interest. Ferment in the ranks. From what he'd heard, that was the Chelonians' big problem of late. He turned to Christie, ushering her to her position. 'Ready, my dear?'

She nodded and managed a weak smile. The poor girl had turned completely white. One of her blanched fingers pressed the activator.

'On its own, number three,' said the game voice as the first ball was drawn. 'Three and four, thirty-four.'

'I see, a lottery,' Hezzka murmured. 'The numbers are matched with the player's random selection.'

'You have the basics, sir,' called Taal.

'Lotteries are for idiots,' said Ivzid quietly.

'Clickety-click, sixty-six. Eight and one, eighty-one. All the fives, fifty-five . . .'

Alone in her office, the Secunda flicked through available viewpoints on her Outscreen. For months the Management had restricted the interior of yard six while the new ship was constructed, and she had wondered occasionally if the rebellious Zamps had done any work on it at all. The test model had been completed last week and fired last night, some time ahead of schedule, an achievement she regarded sceptically. The Management had rushed the test in order to assure his staff that all was well. She wasn't fooled.

She watched as half of the working herd of Zamps scaled the conical tail section of the ship, burbling and wiggling their feelers at a smaller group crossing their path on a downward-slanting walkway. The second group reached the end of the strut and without stopping secreted strings of slime that secured them to the metal beneath, enabling them to curl over the edge of the strut and descend to safety many feet below.

A servitor entered the office, carrying a thin sheet of silver paper attached to the tip of its probe. 'There was an equipment failure earlier today,' it reported. 'In the gaming centre. The faulty component has been replaced and the incident recorded in the technical log.'

The Secunda was used to reports of this type. It was part of the servitors' way to have her informed of almost everything that went on, no matter how trivial, as an insistent, irritating reminder of her duties. The Management used the servitors for matters he considered of lesser importance, not worthy of a personal appearance. Or, the Secunda reminded herself wryly, for matters he wanted her to think of as of little importance.

This was the sixth equipment failure in a week, the eleventh since Nula's death. It was enormously significant.

She nodded, concealing her reaction.

'There is also a report from the test site, madam.'

'Proceed.'

'Test flight terminated at 09.26 hours at map point 45, sector 14. A team of servitors has been despatched to examine the wreckage. Available results are as expected, except that two of the ship's six escape capsules were dropped ahead of program, including that containing the flight log.'

An unusual fault, and more proof of the Management's erratic behaviour. 'Is that all?'

'There was also a slight deviation in the expected flight path of the test model. This may have been caused by atmospheric influence from the ship of the new buyers. Also, latecomers from the buyers' party have now been escorted through the germwash.' The servitor turned to go.

'Latecomers?' The Secunda's voice halted her servant. 'More Chelonians?' Hell, the Management was supposed to check each ship as it came through. If he'd fouled this up they might all be endangered.

'Two latecomers have been escorted through the germ-wash, madam.'

The Secunda flicked over her Outscreen. The germwash was empty. The lift, then. She selected the interior viewpoint.

Standing in the lift were two humans, a woman in her forties and a much younger man. For the first time in the history of Zamper intruders had come. Had they come in on the Chelonian ship, stowed away somehow? If they had, and the Management had overlooked them, his power was finally over.

And her time had come.

Smith's ointment had worked a treat, and Bernice woke and stretched on the bed with renewed vigour. Time to find out what the Doctor was up to. It was their distance from the TARDIS that was now her primary worry, along with the fate of Cwej and Forrester. Even if they had got back to the TARDIS, the impact of the crash wouldn't have done them any good.

The lab area was empty. The voices of the Doctor and Smith came from the kitchen through the far door. Smith was asking, 'Your ship transcends dimensions?'

'In many ways,' the Doctor replied chattily. 'And I think that may have something to do with it stalling here. Travelling through that spatial barrier of yours may have confused the orientators.'

'It's still difficult to believe you came here by accident.'

'I go everywhere by accident.' Bernice raised an eyebrow at this statement, and was preparing to shout an eminently witty remark through the door to cap it when one of the two blank screens in the lab flashed up an image. The caller was a handsome, middle-aged man in the ages-old suit of the business community.

No use in hiding. 'Hello,' she told the caller brightly. 'You don't know me, my name's Bernice Summerfield, a lot of people call me Benny, well I try to encourage them to –'

The caller's reaction was immediate and strange. After glaring at her in what she took to be confusion, he pressed his fingers to either side of his head, opened his mouth wide, and screamed and screamed.

Chapter 5

'Their security's not good,' said Cwej as the lift continued its slow descent. 'We've walked in to this place.'

Forrester shrugged. 'Doesn't prove anything. And when we get down there, the odds are that somebody'll be waiting. With a gun. A list of questions, at least.' She moved closer to Cwej and hissed in his ear, 'There's a camera behind you, in the plant pot to your left. Don't look now.'

'I don't think we're in any danger,' he whispered back. 'The people here are only shipbuilders.'

'And they're most probably going to think we're spies. We don't know how protective they are.' Her young partner's crushed expression gave Forrester a warm feeling. For the first time that day she felt like she was back in control. It lasted only a moment, until the lights flickered and went out, and the whine of the lift's descent mechanism spluttered and died.

Forrester swore, fearing that the lift would topple unsupported down its shaft. To her almost immediate shame, her reaction was to grab Cwej, as his was to grab her. But the lift steadied. A loud clunk came from the other side of the door; Forrester reasoned that it had settled at a floor intermediate to their destination.

'We're all right, we're all right,' she told Cwej as they disentangled.

'Power failure,' he said optimistically.

'Or somebody's seen us.' She looked towards the camera, but the red light on top had gone out with all of the others.

* * *

The tension in the gaming centre increased as the third set of numbers was calculated. Taal observed several of the signatures signing off as the stakes got higher. 'Can't take the pace.'

Even the Chelonians seemed to have been caught in the spell of the game. Taal heard the General say, 'These games of chance must increase the parasites' adrenal level.'

'Then they should reduce it,' Ivzid replied peevishly.

Taal and Christie exchanged an amused glance. Taal's heart went out even more to the girl and he gave her hand a gentle squeeze. Her nervousness in the presence of aliens was more evidence of her unsuitability for the job of hostess. Why had the Management chosen her as hostess? More to the point, who was she?

Mr Jottipher gave one of his nervous coughs. 'Er, gentlemen,' he said to the Chelonians, 'shall we inspect your quarters?'

'The General wishes to observe the game,' Ivzid growled, 'and so we shall remain, para– Mr Jottipher.'

'Let's get on, shall we?' said Taal. The register for the third round had now stabilized, and he threw the lever to recommence the game.

'Bingo game three commencing now,' said the network, its voice reaching the signatures simultaneously, traversing half the galaxy along hyperspatial compu-link to address the data-coil competitors in their own tongues. It really was a most impressive system, thought Taal. 'Eyes down for a full house.'

Taal checked the monies staked on the tabulator display and whistled. 'Forty-five thou. This'll sort the men from the boys, no mistake.'

'Oh?' The General said. 'You are unsure of the maturity of the male competitors?'

Taal had barely begun to formulate a response to this enquiry when the list of signatures fragmented, the voice of the network issued a sharp, sudden intake of breath, and every light in the gaming centre went out.

74

'What is happening?' Ivzid shouted, with all the vigour of a cynic proved right.

A shudder ran through Taal's portly frame at the thought of being so close to the Chelonians in this pitch blackness. Christie whimpered and caught his arm. Despite the desperate nature of their predicament, he couldn't help feeling happy about that, but then he'd always been a mercenary swine.

'A temporary equipment failure, I'm sure,' Mr Jottipher said with transparent confidence.

'Another total blackout.' Taal scrabbled for the secondary system controls on his console. He flicked the row of switches to the 'on' position, and nothing happened. 'On primary and secondary systems.' He turned his head to where he guessed Mr Jottipher was standing, and said, 'How many equipment failures would it take to cause this, eh?'

'You mustn't talk like this, Taal,' hissed Mr Jottipher.

'Why not? He can't see or hear us now. Here, Jottipher, perhaps the end has come, d'you reckon?'

'It's merely an equipment failure!' Mr Jottipher shouted back.

'I take you to mean that your Management is failing.' Taal realized, with a sudden shiver, that the Chelonian General was addressing him. 'That is your belief?'

'We have total faith in the Management,' said Mr Jottipher hurriedly. 'I assure you, gentlemen, that this is merely a temporary equipment failure.'

Taal slammed a pudgy fist on the console. What if this was the end? The Management controlled every system. If he was dead, then he, Jottipher and Christie were locked in the dark with two of the most vicious creatures encountered by humanity.

Ivzid roared, turning Taal's stomach to a wobbling jelly. 'This fault in your equipment must be rectified,' he said. 'I do not like this.'

When the screaming started, the Doctor saw the look of horror that flashed over Smith's face. He followed her into the lab, where Bernice was backing away from the flickering Inscreen. She held up both hands. 'I didn't do anything, honest. I don't think he likes my face.'

The Doctor examined the image. The man he took to be the Management was barely visible between flashes of interference, but the screams, hollow and drawn-out, were agonizing. The Doctor's cluttered memory flashed up an image in response to the sound; a teenage solider in the Crimea, both legs blasted off. coughing up blood, quivering horrors on every side.

'I feared this.' Smith stepped back from the screen, her hands knitted together between long strands of hair. 'The final breakdown.'

'Brought on by our unexpected arrival,' the Doctor surmised. 'It didn't recognize you,' he told Bernice. 'It's learning an important lesson. It isn't infallible.'

Bernice raised an eyebrow. 'Cheesy computer/child analogies aren't what I expect from you, Doctor.'

'The Management isn't a computer. In fact, I'm rather worried about its response to us. It may decide that as we don't fit into the scheme of things here . . .' He mimed a throat-cutting gesture.

'Sir,' Smith called to the Inscreen, illogically slapping her palm on the vision plate. 'Sir, I can explain. These people are friends.' There was no reply, but the screaming went on, losing its human sound and becoming a strangulated electronic wail. Smith told the Doctor, 'Over the last couple of months, there have been more and more equipment failures, a power loss last week. We all knew this was coming, but of course we couldn't discuss it.' She kicked the wall, adding desperately, 'It can't fail. It controls everything.'

As if in response to her words, the Inscreen flashed and fizzled. For a moment it was blank. Then, as if nothing had happened, the screen brightened like an archaic TV set and the Management returned, immaculate and smiling broadly. 'Smith, you have new friends. Would you care to introduce me?'

The Doctor studied the image intently. It was a simple

holographic animation, convincing enough but common-place for the sixtieth century. Merely an outlet, then, for the real Management, the mass of perfectly co-ordinated responses detailed and programmed hundreds of years ago by the consortium. A vast, intelligent network that could simultaneously interface with systems across the length of the galaxy, interact as a personality with its staff, and sustain a complex shipbuilding facility in a pocket universe of its own. It had the wealth and the wherewithal to reach out into space, grab people from their lives, and bring them here to fulfill new roles; it was orientated to create maximum profit for its shady shareholders; it, apparently, was falling apart.

'This is the Doctor, and Bernice.'

'Ah. Doctor who?'

'I'm Professor Bernice Summerfield,' Bernice said quickly.

The Management closed his eyes for a moment, as if thinking. 'Ah, yes, of course, the author of *Similarities in Proto-Cultural Artifacts of the Second Dynasty of the Zyrs?*'

Bernice gulped. 'It was actually published? I only wrote it for a bet. There aren't any similarities in proto-cultural artifacts of the second dynasty of the Zyrs.'

'That's what the critics said.' He smiled at the Doctor, who couldn't resist smiling back. The force of the thing's personality was daunting. 'The Professor's displacement from her own era would seem to confirm my research into your background, Doctor.'

'Really?'

The Management closed his eyes again. 'The Doctor and the TARDIS?'

The Doctor thought. 'I dare say.' He was slightly put out. Being recognized was a rare occurrence, despite his long relative history of interference in the affairs of the universe, and it robbed him of a usual advantage. He was unlikely to be underestimated by the Management.

'Welcome to Zamper, both of you. This visit could be timely.' He spoke as though he considered their presence of little importance. To Smith he said, 'The Doctor and the Professor have access to your research. Full access.'

Smith bit her lip. 'My new findings – '

'Full access, Smith.' He tipped a wink. 'Enjoy your stay, Doctor, and feel free to look around. You may even see people you recognize.' The Inscreen flickered again briefly. 'You must see the – the cave, Doctor.' The Management's smile remained, but his voice was that of a desperate man. 'You must help. You must help. We will – I must – they have – '

He blanked out.

The Doctor considered his position. The Management had taken only moments to overcome its shock and fit him into his scheme of things on Zamper. It would be as well to play this new role, for the moment.

'Well, he seems to have got over the upset rather well,' Bernice observed. 'Pardon me, but I don't know anything about anything.'

'I'll explain later.' The Doctor turned to Smith. 'What's all of this about new findings?'

Smith held up the reader into which she had inserted the tape delivered by the now-departed servitors. 'I've found something. A cave that's appeared from nowhere, in what should be solid rock. Classified as cave 74D.'

'Thank goodness it's a cave and not an item of lingerie,' Bernice muttered.

'This is a recording taken by servitors I sent down there.' Smith hesitated with her hand on the reader's activator and looked the Doctor in the eye. Her directness appealed to him.

'You're wondering,' he said, 'if I can be trusted. If my arrival isn't part of some larger plan of the Management's. A test.'

She clicked her tongue. 'After eight years here, suspicion becomes a habit.'

Moments after the power failure, Hezzka had overlaid his eye-facets with an enhancement membrane, which picked out the inert gaming structure, the sweating parasites, and the sour-faced snarls of Ivzid. As the minutes passed slowly the atmosphere in the darkened room grew more tense, with Mr Jottipher folding his body and gnawing at his hands, and Ivzid threatening all with furious retribution. The stripling was becoming tiresome.

'How can we trust this ship we are to buy, General?' he said loudly. 'These parasites are stupid. Their technology plainly backward.'

Hezzka sank inside his shell. 'You forget their sensors, which cracked open our auto-log. You want them to be stupid, yes Ivzid, but you must realize that they are not.'

Ivzid spluttered, 'With respect, sir, in my grandmother's day, such words would've earnt you a half-week in the pillory.' A line of steaming dribble oozed over his chin, its heat trace flaring in Hezzka's enhanced vision-field.

Hezzka forced down his anger. 'And even today, Ivzid, your words could put you up on a charge.' He shuffled closer to his insubordinate First Pilot, and spat in his ear, so as not to let the parasites overhear, 'You must learn to think clearly. Do not underestimate the parasites as your grandmother and his kind scoffed at the usurper. Wars are for winning, boy. And we will win only by understanding the enemy and his weaknesses.'

'I stand corrected, General,' Ivzid said with bad grace.

The lights came back on, and the gaming device hummed, ticked and glowed brightly. Hezzka slid back his enhancement membranes, and noticed for the first time that those called Taal and Christie had laid hands on each other. He wondered if this was part of the ludicrously complex and anatomically vile parasite mating ritual, the lurid details of which had fuelled barrack-pod jests for generations. He hoped not. 'The failure has been rectified?'

Mr Jottipher hurried over. 'Yes, General. Everything is back to normal. I must apologize for the inconvenience.'

Ivzid laid a foot on Mr Jottipher's leg. The clerk flinched at the touch, and for a moment, as the parasite's face twisted with fear, Hezzka's heart beat faster and his internal organs were suffused with sensation, a feeling akin to rapture and almost religious in its intensity. Yes, the sensation urged Ivzid, destroy this puny creature, rip its head off, let us see the life-juices spurt from its severed limbs.

'Then apologize,' said Ivzid.

'I – I – I, er, I apologize for the inconvenience.'

'Good.' Ivzid removed his foot, licked his chops, and said, 'Our rooms, Mr Jottipher?'

He beckoned them away. 'Yes, gentlemen. This way, please.'

'Heck.' Taal much preferred sitting to standing, and surely no chair had ever felt as comfortable. The slavering jaws of the younger Chelonian surpassed all of the ugly sights upon which he'd set eyes. It wasn't the creature's savagery that unsettled him; after all, he'd faced the Sprox in his time. But the Sprox and the Hotris and the human race, come to that, shared the denominator of corruptibility. In Taal's experience, everybody and everything had a price; he himself had traded his freedom for twenty years in exchange for a payment he now very little expected to see. But the Chelonians were an exception. There was no way to reason with such beasts, nothing to be haggled. And the Management, if it lasted, was going to hand them a Series 336c Delta-Spiral Sun Blaster, packed with enough technology to rip a system apart.

He realized that Christie's hand was still held in his. 'They're worse than I ever imagined,' she said. There was a high colour in her cheeks that brought out Taal's deeply-buried protective streak. He passed her his hanky. 'I've seen tapes of Chelonians, but only the friendly ones. My friend Billie said that there were – oh.' She looked up fearfully. 'I forgot, we mustn't talk about our lives before.'

Taal considered a moment, then abandoned the last of his doubts. 'Stuff him,' he said, shaking two fingers upwards but still keeping his voice low. 'That's the second total power loss. This place is cracking up.'

Christie withdrew her hand and looked away from him, her mistrust obvious. She must think this a test, Taal realized. He thought back fourteen years to his first weeks on Zamper. The hostess, Lotte, had been older than him, the Secunda bearded and aged, Jottipher as he had always been. Taal had been suspicious of all about him. So Christie's behaviour was understandable.

'Listen, love,' he said, edging closer. 'We've got to trust each other. What if I tell you something about the time before, then you?'

She stood and backed away from him, towards the exit. He sensed that she wanted desperately to believe him, but couldn't be sure. He tried to look honest, but he'd never been very good at that. 'I'm going to my room,' she said, and left.

The Secunda was in her office when the power loss struck. Immediately, she forced herself to remain calm, and simply to wait. She counted the minutes. If the Management was absent for twenty minutes, then she could proceed. Until then, best to wait.

The darkness was total. She rested her hands on her desk, and re-ran the details of her plan. If this was the end she couldn't have wished for better timing. For the first time in many years, a feeling of real hope surged within her. In just a few hours she could be free.

Free, or dead.

She remembered space, the sensation of leaving one world and travelling to another. In the time before, as head of Gilby Co, she'd grown used to the wonders beyond the portholes of executive class cruisers; the dust cloud, covering like a muslin veil the sparkling jewels of clustered red dwarfs that looked near, but were in truth scattered between separate systems, joined only by perspective. She'd not even noticed them, turned her eyes back to the reports and profit charts resting on her knee. She'd taken as much account of the glories of space as she had the faces of her servants.

When the lights returned, she exhaled deeply. Seventeen and a half minutes. As if nothing had happened, she straightened the papers on her desk and returned to work, signing the certificate of authenticity for the scanner report on the Chelonian shuttle. Inwardly she was cursing bitterly.

Next time, then.

'The equipment failure has been rectified,' were the Management's first words to her. 'Everything's up and running.' He was daring her to question him.

'Good,' she said, not looking up.

'And we have new visitors.'

'Sorry?' She rested her pen.

'New guests. They must be made welcome. I know you've seen them.'

'Yes, in the lift. I assume they're here at your invitation. More specialists, friends for Smith?' She wasn't trying to keep the bitchiness from her voice.

'Treat them well.' The lines of distortion across the Inscreen's image was enlarging, making it difficult to see the Management's eyes through the interference. 'There are two others with Smith now, the Doctor and Bernice. Treat them well, treat them well, treat them well.'

'The Doctor and Bernice.' The Secunda rolled the names around her tongue as the flickering Inscreen faded. Damn them. Random elements, specialists that could throw her plan into disarray.

Mr Jottipher led the Chelonians into the luxury twin suite, feeling sure as he did that they were unlikely to appreciate the vital colours of the trailing damask curtains, the complementary vastness of the valley of Yollofos captured in the holo-window, the pleasurably puffed pillows at the heads of the beds, or the inbuilt walk-in shower unit. 'Here we are, gentlemen. This is compartment fourteen, our luxury suite.'

The vulgar Ivzid snapped a plant from its pot and the thing disappeared down his gullet with a splintering crunch. 'There will be no more power losses?'

'A most rare occurrence,' Mr Jottipher stuttered, shaping the truth to suit him. 'Zamper prides itself on its efficiency.'

Hezzka rested one of his front feet on the nearest bed and tested the springs. 'What are these objects?'

'They are beds, on which to rest yourselves.' Mr Jottipher felt very sick. He couldn't picture a resting Chelonian.

'Ah yes.' Hezzka nodded. 'I have heard of this. It is our custom to rest suspended.' He used his front foot to indicate a swinging motion.

'Sir means a hammock.'

'That is usual.'

'But,' said Ivzid, 'officers have no need for webbing when they rest. A good officer withdraws, but maintains his alertness.'

Mr Jottipher wasn't at all sure what Ivzid meant, but wasn't going to ask for clarification. For a few moments back in the gaming centre, with that idiot Taal shouting recklessly up at the Management and trying to pull them all down, he'd really thought Ivzid was going to spring. It was only his professional detachment that had prevented Mr Jottipher from bursting into tears or running for his life. 'Very well,' he told the Chelonians. 'Now, the food unit is there,' he pointed to the corner, 'and if you require anything else, please call,' he rang the bell that dangled on a long string between the beds, 'and a servitor will be with you instantly.' He backed away as he spoke, not expecting any thanks for the day's efforts.

None were offered. Mr Jottipher babbled, 'Well, until tomorrow, gentlemen,' and hopped through the door before they could stop him. On the other side, alone at last, he collapsed against a wall, chest heaving in and out, heart pumping fast. He felt as if his eyes were going to pop from his head, and his legs curled with cramp. This had unquestionably been the worst day of his career. And the worst thing of all was, it wasn't over yet.

Hezzka tapped his chin thoughtfully as he re-examined the bed. 'I think I understand the parasites' rest system.'

Ivzid was investigating their quarters. He scoffed at the lurid hologram – 'revolting vista' – and closed the heavy drapes to block it, then shuffled over for a look at the glass cabinet in the corner. 'This apparatus seems to be some kind of weapon,' he said, unhooking a slim white device at the end of a twisted silver cord.

'It is a sprinkler.' Hezzka took it from him and returned it to its fitting. 'Parasites need regular sprinkling, you will remember. Else they become infested by carrion insects.'

'Infestation upon infestation.' Ivzid looked around the suite, then came closer to Hezzka and whispered, 'Their Management thing, is it watching us here?'

Hezzka increased the sensitivity of his ocular enhancements and turned a slow shuffling circle, keen to detect any trace of a recording or spying device. The walls beneath the hangings were bare, and the corners of the room were clean and empty. He stopped. There was an object he could not account for, lying on top of the resting-bed sheets. Hezzka held up a foot to motion Ivzid to silence, and advanced cautiously. The object was small and rectangular, and seemed to be composed of shredded cocoa solids encased in a metal wrapper. Gently, he opened the wrapper. Revealed was a collection of thin wafers. Embossed on the front of each was a golden Z.

'It is perhaps a gift,' Hezzka theorized. 'Think of our own custom of leaving a meal for the next user of a withdrawal pod.'

'It is very small for a gift,' said Ivzid.

Hezzka munched on a corner of the thing. 'It is too sweet,' he said, spitting pieces of the thing out. 'If such things are the delicacies of parasites, small wonder they do not thrive.' He threw the thing aside, yawned and crabbed closer to the bed. 'Ivzid, I am near my withdrawal time. Perhaps I should use this resting bed of the parasites.'

'Their ways are of no interest,' said Ivzid. 'Why make a study of vermin? They are a blight, a nuisance.'

Hezzka stretched his limbs and yawned again. He'd been on edge for the past week-length, and a few hours' withdrawal was long overdue. Ivzid's query was typical of the thinking of the officer class. 'Why bother to study

84

anything?' he replied. 'It is a good thing to be curious, to enquire.' As he spoke he climbed up on the bed. Far too soft a surface, but suitable for the puny frame of a parasite. How could the things stand to be wrapped in softness like this? Most unnatural. 'If all thought as you do, Ivzid, we'd still be living in mudflats.'

The reply was a grunt. 'There's nothing to be learnt from parasites.'

Hezzka withdrew his back feet and put his shell temperature up a notch. 'Nothing we can learn from their ships, their technology?' He fixed Ivzid with a significant look. 'Nothing to be learnt from their shipbuilders?'

'The slime-beasts?' Ivzid recoiled. 'All slime-beasts are vile.'

'But these have a strange power. A power that we could put to good use. Withdraw on that, First Pilot.'

The lift stopped at last, the floor settling with a definite-sounding thump. Forrester grimaced. 'Here we go, then.' Cwej smiled back, and she was glad to see him looking jumpy.

The door slid back and they emerged into a bright white spherical room. Some kind of reception lounge, thought Forrester as she looked around the deep leather sofas. Oddly, the neatness of the room was spoilt by the disfigurement of the potted plants that lined the holo-wall. Branches and leaves looked as if they had been savaged by some ferocious creature.

Hovering in the centre of the room was another of the flying discs. 'Welcome, friends of the Doctor,' it told them. 'Welcome to the Complex.'

Forrester felt almost disappointed. Stupid. If the Doctor was alive, and it looked that way, things were a lot better than she'd anticipated. It felt wrong, really badly wrong, to have her pessimism thwarted at every turn. In a few hours, she thought, she'd be proved right.

'Can we see him?' Cwej asked the disc.

'Later. The Doctor is busy.'

Probably having his arms torn out. 'There's another

member of our party,' Forrester began, instinctively advancing.

'Professor Summerfield is with the Doctor.' Something inside the disc clicked and beeped, and the door leading from the room slid open. Forrester caught a glimpse of a travelling pavement just outside, and the edges of some large structures.

Cwej followed the disc with an expression of complete trust and a relieved smile. Forrester fell into step, shaking her head.

'These are the deeper caverns.' Smith licked her lips in anticipation of what might be revealed, and checked the recorded images with her mapscreen. 'Coming in to cave 74D.'

Bernice was unimpressed. Blurred and distant and dark, the reader's inbuilt holo-projector showed a herd of the Zamp creatures slithering through a split in a looming batholith. She studied them more closely. It appeared that the Zamps at either edge of the herd were being squashed against the sides of the gap. The pictures were so bad it was hard to be sure.

Smith tutted and shook her head 'The servitors run on a basic reaction program.' She tapped the side of her head. 'Not too bright.'

The Doctor looked up from the eyepiece of the microscope, and absently slid in another slide. 'Hmm. Has anybody ever taken a look inside one of these servitors?'

'None of the staff would even try, and the buyers would lose their deposit instantly if they did. Although we're all curious.'

The servitors' cameras zoomed close in on a smaller group of Zamps squeezing themselves through a cavern wall. 'They're going to spawn?'

'No,' said Smith, 'their egg chamber is on one of the higher levels. The cave in those pictures is 72 on level D, not that far from the construction bays. The Zamps are heading across in their droves, after centuries of inactivity.'

The projector blanked out, then flashed up a picture so

86

strange and unexpected that it took Bernice a few moments to accept it. There was no visible point of reference, nothing to put the scene in perspective, and that reminded her of the concealed patterns in trick three-dimensional pictures. She looked away, looked back.

At the borders of the projector's range were recognizable strata of rock, bulging outward to form twisted, jagged shapes that fringed the scene within like a frame. Bernice shivered. Trickling through crevices in the cave walls were slow-moving herds of Zamps, their feelers twitching feverishly. Trails of slime formed a sticky underlay that coated the surfaces of rock. The cave, which she estimated to be about five hundred metres high, was swarming with Zamps, their shining black bodies glistening, one on top of another. Squelching and squirming and writhing wetly, packed into the available space, clinging like abandoned sea shells along the walls and the roof of the cave. And crawling all over the artifact in the centre of cave 74D.

The artifact was two thirds the height of the cave, and bulged to either side until, at its widest point, it almost touched the sides. From what she could see under the mass of Zamps, Bernice judged it to be vaguely cylindrical. It was metal and irregularly arranged, a random shape that suggested a mindless, purposeless natural growth. There was something of the crystal about the way its metal planes might abruptly jut out to a sharpened point, or flatten and then loop, or taper into small spines. It was decidedly alien.

The Doctor squinted at the image, his face creased with curiosity. 'What is that?'

The travelling pavement was several hundred meters long, and sloped at a gentle angle from the reception sphere. Forrester allowed herself to be carried along, and used the journey as a chance to orientate herself. The Complex was vast but empty. There were many more such pavements, every one encased in a clear plastic tube, ranged between tall windowless structures.

'Where are your masters?' Cwej asked the disc awkwardly. 'I mean, are there any living beings here? Flesh and blood?'

The disc didn't answer. Cwej turned to Forrester and shrugged. 'Not very talkative.'

Forrester waved a hand in front of the disc. It didn't react. 'It's a basic function model. Which means there must be a controlling force. More adaptable machines at least.'

'An automatic shipyard?' Cwej nodded enthusiastically. 'But then why do they need an atmosphere? But then who's to say there was an atmosphere down here before we arrived? It all makes sense. Shame you've got it wrong, really.'

'I'm sorry?'

He pointed through the clear tubing. Across, in the pavement running upwards next to their own, a short, fussy-looking bearded man dressed in a crumpled grey suit was staring at them with a look of sheer terror. That look couldn't have been reproduced by any android, no matter how sophisticated its innards.

Forrester was rather relieved to be proved wrong on this occasion. She'd had visions of a malevolent blob of green jello at the centre of the Complex, directing its servants with monstrous glee. The Doctor had been through some mementoes of previous adventures with her, and confirmed her long-held suspicion that the most cliched solution was usually the correct one. But no robot-controlling mastermind, this fellow, just very scared and very ordinary. Very human. Cwej scissored his arms over his head in the recognized sign of galactic greeting. The short man disappeared from view, looking even more horror-stricken.

'Not used to visitors, I suppose,' said Cwej.

The pavement slid into another section of tubing and juddered upwards a few hundred metres. It stopped before a plain metal door. The disc ushered them forward. 'Please step forward, friends of the Doctor.'

'Er, what's through there?' asked Cwej.

'Please step through, friends of the Doctor.' The door slid apart.

After a few seconds, Forrester slapped her hand on Cwej's shoulder. 'Might as well.'

Beyond the door was a short dark passage. Another set of doors slid apart, admitting them to a large room decorated in the Complex's prevailing style. Bare and white. In the centre of the room was a machine that Forrester recognized immediately. The exact model was unfamiliar, but the flashing multi-coloured lights, whirling spiral displays and winking bars of neon signalled its status as a larger than average fruit machine. A larger than average man in his middle fifties stood before it, dressed in a bright red suit that only just met about his middle. Its colour matched his ruddy cheeks, and there was a kind of jolliness about him that complemented the machine perfectly. He could have walked into any pleasure park in human space and not looked out of place. But there was something false about his welcoming smile, a suppressed anger that Forrester's experience marked as dangerous.

'Welcome to Zamper,' he said, with open insincerity. 'You're guests of the Management, I hear. Specialists? Repairmen? I think you might be a little late.'

The frantic rapping on her office door could not have been made by anyone other than Mr Jottipher, thought the Secunda. It was hesitant and insistent at once, nervousness overcome by simple devotion. She admitted him.

He burst into the room. 'Madam, I've just seen strangers!'

It was her task to calm him, as always. 'Relax, Mr Jottipher. The strangers are guests of the Management.' She nodded to her Outscreen, which showed the newcomers – from their overheard conversation as they were escorted in, she had gathered their names were Cwej and Forrester – talking to Taal in the gaming centre. 'They are specialists.'

Mr Jottipher's shoulders slumped with relief. He dabbed

at his brow with a handkerchief pulled from an inside pocket. The Secunda gestured for him to sit. 'I'm deeply sorry, madam, but today has been rather stressful.'

She regarded him with a degree of affection. 'The Management is in total control.'

'I am glad.' He sat up, tried to straighten his collar. 'What with the new buyers, and the equipment failure, and poor Nula, and the strangers, I was rather worried.'

'Understandably.' The Secunda came to a decision. The time had come. She took a sheet of blank paper from the file on her desk, picked up her fountain pen and began to write with the scratchy nib. It was a simple message, four sentences. She passed it over the desk. Puzzled, Mr Jottipher took it.

This is NOT a test. The Management is dying. I intend to leave. Will you join me?

Bernice stood outside the hut, watching Zamper's purple sun setting between the peaks of a distant mountain range. The beauty of the view made her feel drowsier still, and she yawned and stretched, the muscles in her arms and legs aching with cramps. All at once she realized how tired she was, and she slipped back in to the lab, where the Doctor and Smith remained engrossed in a huddle over the specimen cases. Bernice was surprised to feel an odd pang of envy. She was used to being the Doctor's *confidante* on scientific matters, and it felt strange to see him chatting away to somebody else.

'So, the caverns, the construction yards, are directly beneath the Complex?' he was asking, tapping a finger on his chin. 'The sub-herd of Zamps leaves the yards and swarms off to this new cave of theirs.' He was crackling with energy. 'You see, I think we really need to see that object or whatever it is, up close. It really is fascinating, fascinating.'

Smith grunted. 'It's too dangerous, old chap. Those caverns are treacherous.'

'I've seen a lot of caves in my time,' the Doctor assured her.

Bernice said, 'Doctor, I'm tired, and I want to see how Chris and Roz are.' She turned to Smith. 'May I borrow your buggy? If you give me directions I'm sure I can find my way to the Complex.'

'Better than that. You can program it to take you there,' Smith replied kindly, sliding from her stool and leading Bernice back outside by the arm. Next to the steering wheel of the buggy was a series of colour-coded controls and a mapscreen. Smith pressed a blue button, the map screen crackled and glowed, and the motor started, lifting the chassis of the vehicle a metre off the floor. Warm air blew from twin vents on the dashboard, reassuring Bernice as she climbed up, swung herself in and settled before the wheel. 'I use it to bring my supplies over from the Complex. It should take you about fifteen minutes to get across.'

Bernice smiled. 'Thanks. Look after the Doctor, won't you?'

'I will.' Smith patted Bernice on the back, then the nose of the buggy clicked up, and it zipped off across the darkening plain. Bernice turned to wave goodbye to Smith, but the woman was already a tweedy dot. It took a while for Bernice to adjust to the buggy's speed, and its ability to navigate itself over and around clumps of rock just when it seemed that to crash was unavoidable. As the minutes passed, the tensions in her exhausted body unknotted. Her head fell back against the padded rest, and she slowly fell asleep, lulled by the warm air blowing across her face, her eyelids closing as the buggy carried her smoothly through the twilit landscape.

Smith found the Doctor hunched over her workbench, an inky fountain pen gripped in his right hand, her own stylus gripped equally tightly in his left, both hands writing at a furious pace over sheets of scrap paper. He muttered as he worked, occasionally tapping his temples in exasperation and leaving inky streaks across his brow. From time to time he looked between his work and a series of her specimen slides that he had lined up in an order that to her made no sense. She came closer, looked over his shoulder. In the fading twilight she saw reams of an unfamiliar notation. Gently she said, 'Bernice has gone off to the Complex.'

He nodded, but said nothing and continued working. Smith turned on the desklamp; in its white glare the Doctor appeared quite mad. She put the kettle on, and as she spooned tea into the strainer, found herself smiling. There was something very reassuring about the Doctor's presence. Other people tended to make Smith rather uncomfortable. The basic problem was that they weren't enough like her. The Doctor was. What they shared was dedication to science.

He was suddenly at the divider of the kitchenette, waving his notes at her. 'My admiration for the builders of Zamper grows ever greater. The brain has been enlarged, either through selective breeding, or hormone stimulation.'

'Or both,' she said, attending to the whistling kettle.

'Yes, yes. Now,' he consulted his notes, 'a series of thick ganglions connect the cortex to the section of the brain that regulates the creatures' psychic powers.'

Smith nodded, pouring the boiling water.

'So. What we have here is a custom-built component. Part of the construction process. An essential part. Alone, a Zamp would be helpless.'

'Isolate them and they die in only a few hours.'

'I thought so. But in a herd, their concentrated powers are put to use.' He took one of the slides from his pocket. Taped to it was a tiny silver strand. 'Do you know what that is?'

'Each Zamp has one, coiled around its cortex. I can't be sure, but I think it's what links them to their herds, what keeps them together. A sort of transistor, you might say.' She led the Doctor back into the lab, put down the tea tray, and fished out some holo-pictures from her desk. Handing them to the Doctor, she said, 'At almost each hatching, there are a couple of runts. They're left to die. The others move away from them, start to orientate, and then form a herd.' She pointed to a detail on one of the shots, the halved section of a brain. 'Every runt that I've examined has a lesser developed or malformed transistor strand, see. I don't think the healthy Zamps regard the runts as part of the species.'

The Doctor nodded. 'The strand is essential, because it's the supreme addition to the original creature. A magnificent feat of genetic adaptation. It keeps the herds together, yes, but that's not its only purpose.'

Smith felt like jumping up and down and punching the air. It was such a joy to discuss these matters, freely, with somebody who understood. The Doctor's dropping from the skies was like an answer to a prayer. 'Go on.'

He smoothed out his notes on the bench again, and ran his finger down to a particular section. 'A Zamp's motivation is to form a herd. To form a group of components. When enough are gathered, there is sufficient shared telekinetic power to proceed. That could be when the ship designs come through.'

'A telepathic image, a telepathic instruction, conveyed by electronic means?'

'I would say that's almost impossible, even for the miraculous level of technology behind this place. There would have to be an organic component, a thinking component, in there somewhere.' He leant closer, and whispered, 'It's not what that tells us about the Zamps that's important, really. But it reveals quite a lot about the Management.'

'It's organic?'

'Part of it has to be.'

As Taal assigned the two new specialists to quarters, he was aware of a long-dormant instinct reviving. Whenever one of them was behind him he felt a tension in his back and an itch between his shoulder-blades. He strained to identify this almost forgotten feeling.

'I can give you a place in apartment thirteen,' he told

them, consulting the room roster. 'It's ready for occupation, fortunately. Running water, breakfast facilities.'

The male, the boyish Cwej, was examining the gaming network. 'And you play games on this?'

'There is an in-house facility for visitors, yes.'

'Can you switch it on? I'd like to try.' The lad was bursting with youthful enthusiasm. He nipped quickly between the input stations, examining the differing attractions of each console with a knowledgeable air.

'Unfortunately,' said Taal, steering him towards the door, where his colleague was waiting, 'the network's gone off-line for the day. We'll be opening up again at nine tomorrow morning. If your schedule permits I'll be glad to show you about the system.'

The woman, Forrester, spoke. Her diction was clipped, and Taal couldn't imagine her without her frown. 'Every day you run this casino?'

'Every day.' Taal wondered why she made him feel guilty, as if he was being interrogated. The woman had a powerful air of authority. 'Here on Zamper we're neutral, you see. Outside the revenue laws.'

Laws. The word prodded his searching subconscious, and he realized. These two were police. The way they looked everything up and down should have made it obvious. When Forrester had walked in, the first thing she'd done was run her eyes over him for concealed weapons. It couldn't have been more obvious. Taal felt a little disappointed with himself.

They weren't technicians, then, as he'd assumed. But why would the Management give access to police?'

He indicated the inner door. 'Yes, now you want to go through there, along the hall, and through to apartment thirteen.'

Forrester sneered, as if she could see right into his mind. 'Thanks, Taal.' She left. Cwej smiled and shrugged, an apology for her behaviour, and followed.

Mr Jottipher's bearded mouth twitched and he rubbed the back of his neck. The Secunda's suggestion had startled him. He was certain that her desire to leave was genuine, because over the years of their acquaintance he had learnt that she was resourceful and determined and usually right. If he had thought to consider the situation and her response, he might have predicted this. What he couldn't understand was her eagerness to involve him, and her apparent disregard for her own safety. The eyes of the Management could be on them, even now.

'Madam,' he said quietly. 'Is it wise to discuss these matters so openly?'

She smiled confidently. 'Do you trust me?'

'Of course, madam.'

'My loyalty to Zamper is beyond question?'

'Yes.'

'As is yours. If you were the Management, then, would you think to spy on a meeting between your two most trusted employees?'

Mr Jottipher shook his head. 'But, madam, our loyalty is to the Management. We cannot plot against him, he is our employer. It is his duty to protect us.'

She reached across her desk and held his hand tightly. 'In the normal run of things, indubitably. But how far are we prepared to extend our allegiance? Nothing lasts for ever. The Management is dying; the power losses, the equipment failures, the arrival of these strangers.' Her large eyes stared directly into his. Mr Jottipher thought she had never looked so impressive, so inspirational. 'How much longer can this last? We have a duty to the Management, yes, but also a duty to ourselves. Ask yourself what will happen when he dies.'

Her words perturbed him. For the last few weeks, he had been deliberately attempting not to think about that. 'But there isn't anything we can do, surely?

The Secunda withdrew her hand and passed over a sheet of paper. 'This is the hard copy of a routine technical report on the strength of the defence outposts.' Printed on the paper was a continuous wave form that weaved smoothly up and down in a sine pattern. The Secunda pointed to certain irregularities in the formation. 'These breaks occurred during the power losses. On both occasions they lasted for several hours after the power here in the Complex was restored.

Mr Jottipher shook his head. 'I've no technical training.'

'For a few hours after each power loss here, the defence outposts are off-line. The Management's first priority is to restore power to the Complex. It's only later that the defences come back on-line. Don't you see what that means?'

'It means that for a few hours Zamper is defenceless.'

'More than that.' She took back the report and tapped it for emphasis with a finger-nail. 'If we time it correctly, come the next power loss we can fly a ship away from here, wait until the system breaks down totally, and then go right through the gateway.'

'But we have no ship, madam.' Mr Jottipher could hardly believe he was involved in such treachery. 'Only the cruiser under construction, and that is inaccessible until its completion.'

The Secunda folded the technical report and returned it to its file. 'There is the Chelonian shuttle,' she said. 'Now, are you with me?'

He considered. 'The Management might find a way to continue.'

'Do you really think so? When strangers can breach our defences?' Her voice demanded respect. Mr Jottipher realized how much she terrified him. Perhaps more than the Management. In that moment, he decided. It was always better to follow the strongest party.

'I'm with you,' he said.

Ivzid stared at the wall and let his thoughts go where they would. Behind him, up on the resting-bed, the General's shell shifted slightly to the steady tempo of its occupant's snores. That sound, like the suck of a breaking tide, offended Ivzid. It typified Hezzka's spinelessness in the face of the enemy. It was Ivzid's opinion that Hezzka should have been retired from the service years ago. The patience of the younger officers could not be extended indefinitely. All this talk of caution, of long-term planning, was so much manure. That was not the way the Chelonian empire had risen. It was insanity to talk of compromise with parasites, in any circumstances. The creatures stank of curdling milk, for Buf's sake. Ivzid's nostrils had been clogged by the unhealthy mammalian stench since his arrival on Zamper. How could Hezzka withdraw in such a place? He was unfit for command. Hafril would not have stood for this nonsense.

Ivzid shook himself, realizing that he was slipping into dreams. He must remain alert, for the sake of his race. Now, there was a thought. His name would go down in the history books. Ivzid, begetter of great deeds, who led the way to the demise of the usurper! A prime role, of which he was deserving. There would have to be changes to the record, of course. No mention would be made of these dealings with parasites. Instead, he would pen an account in which he led a raid on Zamper, raining fire on the vermin! That was how it should have been; that was the way he would tell it. And Hezzka? His part would have to be rewritten, upgraded, to conceal his sordid compromises.

There was a noise from the next room. Ivzid attuned each of his sensors, diverting a little power from his heater unit to increase his ocular and tympanic capacity. The wall was composed of a thin metal, and the warmth traces of two parasites registered clearly. They were conversing. Ivzid strained to overhear.

' – if we accept a bit of hospitality. That old guy was just doing his job.' This voice had all the naivety of a hatchling.

The other parasite, from the look of her a female, replied, 'He was holding something back.'

The male folded himself and lay on a resting-bed, his hands knitted behind his head. 'I'm tired. I can't be bothered to argue any more, Roz. If they wanted us dead, we'd be dead by now.'

Ivzid frowned. The Zamper brochure had stated that only five parasites lived here. They had seen four. Now there were two more, and from their conversation they were strangers to the planet. Most strange. He would wake the General and report this odd development.

Ah. But no. Perhaps this was a discovery better kept to himself. A chance to prove his initiative.

He shuffled closer to the wall and spied on.

When she opened her eyes, roused by a faint vibration, Bernice found that the buggy had reached its destination, and was descending a ramp that ended in a small and very clean garage that was illuminated by strips of fluorescent green. A door swung open by itself, admitting her to the Complex. She made sure the flight recorder was still inside her half-melted jacket, and passed through.

The pavement's rollers activated the moment she stepped cautiously into the connecting plastic tubeway, and carried her up through the network of connecting walkways that criss-crossed the heart of the Complex. The silence and grand cleanliness of this environment stirred memories of the optimistic future scenarios of mid-twentieth-century Earth culture. On one of the Doctor's regular trips to England in that period, she'd sneaked off for a look around Milton Keynes, keen to settle some of the archaeological debates it was to spur hundreds of years on. Hours later she'd returned to the TARDIS with an air of being proved right, and boxes full of shoes. The high deserted tubeways and the gently moving escalators of the Zamper Complex left a similar impression of a place not quite suitable for habitation. Whichever way she turned her head, the view was about the same. Her ascent of the travel tube took her to an intersection, and she was gently tipped onto another roller and sent a different way. Half a minute later the journey was over, and she faced a door set in to a blank grey metal wall that slid open as she approached.

'Another one,' said the tired-looking, red-faced and red-suited man on the other side.

'Yes, hello.' She held out her hand. 'Bernice Summerfield. Expecting me?'

'No, as it happens.' He made a swift appraisal of her and chuckled softly. His thinning, straw-coloured hair was combed back over his ears and he had a healthy outdoor look about him that was entirely contrary to the sterile historylessness of his surroundings. 'But you're welcome. I am Taal.'

After shaking his hand, her attention was drawn to the brightly-coloured structure in the centre of the room. 'That's a gaming grid, isn't it?'

He held up the palms of his hands. Bernice could tell that he was suppressing his curiosity, and was naturally suspicious of her. Her status as a guest of the Management was not, in the current situation, conducive to easy social dealings with the staff here. Still, it made a change to be feared and not shot at. 'Just closed up for the night, I'm afraid. Now, you'll be with Mr Cwej and Ms Forrester? A guest of the Management?'

'That's right. I'd like to see them.'

'You'll want apartment thirteen of the guest block.' He pointed to the inner door. 'Away through there. I'll see you tomorrow.'

Bernice stopped him as he moved to return to the gaming centre. 'Taal. I've spoken with Smith. I know the way things stand here.'

He didn't react.

'Believe me, my friends and I came here to Zamper by accident. We're not here to cause any trouble. This time yesterday I'd never heard of this place. But we'll help if we can.' She smiled hopefully.

'You just appeared, eh?'

'Yes. We just appeared.'

'Typical of the commercial philosophy,' said the Doctor. He was leaning over the specimen case, watching the Zamps curled up in their rest position. 'Zamper was constructed to be a short-term success. Any later problems weren't accounted for.' He tapped the case. 'It's all so complex. Industrial security, I suppose, but very irritating now things have started to go wrong.'

In spite of the enthusiasm he had reawakened, and her growing anxiety over the future of Zamper, Smith was finding it hard to keep her eyes open, and looked regularly over at her bedroom door, beyond which her self-warming blanket would be heating up nicely. The cool clean air of this planet increased the body's need for sleep, although it didn't appear to be affecting her new colleague. 'The question we should be asking, perhaps, is where has the design for this object of theirs come from? The same place as the ship designs?'

Smith yawned. 'Doctor, would you mind if I– '

'But the Zamps have no creative ability of their own. Their brains just don't have enough room for it. If we presume that some sort of imagination, an ability to visualize a future event, was once in their nature, then we must also presume that the consortium bred it out. Such a thing is not there. So how are the ships designed?'

Smith yawned again. 'Doctor, it's gone midnight, I really think I – '

'It just doesn't make sense. The designs must come from somewhere. Within or without.' He nodded to the projector screen, which he had paused on an image of the artifact. 'There must be a purpose in its construction. Strictly speaking, the Zamps have no consciousness of their own. They may breed and feed, but those are automatic reactions, and unnaturally reduced anyway.' He clicked his fingers. 'What if the construction of such an object is a subverted part of their subconscious, autonomic behaviour pattern?'

It was difficult to follow his arguments through her tiredness. 'Not likely. I've examined the brains of several Zamps. You can see for yourself, there's no part of the Zamp brain that can think for itself like that, even on the unconscious level.' She stood up and made for her bedroom door. 'You've reached the same *impasse* as I have. There's simply no logical explanation for why they are building that thing. Now, I really must get to bed. I'm afraid I haven't got any extra bedding, but there are some blankets in the kitchen cupboards.'

He wasn't listening. 'The instinct we're searching for. We can't see it in the dissected brain of an individual Zamp. But we've already established the strong, co-operative telepathic link in their herds.' He paced the lab anxiously, drumming his fingers at his temples. 'It's hard to credit, but what if the instinct functions on that level? And if so, why?'

'That's silly. Goodnight, Doctor.'

She closed the bedroom door, kicked off her boots, and climbed into bed. There'd be plenty of time to discuss his wild theories in the morning. If, she thought grimly, there was a morning.

Hezzka was dreaming. He was back on Chelonia, and the place had changed. Gone were the multi-levelled island cities, and the congested sky pedways were cleared of traffic, reclaimed by the giant thrusting flora that sprouted from the cracked asphalt below. The equestrian statue of the fourth Big Mother had been toppled, the stone head of the raptor he rode split in two, and corpses lay plastron-up in the streets, shells frying in the heat from the unshielded suns, the organs inside baking and issuing smoke. There was a repulsive odour of cooking flesh.

The last Chelonian, Hezzka dragged himself forward on three limbs, each movement sending a shriek of pain through his weary bones. He felt that the suns were descending through black burning clouds, twin spheres of coruscating energy absorbing the last of the planet's atmosphere. The angry Goddess was redeeming her gifts. Destruction came also from below, in the shape of crushing hands of bark, curling woody metatarsals to pierce the moaning dead with nightmarishly sharp-tipped thorns. Hezzka slithered forward, resisting death, searching for an impossible sanctuary, one eye flowing where a thorn had scratched. A fang-bird dropped from the sky, its vestigial wings flapping helplessly, its body caught in a nimbus of fire.

The moon passed before the suns.

Hezzka fell; his heart pounding, the ground opening, feet flailing, he dropped into a freezing darkness.

His fall was cushioned by cold mud, into which his feebly protesting form was submerged. In less than a second, he had sunk through a thick barrier of the sludge, and plopped out into a tunnel. His remaining eye increased its range, and he saw that he was enclosed between solid walls of earth. A prisoner. The walls on either side were streaked with a glowing white substance and a fetid odour came from the end of the tunnel. That and a hideous tapping sound.

Centuries of evolution and civilization were stripped clear and Hezzka knew primal fear, a pure animal terror. A shadow reared against the facing wall, the tapping grew louder, now accompanied by a dragging sound as something indescribably horrific pulled itself along. It came into sight. It was a merciless, evil, slithering thing, twice the size of him; its feelers, dripping with Chelonian blood, drooped obscenely from its head. His frantic efforts to retreat were halted and he went limp. The beast's mouth opened wide, revealing a hideous black gullet and a circular digestive tract that glistened with oil each time the muscle inside winked hungrily.

Hezzka screamed as the thing came closer, whistling, clicking, slithering, and lowered its head to feed, to feed on him, its final victim, the last of the Chelonians –

He woke to the sound of his own frantic murmurs. He was rolling from side to side on the lumpy uncomfortable resting-bed. The room was now in darkness.

'General?' Ivzid was at his side now, his eyes night-lit. 'You are troubled?' he enquired with heavy sarcasm.

Hezzka shuddered. He recalled the mission to Zamper and the odd events of the day. The dream images lingered, and he could almost see the ravenous beast before his eyes. In his mind, he was still trapped in the monster's underground lair.

Ivzid's eyes, all that was visible of the lad, seemed to be mocking him. 'A bad dream, that is all,' Hezzka said, aware of the flutter in his voice. 'Nothing more.' But perhaps his mind was trying to tell him something. In his heart, he was unhappy at coming to this place and dealing with parasites. The dream could have been the result of his guilt rising, unchecked, to the surface.

'General, there are two more parasites in the next room,' said Ivzid. 'I was about to wake you. Surely there are supposed to be only five workers here?'

Hezzka barely heard him. He remained dazed, adrenal-amyl pumping through his bloodstream. Somehow it had been more than a dream. His automatics struggled vainly to relax him. 'Ivzid, I . . . I saw – ' he searched his mind for the word, dredged it up from his schooldays, ' – an Arionite.'

'An Arionite?' Ivzid scoffed. 'The Arionites are long dead. The Book of Time tells us so: "Fiftie generations of the houses of Chelonia hath passed since the last Arionite bog was salted".'

'But I saw one, Ivzid. I saw them return to destroy us, to bring death on all our families.'

Ivzid growled. 'In your dream, General?'

'Yes. In my dream.' Hezzka glared back at him.

'How could you tell? The appearance of the Arionites is not recorded. It is a scholars' battle to prove that they even existed.' He motored away from the bed, and raised a foot to indicate the far wall. 'Sir, I consider it more important to examine these new para– '

A fresh terror struck Hezzka. 'I know what an Arionite looks like Ivzid, because we saw such creatures this very day. In the construction yard. The Zamps!'

'Unpleasant creatures but plainly harmless,' was Ivzid's summation.

As he emerged from his shell, Hezzka felt the beginnings of shame. His previous outbursts now, even to himself, appeared unseemly, and surely not fitting for an officer of his rank on a mission of such import. Mumbling of mythic terrors, indeed.

Yet the vision had been so vivid that in the few seconds' confusion between sleeping and waking, the dream world had possessed more certainty than this one.

Casting his doubts aside, trying to assert the dignity of rank, he said. 'Think nothing more of it. The food we have eaten here,' he belched for effect, 'may have a mild deranger effect. What of these new parasites?'

'In the next room, General.'

'I can hear something.' Forrester motioned Cwej to silence and pointed to the wall. 'Voices, through there.' They came again. A stream of bass rumbles.

'Taal did say there were visitors here besides ourselves,' Cwej pointed out.

'He didn't say they were aliens.' She listened again. 'I can't make out the words.' She pictured the owners of the voices as hairy, as broad as they were tall, with flicking tails and savage fangs.

Cwej fell back on his soft, springy bed. 'Just relax, Roz.'

'How can I? There's no lock on the door.' Her eyes cast around the room, searching for a tool for the task she had in mind. In the drawer between their beds she found a couple of crystal tumblers. 'Excellent.' She hurried back to the wall, pressed one of the tumblers against it, and listened.

Cwej yawned and buried his face in his pillow. 'I don't believe some of the things you do.'

The female parasite was holding something to the wall. Ivzid scanned it. A non-electronic device, composed of processed silicates. Hardly useful. 'What is the purpose of this?' he wondered aloud. 'Could it be a form of res-onator?'

'A primitive adaptation of the principle,' said the General, who had clambered down from the bed and joined the inspection. 'They mean to amplify our conversation.'

'They dare to spy on us?' Ivzid considered the two parasites once more; the female was warmer, her muscles tensed. The male, lying back on one bed, was more relaxed. It followed that the female was the commander, as the parasite custom seemed to be.

'I can just make out what they're saying,' he heard her say.

He shook with anger, took a deep breath and bellowed, *'Oh it's hard when you're in space, and there's no green about the place, and the journey's end seems ever further on-on-on . . .'* To his delight, the General took up the song, clearly determined to assert his character after his silly nightmare. *'But when it comes there's lots to eat,'* they harmonized, *'and parasites to greet, before you blast them from existence with your gun-gun-gun.'*

The martial metre lifted Ivzid's heart, and he remembered how good it was to be a Chelonian. To be made of the best stuff. He and the General laughed heartily as the parasite leapt back in alarm.

Bernice walked through from the gaming centre into a long high corridor with numbered doors on either side. The lighting was dimmed for the night, and she was forced to squint to make out the numbers. She counted off the numbers, only giving the task half her attention.

This was apartment thirteen, wasn't it? Probably. She opened the door, sensing the presence of others in the darkness. She slipped off her boots and tucked them under her arm. Cwej and Forrester were, by the look of things, fast asleep. If their day had been anything like hers, they needed the rest.

The room was very dark. She felt her way forward, and the tips of her fingers brushed candlewick. Good, a bed. Occupied? She listened closely. The occupant of the bed was breathing deeply and snoring loudly. It had to be Cwej.

Oh well, room enough for two. And in the morning he'd get quite a shock. Childish, admittedly, but Bernice had learnt over the last few years to enjoy the simple pleasures life offered whenever she could. Careful not to wake him, Bernice put her boots under the bed and climbed in. She really was very tired and as soon as her head touched the pillow she fell asleep.

She was disturbed. Cwej was hogging the sheets. Each

time she tried to pull them back he shuffled about and took more. The bedsprings creaked under his weight. But then, Bernice reflected, he was a big lad.

She dreamt.

An ordinary sort of dream. Edwardian London, being knocked on the head, being strangled by Ace, being half-eaten by carnivorous plants, being menaced by a glinting octopus with the sea inside-out above it, being spat at by pink-haired youths, being chatted up by Dr Watson, doing a jigsaw at Allen Road, painting a picture of a lady with a shopping basket, shopping with President Flavia, entering Paris on a haycart, being . . .

Being stared at by a Chelonian.

Being stared at by a Chelonian.

Being stared at by a Chelonian.

She hadn't been sleeping next to Cwej.

Bernice screamed. The Chelonian blinked in outraged astonishment. Bernice leapt from the bed, still screaming, and ran from the room.

In a file on Smith's computer, the Doctor found a detailed map of this region of Zamper. With his fountain pen he copied down the important details. X marked the point of access to cave 74D.

He turned of the screen, scribbled a note for Smith, and slipped out of the hut and into the night, heading west.

The specimens watched him go.

Chapter 6

Hezzka ignored Ivzid's petty smirks in the morning. He refused to allow the brat any satisfaction from his discomfort, although the unformed fears of his nightmare remained. The feeling was hard to pin down, and seemed to disappear whenever he tried. It was rather like, he thought, coming across an old letter penned by oneself, in an associate's belongings; the writing is one's own, the words are one's own, but the content is forgotten pieces of tittle-tattle and outgrown habits. The creeping repulsion he felt at the thought of the dream was operating on a level of his mind beyond conscious control, as a background murmur to his ordered waking thoughts.

One of the servitor disc-machines entered their room, buzzed, and announced that a morning meal was shortly to be served in the dining room at the end of the accommodation hall.

Ivzid lurched forward, raising a foot to prevent its departure. 'You, machine. You will explain the events of last night.'

'It is not in my function,' the disc replied. 'Refer your query to the host.' It buzzed again, turned smartly and glided out.

'Here, as on Chelonia, it is always somebody else's fault.' Hezzka tapped Ivzid on the shell in a gesture that he hoped would reassert his authority. 'We will take our morning meal.'

Ivzid hissed. 'I do not like this, General.' He gestured next door. 'Who are these new parasites? Why did one of them enter our suite? I grow warier by the moment. I say

107

we should go to the Secunda parasite and demand the return of our monies until our questions are answered. Also, the weapon, I feel need of it – '

'Hold your tongue. We will discover more by subtle means than by force.' He motored forward. 'We will take the morning meal.'

Ivzid muttered something, loud enough to be overheard. 'Pah. Cowering like an aged crack-shell in the night, babbling of bad dreams . . .'

'Ivzid!' Hezzka controlled his anger with difficulty. 'To what do you owe your allegiance?'

'The glorious empire of the Chelonian race,' he replied bitterly.

'That is so. Do you know what sustains the empire? Respect! To speak dishonourably of a superior, that is the credo of the usurper's mutinous rabble, and the way of the parasites you so much detest! If you have thoughts on the handling of this mission, you will address them in a manner suitable for an officer of your rank. Do you understand?'

Ivzid looked away. 'Yes, General.'

'In the meantime, I am placing you on report.'

'What?' Ivzid's nostrils flared. 'Sir, you can't – '

'I already have. When we return to the fleet your appointment will be subject to a full appraisal.' Hezzka weighed up his decision. The words had come before he'd had time to consider, but this had to be for the best. Little more than a hatchling scout, Ivzid had been promoted too far and too fast. Disloyalty had to be weeded out, strength of character built. 'Now. No more shall we speak of this. To the morning meal.'

Briskly he left the room, aware of Ivzid's eyes burning on his rear.

Forrester had insisted on staying awake all night. When Bernice had revealed that Chelonians possessed X-ray eyes and cyber-enhanced hearing, she'd pulled her into the shower cubicle, drawn the curtain, and switched on the flow, then demanded a full explanation. In spite of her unexpected encounter in the next room, Bernice was very tired. Yes, the Doctor was all right, yes, the TARDIS was all right. Probably. Promising to reveal more in the morning, she collapsed next to Cwej and got some sleep in. She found Forrester asleep in the jacuzzi as the lights came up for morning, still wearing her jacket, her boots dangling over the sides. She was muttering something about betrayal and aliens. In a strange way she looked rather sweet.

Cwej availed himself of the range of toiletries provided in the room's cabinet. As he shaved he asked Bernice, 'You've met these Chelonians before, then?'

'They're old enemies of mine. The Doctor and I bumped into some quite a while ago.' Briefly she was lost in the distant memory. Her first few trips in the TARDIS had been almost fun, the Doctor the friend she'd always wanted. 'There's been a lot of water under the bridge since then. Goodness me, yes. Sorry, you were asking?'

'Chelonians?'

'Oh, right. Well, they're just an average bunch of cybernetically-augmented hermaphrodite giant tortoises who want to destroy the human race, and came closer than most. Or will come close, or did come close. Tenses are a bit of a problem when you've travelled as much as I have.' Cwej was staring at her oddly. She realized how much she sounded like the Doctor. 'The lot we met got trapped in a time loop, poor things, but much the safest place for them.'

'I suppose they've come to buy a ship from this place.'

'Hmm. I don't think any Chelonian worth his shell would do deals with humans. They regard us as parasites, you know.'

Cwej finished his shave and got dressed. 'That'll make Roz's day. She's been looking for an alien to beat up ever since we got here.'

Bernice had an idea. She put a finger to her lips, then tiptoed over to the jacuzzi. Holding her nose she grated, 'You-are-an-en-e-my-of-the-Da-lek-race-you-will-be-exter-min-a-ted . . .'

Forrester leapt from the jacuzzi, hitting her head on the shelf above and dislodging a row of perfumed shampoos. She regarded the laughing Bernice and Cwej with undisguised venom. 'If you could see how childish you look.'

Violet artificial sunbeams shone through the slats of the blind in Smith's bedroom. As dawn broke her sleeping form was revealed. Still dressed in her day clothes, she lay with her face in her pillow.

A voice came from her Inscreen. 'Smith. Smith?' The Management crackled into existence on the screen, his face obscured by a widening pattern of interference. 'Smith, where are you? I can't see you.'

She mumbled something, turned over and over.

'Smith, I must talk to you. We have lots in common. I can't talk to the others. It's urgent. Where is the Doctor? Smith!'

There was no reply from the sleeping scientist. In their cage, the three specimens burbled urgently to each other.

'Smith, I can't – I can't hold on much longer. This manifestation is ... failing ... You must find the answer. My power is weakening ... They're taking my power. Please, Smith. Smith! You must find them. Only you I trust. The others, I can't trust them. First Nula, now I'm sure the others plot against me ... They're using ... Zamper must continue, you must help me!'

The picture faded.

Smith slept on.

The Zamps fell silent.

On foot, it took the Doctor a couple of hours to reach the area marked on Smith's mapscreen, which was west along the border of the big lake. Walking through the darkness, swinging his umbrella as he went and whistling to keep himself company, he was brought up several times by movements in the water that turned out to be his reflection, ghostly and white. The starless sky and the clear atmosphere created an eerie effect.

When he was certain of his position, he cast about for

the particular rock formation that had been marked on the mapscreen. In the night it was hard to orientate, and he wandered along in the gully formed at the base of the undulating hillocks, stopping now and again to get his bearings. After a few minutes occupied in this manner he came to what looked like it might be the correct opening. With the sharp end of a piece of rock he marked the site with a question mark, and slipped through, umbrella forward, squeezing his shoulders and taking a deep breath.

The darkness beyond was cold and wet. The moisture from the lake had seeped through into the caves in this area and he could hear water flowing in the distance. Probably an overflow tide. He pushed himself through the narrow channel that led downwards, compressing his slight frame using a trick he'd learnt from . . . well, from somewhere he couldn't remember. His torchlight he extinguished, thinking that a later moment might present a greater need for it; and besides, he could navigate almost as well by hand and through use of his well-honed senses.

Some way further down the channel grew too narrow to traverse, and he was forced to climb back up and lift up his arms before going down again. Stretched out, he pushed himself downwards like a worm. His face was streaked with dirt as he pushed it through the foot-wide space. It would be rather undignified, he thought as he pushed himself down again with a shove that scraped the skin off his legs where his trousers had rolled up, to get stuck down here.

'This,' he muttered, 'must be something of how it feels to be a Zamp.'

After an anxious night, which she spent watching the wall-light for any signs of a further power loss, the Secunda carried out her morning routine without deviation, taking coffee from the servitor and settling back to view the new day's market reports. The data-coil link inset in her desk did not respond to her request for an update. She knew at once that this wasn't an equipment failure. The thing was inert. But the internal lighting was on, and the servitor was unaffected.

She turned in her chair to her Inscreen. Only rarely had she made use of her right, as Secunda, to summon her superior. 'Management. I request your presence.'

There was no response.

The Inscreen flickered and he was there, in monochrome. His face had frozen in a frown and when he spoke his voice was thin and reedy. The image could have been a transmission from three star-sectors away. 'You called?' He was, she realized, trying to sound confident.

Keeping her expression and her voice calm and steady, she asked, 'I'm having a spot of bother with my data-coil link.'

'Just-just an equipment failure.' Static flared.

'Oh good. That's all it is. Only there doesn't seem to be any power.'

'There is just-just a fault in the-in the power distributor-tor links. Power is being reserved for esse-essential functions. Business can proceed smoothly.' A thick bar of colour superimposed itself over the top third of the screen, and his eyes switched from red to green to blue. A brief moment of confidence that soon faded; he must have realized he was lying to himself. 'Business can proceed smoothly. Business must proceed smoothly. Business-ness must proceed-eed smoo-oothly-ly.'

And he was gone.

The Secunda took a deep breath and called up the operator. 'Madam?' The simulation sounded as calm as ever. She asked for Mr Jottipher.

The dining hall's numbered tables, napkin rings and toast-racks put Bernice in mind of a provincial guest house. A couple of servitors buzzed over as she, Cwej and Forrester took their seats, and hovered with an air of waiterly deference.

Forrester shook her head as Cwej handed her a plastic wipe-clean menu. 'I can't read that.' Although the format

112

of the menu was familiar the notation was in rows of aggressive-looking hieroglyphs.

One of the servitors reacted to her words, chimed, and the menus instantly rearranged themselves in English.

Cwej chuckled. 'There you are.'

'If somebody's treating you well, they're expecting something,' she said. 'I wonder whether we've got it to give.'

'Robots don't need tipping.' Bernice examined the menu. 'Coffee and croissants all round okay?' The servitors took this as a command, dipped and buzzed away.

'We can't pay,' said Forrester.

'We're guests, we don't have to. Relax.'

The door crashed open and the Chelonians ambled in, their internal mechanisms grinding and clanking. The younger one glared at them and growled ferociously. Bernice reached across the table and laid her hand on Forrester's arm to warn her against replying in kind. 'Morning,' she called chirpily to the newcomers.

'You are the one that entered our room last night,' said the older Chelonian. Bernice noted the red stripe on its shell.

'Yeah, sorry. I've had a bit of a knock on the head and I got our room numbers mixed up, General.' She could smell her own fear mixed in with the unmistakable odour of the Chelonians. They smelt like old leather upholstery.

'We were not expecting more humans,' said the younger Chelonian.

'We weren't expecting to be here. We got lost,' said Cwej. 'Just passing through.'

The younger moved closer, clicking its teeth deliberately to scare them. Bernice fingered her tablemat. Forrester looked as if she was about to burst. 'You got lost?'

Cwej said 'yes' in a small voice.

There was a distraction that fortunately took away the Chelonians' attention. Taal appeared, grinning obsequiously at them all. His cheeks were ruddied and the strands of wheat-coloured hair plastered over his head were sticking up, making him appear faintly ridiculous. He'd been drinking. 'Morning all.' The cynicism beneath his words did not go unobserved by Bernice. 'All well?'

'Who are these new humans?' the General demanded. Bernice looked into his eyes and registered a quality she'd not previously accounted a Chelonian. He was curious, and unlike his junior seemed unwilling to reach conclusions. 'We were told only five of you lived on Zamper.'

'Guests of the Management, General Hezzka,' said Taal. 'Quite unconnected to your visit. I'm sure you have nothing to fear.'

The wrong thing to say. 'We do not fear parasites!' The younger Chelonian reared up, showing its teeth again and a glimpse of its bright red tongue. 'You intend to deceive us!'

'Not at all, Mr Ivzid.' Taal spoke with an air of experience. 'No need to concern yourself. All is well.'

'Come away, Ivzid.' Hezzka beckoned his junior with a motion of one claw. 'We will take our morning meal.'

Snarling, Ivzid followed the General to a table on the far side of the room. A little confused by the chairs they pushed them aside and examined the menus.

'This is crazy,' said Forrester. She shook Bernice's hand away and sneered at Taal. 'You're going to sell those – those things a battle cruiser?'

'It's not for me to make a moral judgement.'

'The eternal excuse of the arms dealer.'

'If it wasn't us it'd be somebody else, love.'

'Likewise.'

Bernice was relieved when the servitor-discs returned. Suspended between them was a tray laden with a coffee pot and cups and a plate of croissants, which they lowered on to the table.

'There must be some sort of penal code out here,' Forrester went on, twisting in her chair to keep up with Taal as he moved away. 'You're selling out your entire species.'

'We're neutral and I couldn't care less.' He turned to the Chelonians. 'Gentlemen. Your orders?'

The General lifted his heavily lidded old eyes. 'I will take the smasti nuts.'

114

'Twice,' barked Ivzid.

Taal nodded graciously and waved the servitors off on the errand.

There was a long and terrible silence. Bernice looked from side to side. Both sets of diners stared at each other, with Taal hovering inbetween. Forrester locked eyes with Ivzid. Cwej and the General shuffled uncomfortably. If the Doctor were here, she wondered, what would he do?

She reached for the coffee pot. 'Shall I be mother?'

Ivzid roared. 'You mock us!'

'Sorry. Just an expression. No offence given.' She poured. The coffee slopped out, lumpy and cold. 'Er. Taal?'

Cwej waved a croissant. 'Are these meant to be frozen solid?'

All eyes were now on Taal, who shrugged. 'Small equipment failure, I'm sure.'

Bernice wasn't quite sure how to respond to that. Hezzka rumbled. 'Another power failure? I am suspicious of these failures of yours.'

'Yes.' Ivzid tapped his front feet together. 'We demand an immediate explanation. A full explanation.'

'I will personally look into these matters right away,' Taal said as he backed hurriedly from the dining room. His fingers fumbled for the door handles and he was pushed aside by a young girl, dressed in an identical red suit with Z emblem, on her way in. They collided, apologized, and Taal was gone.

The girl smiled hesitantly. 'Hello, everyone,' she said with little confidence. 'I'm Christie, your hostess.'

Hezzka tapped Ivzid on the shell. 'Come, First Pilot. We are leaving.'

'Yes. These parasites insult us.' As they passed by the humans' table, Ivzid fixed Forrester with a contemptuous glance and let fly a string of blobby mucus that landed on the shoulder of her jacket. 'Parasite scum!'

Forrester beat her fists on the table. 'I don't believe this. What I'd give for a gun!'

Cwej dabbed at her shoulder with a handkerchief.

'You'd probably miss. Try not to get so worked up. They're only giant turtles.'

Bernice examined the new arrival. The girl had tried to cover up her unhealthy complexion with layers of blusher, giving her the aspect of a painted doll. Strangely, the muscles of her arm bulged against the fabric of her suit. After introducing herself, Bernice waited for a reply. The girl grinned feebly but said nothing.

'You must see a lot of alien races here,' said Bernice.

The girl performed a shaky gesture with her hand, half indicating herself and half pointing to nothing. It seemed to describe her relationship to the rest of the universe. Her eyes were checkout-dulled, thought Bernice. 'I'm new,' she said. 'I've never met Chelonians before.'

'Let's go and find the Doctor,' Forrester said, standing. The shoulder of her jacket was bleached where the Chelonian mucus had landed. 'It's time we got away from this place.'

Christie waved one of her fingers again. 'Actually, I've got a message for you. Well, it's specifically for Professor Summerfield. The Secunda says would you like to take tea.' As she spoke, something in Cwej's body language drew Bernice's attention. He was standing unnaturally, his legs slightly bent, and his dopey half-smile was dropping as fast as his blink-rate increased. Oh, surely not.

'I'd love to. Where can I find her?'

'I will escort you.' One of the servitors emerged from the kitchen and came level with Bernice's head.

'Right. I'll be off then. Hope the tea's better than the coffee.' She waved to Forrester and Cwej, whose eyes were darting about the room in every direction apart from Christie, and then skipped out after the buzzing disc.

The Doctor estimated that he must be almost a mile below the surface of Zamper. Thankfully, the cave system had widened out, and after an hour's painful navigation through the confined channels nearer the entrance, he had been glad of the chance to stretch his cramped muscles. He stopped often, his head cocked to one side, sensitive

116

to any changes in the rumble of the distant water flow. As he dropped down over a thin spar of rock, the ferrule of his umbrella hooked over the end to take his weight, another noise echoed to his right. At first he was uncertain. In his experience caves were not uncommon, and he knew well their ability to confound the senses. After a couple of seconds, the noise, a high-pitched burble, came again. He brought out his torch, and in its beam he saw an arch-shaped opening leading right. The walls beyond sparkled as the light passed over them, being coated in thin strands of a colourless substance that was tacky to his touch. Wiping his fingers on his handkerchief, he advanced under the arch, noting the small piles of heavy stones arranged neatly on either side of the passage. At least one Zamp from the mysterious sub-herd had passed along this way, lost.

When the burble sounded a third time, he stopped to consider. He told himself that there was no logical reason why the call of a Zamp should mean anything to his ears. It was a simple animal cry, made for the senses of another animal and not for him. But there was something in the tone that suggested pain. Not a physical pain, but an emotion. Regret?

He shook his head and chastised himself.

Walking on, he presently came to a small triangular cavity. Ducking his head he entered and shone the torch around. The source of the regretful burble, three notes descending in scale, was near.

The cavity contained three slime-coated eggs about the size of footballs. The shells were muddy brown, opaque and ribbed; thick turquoise spreading veins pulsed every other second. They looked unhealthy. The Zamp eggs he had seen in Smith's holo-pictures were sturdier and shelled. These reminded him of frogspawn.

He was alerted by a twitching movement in the darkness opposite. He shone his torch and the beam revealed a Zamp. It was trapped by a piece of rock that lay across its mid-section, and was squirming pathetically to free itself, twisting its tapered rear and wiggling its feelers. The

Doctor's arrival seemed to alarm it further, and it squealed with frustration.

The Doctor raised his hat and said politely, 'Good morning, madam. You appear to be in some trouble.' It had not used its telekinetic powers to save itself, he noted. Probably the poor beast was exhausted after lugging its eggs here, and had become trapped by a falling piece of rock dislodged by the movement in the area. He pictured the efforts of the Zamp progenitor to reach a safe place for its young to emerge, away from its herd and unguided, and shook his head in admiration. 'Perhaps that brain of yours isn't as small as we thought.'

There was a slight abrasion in the creature's side, through which issued a thin trickle of grey blood. Kneeling down, the Doctor lifted the piece of rock very slightly and angled the beam of his torch on to the wound. The Zamp burbled and twisted itself, apparently afraid that he intended to harm it further. Satisfied that no serious damage had been done, he hefted the rock and threw it aside. Immediately the Zamp pushed itself towards the eggs, slithering by him.

At the same moment the Doctor felt a slight pressure on his brow, ghostly fingertips brushing past, and he leapt up instinctively, raising his umbrella to confront his opponent. A sensation flashed through his mind, and his legs gave way. The torch fell from his hand.

Sight was gone, smell was gone. There was the trail, only the trail, his mark. Joy made his heart beat faster as he moved forward. The smallest detail of the environment was known to him. He was strong again now, and would not be caught by another fall. He lifted his underside to avoid the small sharp rock that blocked his path to the young. The beautiful young. Three of them, a full litter, and no runts among them. Their auras mingled, he assured them as he felt for the integrity of their containers. No flaws. Each was a perfect sphere, the nourishing jelly healthy and grey. He turned his senses on the other creature in the cave and sensed it meant no harm. It was one

118

of the non-thinkers from above. Perhaps it would like to communicate.

The message faded.

Blinking, the Doctor shook his head to clear it of the intruder and scrabbled for the torch.

The Zamp was circling its eggs, stopping to let its feelers examine each in turn. This time, the musical tone it produced sounded joyful. Curious, the Doctor came closer and put out a hand, intending to feel the surface of one of the eggs.

His fingers froze and a cold pain struck him in the chest like an icy dagger. He pulled back his hand and sucked his fingers. 'Sorry. Very clever. In-built defence mechanism?' The Zamp burbled as if in confirmation. 'Well, that's my one good turn for the day.'

He took out his notebook and pencil, made a quick sketch of the eggs for future reference, then backed along the arched way, feeling rather pleased with himself.

Mr Jottipher had barely slept, his mind thrown into a turmoil by the speed and oddness of the previous day's events. Three times in the night he had gone tearfully to the drinks machine in the corner of his bedroom, and three times had found it without power. There was no Inscreen in his quarters, but still he glanced fearfully around the dark corners, his imagination racing with the possibilities. The more he turned the Secunda's treacherous suggestion around in his head, the more ghastly consequences occurred to him. What if the Management really were testing them? What if the power losses were swiftly repaired? What if they were discovered attempting to flee by the Chelonians? He had always favoured the clearest path through life, preferably in the footsteps of somebody cleverer who looked like they knew where it was taking them. Only the certainty expressed by the Secunda assured him. He couldn't imagine her failing at anything.

Summoned to her office, he took a circuitous route along the tubes, hoping to avoid contact with the Chelonians, or any of the staff. From the mirror of his dressing-table this morning, his red-cheeked, wild-eyed reflection had screamed 'traitor!', and he was certain that others would notice the change in him and start to suspect. He entered to find her, immaculate in red, calling up Smith's lab on her Outscreen.

'Wake up, you silly woman,' she was calling. Mr Jottipher was slightly affronted by the relaxation of etiquette. Rudeness caused him to blush. 'Come on, wake up!'

In the corner of the Outscreen, Smith could be seen lying face down and fully-clothed on her bed. 'Perhaps she's tired, madam.'

'Unlikely. She was never one to lie in. Smith!'

Mr Jottipher leaned over the desk and whispered, 'You're going to include Smith in our . . . in our, er . . .'

'Plan?'

'Er, yes. Our plan.'

'No. It will give me great pleasure to leave her behind, in fact. I was just calling to see if she'd made any breakthroughs with her new friend. Doesn't look like it.' His face must have been letting him down again, because she asked, 'Am I shocking you?'

'I . . . I, er, well, I . . .'

'We attended the same school.'

He squeaked and sat down. 'School,' he said in a small voice.

'School.' She threw her head back. 'School, school, school. It doesn't matter anymore. Why shouldn't we talk freely now? Nobody is listening.' She poured him a drink from the crystal decanter on her desk. 'Here. My name is Margaret Beaumont.'

'I am,' he stumbled and sipped, 'I was with the Telemenary troupe, touring the island galaxies. Lars Jottipher. I was a boy soprano, you know.' He brushed away a forming tear. 'Sorry.'

She smiled and switched off the Outscreen. 'Never mind her. It's you I want with me. May I call you Lars?'

'Oh. Yes, please.' It felt very strange to talk freely again. Twenty-two years. Nearly half of his life. 'May I call you Margaret?'

'No you may not.'

The door of the office slid open. 'Ah,' said the Secunda. 'One of our new friends.'

Mr Jottipher flinched. Another stranger. He was unsure how to react in these altered circumstances. A woman in her mid-thirties, in a black vinyl jacket and blue cloth trousers. Her eyes were also blue, and alive with wit and intelligence. She frightened him. She looked like another one of those people that tend to get what they want. Force of habit sprung him from his chair, which he proceeded to offer.

'Morning.'

'Good morning, Professor Summerfield.' The Secunda indicated the decanter.

The stranger declined. 'Bit too early. Cheers anyway.'

The Secunda reclined in her chair. 'Now then. You just happened to be passing our way, I hear.'

'That's about the size of it. Yes, I know you're going to say that's impossible. But we're not the usual sort of travellers.'

'I gathered that from the report on the test wreckage that came in overnight.' The Secunda tapped a sheaf of print-out. 'An upright oblong, two point six metres by nought point nine metres. External markings suggest ancient artifact of Tellurian origin, but interior resists all datalyzer-patterns.'

'Good to know she's still in one piece.' Summerfield reached for the report. 'Can I have a look at that, please?'

'Feel free. What is "she"?'

'She's the exterior portal of an extra-dimensional patterning matrix. I don't understand it either.'

'A teleporting ship?' suggested Mr Jottipher, sensing the possibilities shifting again.

'Sort of.' She folded the report. 'Can I borrow this copy? Ta. I'd better go and see how my mates are. Nice to have met you.' She stood, nodded cheerfully, and left.

'She seems rather nice,' said Mr Jottipher. 'If a little odd.'

The Secunda looked up at him. 'She's terrified we're after her ship.'

'Oh. Are we?'

'No, no, far too far away. I was right, though. I don't like these new people, Jottipher. Extra-dimensional technology is beyond the predict-horizon threshold of all the major worlds, even today. And you saw the way she dressed.'

Science was not Mr Jottipher's field, and he struggled to catch up with her thoughts. 'You think she's from the future?' His throat ran dry and he sat back down. 'From – from the consortium, perhaps?'

'I think it's likely.'

'But, but,' he finished his drink and steadied his thoughts, 'that means they might have the knowledge to repair things here. And that means that we – '

'Have to make ourselves scarce as soon as possible, yes.' She remained so wonderfully calm; and as if she knew exactly what he was thinking, she reached across the desk and took his hand.

Hezzka marched briskly back to his room, and kicked over his bed. The muscles around his joint implants were sore, and his head felt thick and groggy. Not enough withdrawal-time. He thought longingly of his hatchlings, incalculable millions of miles away, growing up in a state-financed crèche, being fed with Little Sister's lies. Not even knowing his name, their heritage wiped away. He had followed exactly the strategy outlined for this mission, and still was close to failure. There would have to be another way, and then this Zamper planet would yield its secrets. He would return with a battle-formation of Chelonian stealth-cruisers. Yes, blast away their defences by sheer numbers, and ransack this place, take their ship designs, exterminate the slimy and repulsive Zamps.

'You say we are to leave?' Ivzid asked. 'You say we are to leave Zamper?'

Hezzka chose his words of reply carefully. 'I share your suspicions, Ivzid. The power failures indicate that Zamper is not what we hoped for. Perhaps, boy, we were expecting too much. This disorder, these new parasites ... those disgusting Arionite creatures. We did not know of these when the bargain was struck. I say we reclaim our deposit and return to the fleet to consult Big Mother and the strategic council.'

Ivzid turned away from him. He said quietly, 'General, these power failures have made the parasites weak. Surely now is the time to strike and take what we will?'

'There are many servitor-discs, and all are armed. We would be shot down in minutes. I say we return, Ivzid.'

Ivzid reared up. 'Return? I see what lies behind your words. You mean us to flee like raspberry-suckers from puny, defenceless parasites and bad dreams of slimy worms!'

'I have warned you this day, Ivzid. Now return to the shuttle and ready it for flight.'

'You are not fit for command, Hezzka.' Ivzid slouched from the room. 'When we return to the fleet, my account of this mission will damn your actions.'

'Ah, be gone from my sight!'

Alone, Hezzka kicked over the other bed. He released a relaxant, and soothed himself with visions of how Ivzid's pathetic bleating would be dismissed by Big Mother and the council. The lad had a shock coming.

As had the Secunda. He prepared himself to confront her.

Forrester had known Cwej only for what felt like a couple of weeks, but he was easy to read. His mawkishness in the dining room would have been embarrassing enough in more ordinary social conditions, but here on Zamper, separated from the TARDIS, it was embarrassing, dumb and misplaced. Three words that summed him up pretty well.

'Have you got a thing for pretty little waitresses?'

His ears turned red. 'What do you mean?'

She tossed one of the solid croissants between her hands as they walked along the hallway of the residential block, in the direction of the travel tube. 'It looks like we're stuck in the Doctor's pocket for a while, and he isn't the type for sticking around long. It probably isn't a good idea to get yourself involved emotionally.'

'Thanks for the lecture.'

She ignored that. 'I realize you're in your prime, but there are more important things.'

'Or perhaps you just don't want anybody else to have more of a good time than you.'

It surprised her how much that hurt. 'I don't like to be misjudged.'

'I don't like being lectured. Hey.' He raised a finger and pulled her into a corner as a heavy thumping noise overlaid by the whine of an overheating motor signalled the advance of the younger Chelonian. It sped by without noticing them, muttering angrily all the while something about treacherous aliens and cowardice. It stank like a pair of old leather shoes left out in the rain.

They walked on in silence.

At the junction of the hallway with the gaming centre they halted. The voices of Taal and Christie echoed out along the hallway. Forrester grabbed Cwej's arm and motioned him to remain silent as they crept forward, stopping just before the open doorway.

'I'm just frightened, that's all,' Christie was saying. Forrester glanced up at Cwej, and noted with disapproval the dreamy look on his face.

'Anybody would be at the sight of one of those things,' said Taal. 'They're brutes. Don't worry, they'll be gone in a couple of days.'

Cwej moved to enter the gaming centre. Again Forrester held him back.

'It's not just that. It's this place. Why is everything breaking down? Who are these new people?' Her wheedling tones sickened Forrester. Women like that needed a good slap. The girl's voice became a whisper. 'If the Management breaks down, what are we going to do?'

'Well, I've got a few ideas, love, put it like that. Stick with me and you'll be all right.' Dirty old feller.

124

'Thanks. It's all been so sudden for me, I suppose. Nothing much has happened to me before, really. Nothing much at all.' Forrester felt a fist forming automatically. 'I was working at a bar on Rakkelwotts 5. I'd only been there a week when I got brought here. I'd heard of Zamper, of course, everyone has, but I didn't think it would be anything like this.' She burst into tears. 'What are we going to do? The last hostess. You said that she'd been killed. Is that what's going to happen to us?'

'Not if we think straight.' Forrester's suspicions of Taal were confirmed. He was sharp, he'd been planning this one for ages. 'If the power fails completely, there'll be a way out, for a while anyway.'

'But we haven't got a ship,' Christie muttered through her tears.

'No, we haven't,' Taal said emphatically. 'But I can think of a couple of giant tortoises who have.'

It took Smith several minutes to piece together her conscious mind. The first thing she saw was her outstretched hand on the pillow. Another morning, then. Her tongue was dry and felt heavy, her head was throbbing. Time for the specimens' feed. The specimens' feed, the . . .

The Doctor.

She leapt up and through into the lab, her legs tingling. The glass door of the drugs cabinet was open, and the bottle of sedative tablets was unstoppered. On the lab bench stood a line of teacups. The one she'd been drinking from last night contained a residue of leaves mixed in with a white powder. She swore and turned away from the cabinet.

Pinned to her microscope was a sheet of scrap paper.

DEAR S,
I'VE GONE FOR A LOOK AT THE SUB-HERD.
SORRY TO LEAVE YOU BEHIND – I WORK
BETTER ALONE, AND IT'S PROBABLY SAFER.

D

She snatched up and crumpled the message. 'Devious little . . .'

Ivzid waited until the travel tube had deposited him in a shadowy corner of the Complex and stopped. Outwardly calm, he was inwardly seething. He pictured returning to the fleet empty-handed from this mission. Big Mother would laugh scornfully at Hezzka's tale of running scared from power failures and nightmares of Arionites. To face the godhead of the Chelonian empire with such nonsense would be unthinkable, the ultimate indignity. Things would have been much different if Hafril had lived. Hafril, strongest of all warriors, loyal to the last gasp, who had taken seven bullets before dying, oh, he would have rampaged through Zamper leaving none alive. Hezzka might as well be an agent of the usurper. Indeed he was a traitor to his birthright. Ivzid felt the heavy weight of destiny settle on his shell. So, it was up to him. Of all the possible paths fate might have taken, it fell to him alone to secure the continuation of the race. He relished the role. In a couple of cycles, perhaps, he might lead the victory parade down the ancient triumphal archway of the capital, escorting Big Mother's covered carriage, veiled by the interwoven brocades of the inner families, the unblemished scutcheon of Hakifur glinting in the stream of golden rays from the Father Sun, the standard-waving civilian crowds chanting 'Ivzid! Ivzid the hero!'

Pulling himself back to the present with difficulty, he pondered his immediate strategy. As the agent of destiny, he must move swiftly. His eyes swept from side to side, his sensor array amplified to maximum. A circular combat grid cartwheeled into place before his vision and clicked to hyper-sensitivity in seconds. His olfactors he kept at their usual level; the milky reek of parasites infested every corner and he had no desire to enhance it. Instantly, his sensors furnished him with an approximate mapscreen of the Complex. The architecture was twisted and illogical, but a route led through the tubes downward. Most probably to the yards. Yes, that was as good a place as any to start his investigations. He felt almost compelled to proceed there, as if the toes of the Goddess were pushing him gently but firmly on.

The downward route through the tubes led him eventually to a wall of rock. Set into it was an entrance, of metal, and fortunately wide enough to allow access. It remained closed as he approached. Thinking quickly, Ivzid trained his sensors on the door and the devices it contained. In the wall to one side was a metal box that governed the security mechanism. This consisted of a thin film of minute interlocking wafers that could be tripped to release the door only by the transmission of a coded signal attuned to the correct frequency. Ivzid recalled the Secunda's statement that only the servitors were granted access to the construction bays.

He thought hard. The problem was a difficult one, but it was impossible for parasite science, however advanced, to triumph over Chelonian ingenuity. He swept his sensors over the door again. They informed him that the power source to this door was absent; another technical failure, no doubt. Passing through was simply a matter, then, of burning or blasting a hole in the door, yet it was composed of a metal strong enough to withstand concentrated laser bombardment. Perhaps there was another way. He sought an emergency release device; yes, there was one, attached to the far side of the door itself. This, a smaller model of the main box, retained its own power source, independent of external supply. It was active, meaning that it could be overcome.

Angling himself off the floor, he released an internal hinge and his communicator unit, a yellow u-shaped device with a pointed tip, dropped out. Snatching it up, he recalibrated the instrument to function as a transmitter. It ought to be possible to modulate the call tones to simulate the signal required by the release mechanism.

He clawed the buttons slowly and at random, straining his optics to detect any signs of response from the security wafers. He observed tiny changes in the power status of the wafers when certain tones were transmitted in certain patterns. It might have taken a parasite an age to crack the code, but Ivzid placed great faith in the reasoning-screen grafted to the frontal lobes of his brain, which recorded and sorted the sequence over ten minutes. Suddenly the correct series of tones was relayed back to his conscious. Grunting with satisfaction, he keyed in the code. The release mechanism flipped, and with a satisfying clunk the door swung smoothly open to admit him.

'Excellent,' he said. He powered himself up and passed through.

Immediately something moved behind him. He turned his head and caught a glimpse of a hovering servitor-disc. It appeared to have been drained of power, judging from the lessened pitch of its internal workings and the giddiness of its movements.

'State your authori-ity,' it whined.

'I have been given emergency access,' Ivzid replied. He knew the best way to handle machines, he had been trained well. Raising his communicator, he sounded again the tones of the emergency release mechanism. 'See.'

The disc chattered. 'You have no – no – authority.' A probe slide from its side and shot a sizzling energy bolt. The disc's aim was false and the bolt struck the floor. A couple of seconds later the disc died and dropped.

Ivzid nodded, feeling ever more justified in his rebellion, and moved off into the darkness. Before he had gone a hundred metres along the narrow passageway ahead he heard the door clang shut behind him. It occurred to him that he had not checked the release mechanism for a means to return to the Complex. Foolish. But he was an officer, and a good one, and a solution to that problem would present itself, he was certain. For now, he would redouble his efforts to solve the mystery of Zamper.

Trying not to appear worried, Bernice allowed the travel tube to carry her back in the direction of the guest quarters. She was keen to open up the report on the test flight and work out the exact position of the TARDIS, but the presence of a security camera at almost every corner of the Complex was disturbing. Many of them probably weren't working, if the rest of the place was anything to go by, but it wasn't worth the risk. Her priority now had to be to collect Cwej and Forrester, then the Doctor, and to clear out of this place. Unhealthy interest of locals in the TARDIS, she knew from experience, was bound to cause difficulties.

Moving towards her in the next tube was Hezzka, spitting and cursing under his breath. As their paths crossed, she called, 'Off to see the Secunda? I'd better warn you, her teapot's not working.'

He turned his head away. 'Cease your prattling. You are unimportant.'

'Well, somebody got out the wrong side of bed this morning, didn't they?'

Taal fought to control himself when Christie burst into tears on his shoulder. 'There, there, love, you can trust me,' he said. It'd been a very long time since a young girl had taken comfort in his arms and, despite the seriousness of their predicament, his natural instincts were proving dishonourable. Then, of course, she was particularly sweet and admirable, with that lovely little dimpled chin and such charming clear blue eyes. 'I'll look after you.'

'But even if we get away from here somehow,' she said between waves of sobbing, 'we'll be right in the middle of the war zone. And out there we'd get blasted to bits, wouldn't we?'

'We'd just have to take our chances,' he pointed out, steering her towards the seats before the inert gaming network. 'It's a pity the credit that's passed through here in the last fourteen years is all on data-coil, isn't it?'

'Isn't there any money here?'

He thought. 'Only in the strongroom, my duck. And it'd be impossible to get in there, the doors are inch thick megalanium.'

'There must be something of value.' She smiled up at him wistfully. Really she was too young and innocent for all of this. 'What about the ship designs?'

'No. I thought of that years back. Non-starter. The design records computer's linked up to the Management. He goes, it goes.'

She dabbed away her tears with the back of her hand. Ingenuously she asked, 'Well, the designs would be lost, but the computer memory would still be all right, wouldn't it? Without any power?' Noting his curious reaction, she went on, 'Only, well, I've worked with computers, and it seems likely. Maybe I could even disconnect the memory, or something. Then, if we got out, we'd perhaps stand more of a chance, with something to sell. It's just an idea.'

Taal rubbed his chin. 'It's a very good one, my sweet. I reckon we could get away with it.' He patted her on the back. 'We'd better give it some thought. We don't want anybody noticing what we're about, do we? Pretty soon, I reckon the others are going to start thinking along the same lines, you know. Not Jottipher or Smith, but Secunda, she will, I'd bet on it.'

'What'll we do, then?' With a plan in mind, Christie seemed to have perked up a bit. Taal hoped she wouldn't be disappointed. There was still a lot that could go wrong.

'I'll meet you at the end of tube 62 in an hour, all right? That's where the records systems is located. Until then, wait here, and act casual, just in case. If anyone, particularly Secunda, asks you what you're up to, just ... well, just cry, or something. All right?'

She nodded. He muttered 'good girl', chucked her under the chin, and left game control. In her position of hiding on the other side of the internal door, Forrester's shoulders slumped. 'I can't believe he's bought that.'

Cwej wasn't listening. 'Why don't we ask the Doctor if we can evacuate these people in the TARDIS? If Zamper's shutting down, it's only fair.'

Forrester shook her head slowly and backed away down the corridor. She leant against the wall, and chewed on a thumbnail. 'She's a fraud. The broad's a fraud.'

Cwej's eyebrows quivered. 'You're only saying that because you don't like her.'

'I don't like plenty of people, but I can recognize a liar.

She's here for those ship designs. The whole stunt's been planned.' She smirked and looked Cwej up and down. 'Fortunately, I'm immune to feminine charms. No way is little Christie the bubblehead she's making out.'

'She did say that she'd worked with computers.'

'As advanced as the systems here? She'd have to be a genius, and she's not acting like one, therefore she's a fraud. That "only little me" routine is so obvious.'

'You're saying that because she isn't the sort of person you like.' He spoke calmly, as if she was the one at fault.

'Christopher, don't patronise me, thank you.'

The door of the gaming centre hissed open. Expecting Christie, Forrester stopped talking. But the newcomer was Bernice. 'It's time to leave,' she said. 'I suggest we collect the Doctor and get out. The Secunda's rather too interested in the TARDIS.' She pointed behind her. 'I think I can remember the way back to their garage. Coming?'

'No,' said Cwej, firmly.

Bernice walked right up to him, stared at his face for a few seconds, and bellowed, 'Pardon?'

'I think we should help these people evacuate,' he said. 'We've nothing to fear, they're only people.'

'The Chelonians,' said Forrester. 'Even if the Doctor said yes, we'd never get them through the door.' She poked him in the ribs, hard. 'Don't be stupid, Chris.'

'It's not stupid. It's fair.'

Bernice held up a hand. 'All right, all right, let's not get ourselves upset. We'll find the Doctor and then discuss it, okay?'

Cwej looked between the two women and nodded.

Bernice turned to lead them away. They passed through the gaming centre, which was empty. Forrester looked about the room. 'Did you see that Christie girl when you walked through here?' Bernice shook her head. Forrester turned triumphantly to Cwej. 'See? Your innocent little friend is on the move already.'

* * *

For some time, as his descent through the caverns continued, the Doctor had been aware of the echoing signals that were passing between the sub-herd. Cave 74D was close. The sounds increased in volume as he took a fork that went right, and to his astonishment he found that he could see quite clearly all about him. Switching off his torch, he traced the source of the luminescence to a split in the rock wall facing him. The light shone clear as daylight, pure and white. It took his eyes a moment to adjust to the brilliance.

Cautiously, he stepped forward, screwing up his eyes to peer through the split in the rock.

'Bright, isn't it?' asked a voice.

'Yes,' he said. 'I can't make out what's causing the . . .' It occurred to him that he had thought himself alone. 'Ah. Hello, Smith. You got down here very fast.'

She slapped him lightly on the cheek. 'How dare you!'

The Doctor rubbed his wound tenderly. 'How dare I what?'

'Just walk into my lab, steal my research, put me to sleep and come out here!' She punched his chest. 'Well?'

'I did leave a note.' He pointed to the split in the rock. 'I still think this could be very dangerous. And I'm experienced at navigating caves.'

Smith gestured to the length of rope coiled around her shoulder. 'You didn't even think to bring any equipment.'

The Doctor tapped the side of his head. 'All the equipment I need is up here.' He fidgeted, tapping his fingers together. 'I really wanted to be alone down here. It could be vitally important for the future of Zamper. I need my wits about me, I don't want to be worrying about anybody else.'

'I can look after myself, Doctor.'

'I hope so.' He patted her absent-mindedly on the shoulder, and then trailed back to the split in the rock. He tried to make some sense of what was going on in the cavern beyond. At this point, they were looking down at the top of the Zamps' artifact, which stood in all its irregu-

132

lar glory below them, its grey metal sides dripping with the twitching, squelching forms of its creators.

'It's enormous,' breathed Smith. 'About the size of one of the ships. I didn't realize.'

'There's a lot you haven't realized,' the Doctor muttered. He turned back to her, smiling. 'May I borrow your rope?'

Hezzka was jolted forward and back by the travelling pavement inside the tube. He shouted curses against the parasites as he struggled to regain his balance, thankful that he had been moving downward at a gentle angle. The tube juddered, the pavement's pneumatics sighed, and all the lights inside the Complex went out.

There was complete silence. For a few moments, Hezzka thought he heard the high-pitched cries of a female parasite. The sound cut out.

He compensated for the lack of light, and shuffled forward curiously. As far as he was aware, all electrical activity had ceased.

'This inefficiency will be punished!' he shouted, his voice echoing and re-echoing from the glassy surfaces of the tube, and shaking its support structure. 'Hear me, Secunda, I will have our monies returned or my fleet will scorch this planet!'

The echoes died away. For less than a second, stranded in this strange alien place in the darkness, Hezzka felt the rise of that deeply-buried atavistic fear.

What, an inner voice whispered, if the Arionites were to emerge?

Without warning, the screen affixed to the metal rail above the tube glowed and hummed, then returned to working order. At the same time the pavement jerked forward again, and the lights flickered on and off, on and off.

There was nothing on the screen but thick bars of crackling atmospherics, but a parasite voice, distant and strange, as if speaking from beneath a bog, rang out along the walkways. 'Sec-Secunda-da! This-is is the Man-age-age-

ment ... All is proceed-eeding sm-moothly! ... Con-
continue! ... Find the Doc-Doctor! He understands
me ... you must help me ... it is ... I am dying-ing-
ing ...'

The screen washed out with static, the crackling rose in
pitch to drown the voice, and the lights went out again.

Ivzid had proceeded through the darkened tunnels that
led down to the construction bays. After ten minutes he
reached a junction. Etched into the walls of rock were
arrows and identifying numbers. Ivzid used his resource-
bank to translate the notation, and hurried along the
tunnel to yard six.

Green light seeped from the construction yard. He
recalled the image shown in the Secunda's office, and the
faint light plaques built into the structure of the ship's
exterior. Thrilled by the prospect of this history-making
initiative, and mindful of the time it was taking him to
uncover the truth – he had no desire to be stranded by
that old fool Hezzka – he powered up his joints and
engaged his battle-drive. His limbs he flooded with stimu-
lants. It seemed to him that a raging sea roared against
his tympanic membranes, and his heart beat faster, his
head swam, his olfactors flared, every sense was alert,
every muscle in his body ready for whatever might
happen. Ah, the glory of battle-drive!

Something above him creaked. He raised his head –
and sensed the collapse of the roofing struts, dislodged by
his thunderous passage through the tunnel. He screamed
and pushed himself forward even faster as the tunnel
roared and shook, bucking like a beast around him, as if
he was in the throat of some monstrous creature. Large
rocks struck him on the shell, bouncing harmlessly off the
strengthened scutes but increasing his anxiety. He turned
a corner, ran on into the dim green light, his bulky frame
showered with scree and choking dust, his eyes streaming.

At the end of the collapsing tunnel was the construction
yard, its outline dominated by the bullet-shaped magnifi-
cence of the Series 336c Delta-Spiral Sun Blaster. The

ship of salvation. He caught dizzy half-formed glimpses of a few burbling Zamps idling on its surfaces, clicking and twitching their feelers.

At the end of the tunnel was a drop of some five hundred metres.

A hideous crunching noise came from behind, and Ivzid was thrown forward, sent spiralling rear over front through the air. He screamed and yelped, his dreams of glory shattered, his mind filled with terror, his feet clawing pathetically at thin air. His thoughts were of the Goddess. He was praying, no, begging forgiveness for his foolishness.

He tumbled, over and over and over, every detail of the construction yard picked out with terrible clarity. He realized that his internal sensor array, still on-line for battle-drive, was trying to tell him the exact speed and scale of impact he would experience when he hit the ground.

And then something peculiar happened.

Ivzid slowed.

His final thought before he was overcome by darkness was that the Goddess had delivered him.

Having secured the knotted end of the length of rope to a conveniently sturdy stalagmite at the mouth of cave 74D, the Doctor tossed the coil down, tested its strength, and then descended hand-over-hand with the ease of experience. There was a small drop at the end of the rope, and directly beneath was a pool of the glutinous substance used by the Zamps to aid their locomotion. The Doctor had no wish to get stuck, and so twisted himself as he dropped, alighting neatly on a dry flat area. 'Come on, then,' he called up to Smith, having to shout over the increased warbling of the Zamps. There was no response, and he sighed as he recalled his thwarted preference to remain alone. 'Smith!'

He saw her swing over and grab hold of the rope. 'I've never done this before.'

'Oh, really?' Satisfied that she was safe, the Doctor examined his surroundings. The cavern was swarming with

Zamps, their clammy bodies overlapping as still more joined the sub-herd through openings on the opposite face of rock. They moved slowly and purposefully, flocking towards the massive structure. Carefully, the Doctor hopped over a gathering of Zamps to take a closer look. This close the artifact was even more impressive. A white vapour drifted at its base, through which he glimpsed more Zamps, packed even closer together.

'It's incredible,' said Smith, leaping between the patches of slime to join him.

The Doctor knelt down and picked up a handful of stones. 'I'm going to try something.' He threw the stones at the base of the structure. Incredibly they halted in mid-air, then were scattered gently and harmlessly. 'You see, it's protected. Further proof of their independent thought.'

'They're maintaining a telekinetic barrier.' Smith scratched her head and closed her eyes. 'All of this is entirely contradictory to their nature. I mean, I know the Zamp brain to the last cell. They just cannot do this sort of thing.'

'Perhaps,' said the Doctor, moving closer to the structure, 'and I don't mean to be rude, you were looking at it the wrong way.'

Ivzid shook himself awake, astonished to find himself not only still alive, but also undamaged in body and mind. He scanned himself quickly, disengaged his battle-drive to conserve energy, and looked about. He had been deposited at the main entrance hatchway of the mighty star cruiser. In the dim green light, the craft appeared suitably majestic, its neutrino-tickler attachment, a massive studded prong set at right angles from the flank, appearing particularly fierce and daunting. Best of all, the craft looked almost complete. It might still fulfil its destiny as the great tool of vengeance. Ivzid saw himself piloting the vessel, single-footed, out through the gateway and to a tumultuous welcome from Big Mother and the fleet. Yes, he must examine it, now.

As he lurched forward, a slow movement from the

darkness caught his attention. He swivelled his left socket to investigate, and saw two or three of the repulsive mollusc-creatures slithering towards him. They twittered like babes. The macabre sight sent a cold shiver along the joint of Ivzid's neck. He lifted one of his front feet aggressively. 'Back. Back, I say!'

The beasts came closer. They seemed to be ailing, and there were patches of what looked like diseased tissue along their long necks. The noise they made, which grated at his nerves, contained a pathetic pleading quality, rising in scale. Shuddering, Ivzid circled quickly around their path and scuttled up to the entrance hatch of the craft. To his delight, the airlock hatch was unsecured, and he pushed it open, moved through quickly, and slammed it shut behind him. Perhaps it had been foolish; but no, he had been chosen, selected by destiny, and was protected. He had been waiting for this all of his life. He had always been different, set apart, misunderstood. His hour had come. Soon, all who had doubted him – in particular the treacherous Hezzka – would be made to pay, and would have to apologise.

His throat was dry, but that was only natural. A true warrior, Hafril had said, confronts his fears. Only an idiot fears nothing.

He motored along the airlock tunnel. This would most probably lead directly to the flight deck and the battle station. If the controls were powered up, he thought, what was to prevent him activating them and flying up and out through the slipway? A fitting judgement would then befall Zamper. It would be necessary to test the neutrino-tickler, perhaps to boil the core of the system's artificial sun. The parasites, the repulsive shipbuilders, and Hezzka, all would die a slow, agonizing death, the sun would grow to fill the sky, peeling their skins away . . .

Ivzid halted suddenly. His mouth dropped open.

The airlock tunnel led nowhere.

Confused, he carried out a sensor appraisal of the ship's interior.

The ship was hollow.

* * *

Smith and the Doctor reached the base of the structure at last, their feet inches from the strange moat of milky vapour and the slimy mass of Zamps passing, they now saw, in and out of the structure through a ring of seven small holes. Smith took the Doctor's hand. 'Very unscientific of me, I know, but this is making me scared.' She looked away from the slithering mass of cold, clammy bodies. 'They make me feel sick.'

'We probably make them feel sick.'

Smith peered at the gleaming jutting sides of the artifact. 'It's made of metal. They must have brought it here from the yards. There was a ship in construction, in yard six.'

'Then,' said the Doctor, 'most of the raw materials probably ended up here, as part of that.'

Smith shook her head. 'Impossible. The Management would have called our attention to that. He's very keen to maintain the construction rate. He oversees it personally, they just wouldn't have been able to do that.'

'You really have missed the point, haven't you?' the Doctor said kindly. 'I was hoping you'd work it out by yourself.'

'Work what out?'

He turned her to face the screeching slithering subherd. 'They *are* the Management.'

Chapter 7

After the echoes of the Management's final pleas had spiralled away into the darkness, Mr Jottipher's own involuntary whimper broke the throbbing silence. It was as if a part of himself had died. Twenty-two years in unquestioning service, and now the eye that watched and the hand that guided, was gone, with a merciful but distressing swiftness. 'Oh dear. Oh dear.' He sniffled.

'It was only a machine,' he heard the Secunda say. A soft yellow light flashed around the office, making her lined face a hanging spirit-night mask. The illumination came from a large torch she had taken from her desk drawer.

'Emotional of me, I know. Perhaps foolish. He always seemed more than a machine,' said Mr Jottipher, groping in the dark for the arm of a chair. 'Forgive me, Secunda, I need to sit down.' Dabbing his tears with the sleeve of his jacket, he observed her picking up the coder terminal that secured the vault. 'You seem rather well-prepared, I must say.'

'Everything has been planned, down to the last detail.' As she spoke, she examined the coder terminal. 'That is the essence of good business.'

'You'll never find the right combination. It's impossible.'

'You've missed a crucial fact. I don't need to.' She tapped the side of the vault with her painted fingernails, making a tinny sound. 'The power's off.'

Mr Jottipher stood on shaking legs. It felt odd to be contradicting anything the Secunda said. 'It's armour-plated. You'd have to blow it open.'

She reached out and straightened his collar. 'I am going to blow it open. From the inside.' Seeing his doubtful expression, she went on, 'Mr Jottipher, who was it, do you think, that compiled our dossier on the Chelonians?'

'Oh dear.' His throat dried and his tears froze in an instant as he recalled the marauding reptilian twosome at loose, somewhere, in this darkness. 'Well, of course, you did.'

'Correct.' She fingered the numbered pads on the terminal. 'My scrutiny convinced me that their delegation was unlikely to come here unarmed.' She gestured to the vault. 'Their weapons can be operated by a remote signal. Unnoticed, I primed the footgun before it was placed inside the vault.'

'Goodness. But how do you intend to send the signal?'

A heart-stopping cracking and splintering noise came suddenly from the door. Mr Jottipher saw the shadow of fear that flickered over the Secunda's face as she lifted her torch and they saw the claws of one of the Chelonians coming through the partition of the door and pushing apart the slats, the creature's brutish force triumphing over the unpowered security mechanisms. Mr Jottipher put the back of one hand over his mouth, whether to stop himself screaming or because his stomach threatened to turn he was unsure. The Chelonian growled, curled its prehensile foot around one slat of the door, heaved the white rectangle off its hinges, and then thundered into the room. To Mr Jottipher's relief, it was Hezzka, and he was alone. His internal additions rasping, he reared up in front of them. 'Well?'

Mr Jottipher hardly dared to move. Thankfully, the Secunda had regained her composure and was beaming steadily at the Chelonian. 'I'm doing all I can to restore the power supply, General. I really shouldn't worry. These technical problems are very trivial. Why not return to your guest room, and I'll make certain – '

'Cease your prattling!' Hezzka's crocodile eyes swivelled malevolently around the office. Strings of drool on his sharpened teeth caught the light, making him all the more fiercely impressive. He raised a front foot and indicated the vault. 'We are leaving. You will return our deposit. Now!'

'I'm afraid that until the Management comes back online that won't be possible,' said the Secunda. 'I do apologize.'

'Our hands are tied,' said Mr Jottipher. 'There's no way into the vault.' Lying came with surprising ease. 'There's no possible way to open it.'

Hezzka snarled. 'This reeks of treachery. You will open the vault immediately!' He turned to face the vault, and a thin membrane, light blue in colour, slid over his eyes. Mr Jottipher recalled the folder prepared by the Secunda, which had made special mention of the Chelonians' ocular enhancements. A hook-shaped line of lights sparkled under the membrane, augmenting Hezzka's vision with a sensor overlay. 'The security mechanism is inoperative and there is no power. The vault must be blasted open.'

The Secunda turned to Mr Jottipher and smiled. In languid tones, almost a whisper, she said, 'General, I absolutely forbid it.' The sarcasm was lost on Hezzka, who pushed them aside, knocked over the desk, and positioned himself directly before the vault.

'Ivzid's gun has come in useful after all,' he muttered.

The Secunda pulled Mr Jottipher into a far corner, shielding them both behind the leaves of a large potted palm.

Mr Jottipher covered his ears as a shrill electronic tone came from somewhere inside Hezzka's shell. He couldn't fathom this part of the Secunda's plan, which would for sure give Hezzka full access both to his money and the footgun. Her grip on his arm was all that reassured him. If she remained in control, surely nothing could go wrong. The signal rose in pitch, making his eyes water.

A second later, the far wall exploded outwards, showering them with small pieces of rubble. A wave of searing heat rushed over them, and the room was illuminated for a few moments by the pulsing golden glow of the reactivated footgun.

Then silence.

The Secunda withdrew her arm from his and stood. Mr Jottipher remained on the floor, his hands over his face. The first stage of fear had passed, and he felt oddly light-headed. The explosion echoed in his singing ears. He heard the Secunda make an approving noise. 'You can get up now, Jottipher.'

When he dared to look, he saw that the office was showered in pieces of the wall, as was Hezzka. One of the largest chunks of reinforced concrete had settled squarely on the General's head, and his shell was covered in brickdust and oddments of still-glowing shrapnel. In the light from the Secunda's torch, Mr Jottipher saw a trickle of fluid emerge from the flattened section of Hezzka's shell just above his neck. Just when he dared hope that the beast was dead, Hezzka shuffled and moaned, one of his eyes fluttering open for a moment. 'Madam, he's still alive.'

'Unimportant.' She shone the beam of her torch on the broken metal door of the vault, which had been blown half-off its mounting and lay crumpled like a piece of discarded silver foil. The vault itself was shrouded by a thick cloud of dust. Coughing and fanning this away with her hand, she advanced. The strongbox and the footgun lay together on the floor, both barely scratched despite the force of the blast. The Secunda wrapped her hand in her daintily-embroidered handkerchief and lifted the weapon by one of its smoking corners. 'Wonderful.'

'It's still functioning?' Mr Jottipher hopped nimbly around Hezzka, terrified that the thing would wake.

'Oh yes. Chelonian war technology is superbly constitutioned.' She nodded to Hezzka. 'He didn't expect it to be primed and set to maximum, poor thing.' She smoothed her gown, disarrayed by the blast, into its familiar shape. 'We'd better be going.' Playfully she nudged the end of the gun under Mr Jottipher's heart. 'With this, nothing can stop us.'

'Then, er, wouldn't it be safer, er . . .' He gestured to Hezzka.

'Mr Jottipher! A cold-hearted murderer!' She giggled and passed him the torch, then took aim between Hezzka's closed eyes. 'Yes, I suppose it would give me enormous pleasure. I've never killed anything, you know. At least not directly.' She adjusted the settings on the side of the weapon. 'Well, it's never too late to start, eh? After all, it's little more than an animal, really.'

Mr Jottipher closed his eyes. 'No. No, we mustn't.'

Amused, she asked, 'Why mustn't we?'

'It's wrong.' He pushed her gun arm down. 'It's a thinking, living creature. A monster, granted, but . . .'

She laughed cruelly. 'Very well. If it upsets you. We'll just slow him down a little, then.'

When the lights went out, Bernice turned and grabbed Forrester about the waist. 'We'd better stick together. I know my luck, and I don't fancy running into a Chelonian in the dark again.'

'And what difference am I supposed to make?'

A distant explosion echoed suddenly along the tunnel, the repercussion zigzagging over their heads.

Forrester jumped. 'What the hell was that?'

'Something blowing up.' Bernice listened closely to the raging after-rumble of the blast, which was distorted as it passed above, between and around the coiling plastic tubeways of the darkened Complex.

'Something on the surface?' Forrester pushed Bernice gently away. 'It came from above.'

'Wait a moment.' A sinking sensation tugged at her stomach. As firmly as she was able she said, 'I've lost my way.'

'Well, think,' said Forrester. 'You remember the layout, you said.'

'In the light, maybe, perhaps, just about. Not in the dark. We were going up, weren't we, along this tube we're in now?'

'You mean we were going down.' There was a couple of seconds silence, then Bernice heard Forrester slam her fist against the side of the tube. 'We were going down.'

'I thought we were going up,' said Bernice, feeling rather ashamed. 'Chris. Were we going up or down?'

There was no response from Cwej.

'Chris?' Forrester now kicked the tube. 'I don't believe it. Where's he – oh, hell.' She kicked the tube again, once with her left foot and once with her right. 'He's gone after the girly.' She moved towards Bernice and tapped her on the shoulder. 'I'll get him. You get away from here and get the Doctor. Meet you back at the TARDIS.'

'Roz.' She thought for a moment, then took the folded report on the test flight from the back pocket of her jeans and handed it over. 'You have this. Go on, it'll lead you there.'

'What about you?'

'I'll collect the Doctor from Smith's lab and he'll find a way somehow. Now, go and get Cwej.'

'You don't even know your way out of here. We should stick together.'

Bernice gripped her hand tightly, curling her fingers around the report. 'Just let's do it, okay? Do you trust me? I trust you.'

Forrester pulled her hand away. 'You sound like the Doctor.' Already she was walking away back down the tube.

'I know,' said Bernice. She turned and climbed the tube, advancing slowly into the dark labyrinth. 'As long as I keep going up.'

The woman who had called herself Christie reached the computer terminal and set to work. The pace of events since her arrival had surprised her, and she'd been forced to advanced a plan that she'd not anticipated would come about for months. She located the feebly glowing panel that must, she reasoned, control what was left of the Complex's secondary power store, and re-routed with ease a number of subsidiary functions. The panel had been designed for direct use by the servitors, and only by cracking their emergency over-ride cyphers, a chicane of multi-levelled integers, would she be able to proceed. Her advantage was the set-up on Zamper. The consortium had not foreseen the eventual demise of the place, and therefore had not accounted for it in the design of the security systems. That Zamper could be penetrated by an enemy was, to them, unthinkable, an error of judgement that left their most secret designs all but exposed.

As she worked to gain access to the design store, she reflected that her mission could not have proceeded more efficiently. Every freeloader in East Galaxy viewed Zamper as the great uncrackable, its position in the midst of the war zones and its legendarily fearsome defences enough to dampen the ambitions of the most enterprising. Over the last fifteen or so years, it was rumoured that Zamper's rate of production was falling, and in consequence that its role as the spine of the region's finance markets was slipping slightly. Opportunists had taken this as evidence that the conquest of Zamper might now be possible, but none ever returned, and the attentions of the mercenary community had turned back to easier pickings.

On her way back from a raid on a pharmaceutical base she'd come across a vessel that could only have been the Zamper supply ship, marvelled at its ability to pass unchallenged through the disputed borders, and hopped aboard. Killing the girl Christie had been easy enough, taking her place easier still. All the while she'd expected to be challenged and exposed, but as rumour suggested, the Management had been distracted. Getting in was the big problem; once inside, her plan had been to play her part until the end came, however long it took. Things were falling into her hands. Only the arrival of the strangers blotted the outlook. The older woman and the man were enforcers, she could tell that from the way they looked at each other and the questions they'd been asking. It meant East Government were on her back, probably that they'd had the idea of jumping the supply ship themselves and left it too late.

It wasn't important. Even weaponless, if it came to it, she knew she could handle them.

* * *

145

Hezzka lay alone in the rubble. His senses returned slowly and he became aware of nearby movement, of small scuttling upright beasts. Hairless mammals, parasites, two of them. Yes, the Secunda, Jottipher, a small light source flicking around the room, the residue of the blast, the strongbox, the footgun. The footgun. Oh Goddess. A pronounced coldness chilled his extremities and a huge heavy pain pressed down on the left side of his skull. He felt old, tired and stupid, the resounding blast the trumpeting of his failure. The two parasites were talking, but he couldn't hear their words clearly. He felt no anger, and wondered why.

Oh Goddess, he was dying. The relaxant chemical designed to soothe his passing had been triggered. Already he could feel himself being lifted away, leaving his broken body behind in the dust, borne on the flying rug of the host of wing-shelled chorusing angels. And nothing mattered, not the glory of the empire, nor the parasites, and all were as one, and the universe, all of it, galaxy superimposed over galaxy like trickling raindrops, was but a glittering array of ice-cold barbs floating off, a large hot thing of great meaning cooling and reducing to smallness and insignificance.

Minutes passed. He was aware that the parasites had left him. As on the verge of sleep he felt the inner part of him, the soul, turning loose, freed from the body. All he had to do now was to wait.

Then, distant, twisted by innumerable echoes, a sound cut through the blackness. A pipe, a signal? No.

Fear ran through his helpless body, and the pain surged back.

The Arionites.

He pictured them squirming in the dark, their clammy bodies seeking him out, their leech-like mouths sinking into his hide, sucking away his still-warm blood, serrating fresh arteries and absorbing the life-fluids that pumped out. The ancient enemies, cruel and artful despite their size, lured to him by the odour of his fear.

With terror, Hezzka realized that he was not dying.

146

The sound came closer, that awful high-pitched burble, precursor of a bloody and prolonged death. Now very close, coming nearer. He attempted to withdraw, but his head and his rear right foot were somehow blocked and would not obey his commands. He sank down, paralysed and helpless.

He opened one eye and found his vision blocked by a dust-covered membrane. Blinking it back, he saw movement, a figure moving through the darkness, making that awful noise. It was not an Arionite, but a parasite. Tall and slim, he couldn't distinguish its sex in the poor light, and moving closer. It hadn't seen him.

Instinctively, he opened his mouth to utter a warning, although only a gurgling grunt came from his lips. His gums were awash with the iron taste of blood.

'Hello,' the parasite said in doubtful tones, possibly preparing to run.

Hezzka growled again. 'Treach... treacherous... parasites...' Fluid seeped into his eye. He moved his head and a wave of agony flashed along his inner organs; his shell had split at the front. The parasite moved nearer, stepping with difficulty around the fallen chunks of rubble, clearing its lungs.

'Is that the General? General Hezzka?'

Forrester, moving down through the blacked-out tunnels, realized that she was heading back towards the gaming centre and the residential block. Bernice had been right, then.

She reviewed the upward journey mentally. About a minute and a half on their way up, they'd passed through a forked junction that debouched in three directions. Finding herself back there, she felt her way over to the tube that led downwards. Each step she took shattered the stillness like a gunshot. Several times she thought she'd caught a flicker of dim green light, reflected off the upper tubeways hundreds of metres above, and was certain that she'd heard muffled voices, one male, one female, but nobody she'd recognized.

The door of the gaming centre was open. She checked the locking plate, and her fingers curled around an override key that had been slid into the panel. She removed and pocketed it, then stepped through, moving cat-like through the gaming centre, her senses alert for any sign of movement.

There was nothing.

She flattened her back against the wall and felt her way to the door that led to the guest quarters. This also was open. She stepped through, thankful for the deep carpet that softened the fall of her boots as she prowled down the hallway beyond.

The movement, when it came, was too abrupt for her to react. Something thudded between her shoulder blades, a heavy weight that forced her to her knees. Before she could move, a hand clasped around her neck. The surprise of the attack receded, and with relief she registered that her assailant was fumbling and unconfident. It was the fat guy, Taal. Letting him think he was getting somewhere, she went limp for a few seconds, then reared up, knocked his hand from her throat, grabbed his shoulders and kicked him in the groin. He collapsed into her arms, cursing.

'Not very clever, was it?'

'It's you, then.' His voice came through gasps.

'Who were you expecting?'

'Nobody in particular.'

'You've got a date to keep, haven't you?'

He pulled himself from her grip. 'It's rude to listen at doors.' A strong odour of alcohol tainted his breath. 'You're an agent, aren't you? I reckoned as much when I first set eyes on you and the lad. I hope you've got some transport, that's all. Not much hope in hanging about here, eh?'

Forrester never got to give her reply. The light returned suddenly, causing both her and Taal to blink. Oddly, the silence seemed deeper than ever.

Taal paced back to the gaming centre. Forrester now saw that slung over his shoulder was a grey string bag.

He'd been packing. 'Subsidiary support functions only,' he said, waving to the light sources. He patted the sides of the inert gaming machine. 'Nothing else has come back on. Somebody must have re-routed a bit of power to the store.'

'Your colleague Christie, perhaps?' suggested Forrester. 'You did tell her how to find the computer section.'

'Young Christie?' Taal waved a dismissive hand. 'Don't be daft, the girl's barely ... ah.' He ticked his lips. 'I suppose it might be. Must be brighter than she looks.'

'She could hardly be dimmer.' Forrester clapped an arm on his shoulder. 'Let's keep that appointment, shall we?' She pointed to the door that led back out into the tubes. 'Lead on.'

In the pale light of the reactivated ceiling-globes of the Secunda's office, Bernice saw the extent of the damage to the wall and to Hezzka. Most of the debris had fallen on top of him; his shell was covered in a layer of white brickdust, and one large block had smacked him squarely on the top of the head. Her good nature had her heave it off and cast it aside. Beneath, at a point directly above his left eye, there was a deep dent, a kind of groove in Hezzka's toughened skull. Bernice winced.

'Why ... do you help me?' Hezzka asked.

'I'm just a nice person.' Inspecting Hezzka's wounds, she realized that one of his rear feet was missing. It had been shot off. A blackened stump remained, flexing above a pool of congealed blood. She felt a surge of frustration. There was little she could do to help. 'You were attacked?'

'Tricked. Ah, Ivzid was right, the treachery ...' He tried to lift up his front section, but his forward limbs floundered and he sunk back down, making a strange sucking sound with his gums to signify his anger. 'It was planned ... I was a fool to ... believe a word of the ...' His eyes closed and like a dragon he exhaled a cloud of blue smoke through his nostrils.

Bernice crouched down in front of him, and to her own surprise, stroked him gently across the cheek, down which a hot tear was running. 'General, please. Is there anything I can do?'

His eye opened briefly and he muttered, 'Parasite.'

'I don't know how to help you.'

'Leave me. Leave me . . . to die . . .'

Bernice sighed. 'Hezzka, you aren't going to die. Now either you sit here and rot or I try my best to get you moving.'

'I cannot move, parasite. My carapace . . . it is cracked.' Bernice peeked over his head and saw the winding crack that ran across the crest of his shell. 'If I move, I die.'

Bernice thought. 'There must be some way to get you patched up. Come on!'

There was a brief but significant silence. Hezzka looked up at last, and said, 'Sealing salve . . . I have a tank of salve attached to my left mid-under section. But,' she edged back slightly as his eyelids narrowed and his eyes turned yellower, 'only another of my people may touch me.'

'There isn't time to worry about that.' Bernice crawled around him, clambering over pieces of the wall, and peered beneath the left side of his shell. Clamped to his lower half was a thin blue plastic flask. 'Is this it?' she called up, tugging at the clamps.

'To touch me is . . . forbidden . . .' His voice faded.

'I bet you say that to all the girls.' Bernice examined the nozzle at one end of the flask, and worked out that by twisting a small lever it would be possible to release the contents. She directed the nozzle to the thin end of the crack and twisted the lever. Blue, quick-setting foam sprayed out. She applied the jet back and forth along the wound, and was pleased to see it setting quickly. The tension in Hezzka's posture lessened gradually, he relaxed his remaining limbs, and he gave a long groan.

Satisfied with her work – the fast-acting gel had already solidified – Bernice stood up. 'Say thank you.'

'I cannot . . . thank a parasite.' Already he sounded stronger.

'All right. Who did this to you?'

'You talk to me like I was your... hatchling...' He opened his eyes again. 'The Secunda... she tricked me... she has Ivzid's footgun...' He straightened up. 'Ivzid. I must contact him.' He moved his head awkwardly, and an angled piece of wire whirred out from the side of his shell. A gridded unit at its tip swung open before his mouth. It bleeped. 'Ivzid. Ivzid, this is the General. Report your situation.'

Bernice folded her arms. 'Some gratitude. I'll just fade away, shall I?'

'Ivzid, report. Report!' Hezzka moved forward slowly, his rear section sagging to the left where his foot had been blasted off. He looked up at Bernice. 'This is... irregular. It is Ivzid's duty to answer.'

'Why tell me?'

His head slumped. 'Oh, who else is there left to tell?'

Smith followed the Doctor as he leapt nimbly from rock to rock, navigating the massed sub-herd with the ease of a circus performer. It was noticeably colder in this cavern than elsewhere, and Smith pulled her jacket closer around her as they skirted one of the largest flanks of the Zamps' artifact. The evident relish with which the Doctor had dropped his bombshell irritated her; it really was very unprofessional to carry on like that. 'You've had your –' she began, but slipped as she spoke. She found herself wobbling on one leg, her arms cartwheeling wildly. Although they were quite harmless, she had no wish to fall into a pile of the Zamps.

The Doctor took her hand and pulled her clear. 'I've had my what?'

She rattled a finger at him. 'Moment of theatre! I'd like some facts in support of your, your...'

'Theory?'

'Silliness!'

He smiled, and leant against a ledge in the rock wall. 'Describe the colour red.'

Might as well play his game. 'Well it's... it's the colour

of your handkerchief.' She pointed to where it rested, neatly folded, in his top pocket.

'Ah, yes. I agree. Because we agree on the appearance of the colour red.'

Smith was fuming. 'I'm not a child.'

'Do you want me to explain or don't you?' He blew out his cheeks. 'I didn't invite you down here.'

'Get on with it.'

He spoke animatedly, his rubbery features twisting with enthusiasm. He looked to Smith less of the great scientist she'd taken him for; now, as he rambled on, putting emphasis on all the wrong words and rolling every 'r' in his path, he looked more like an entertainer who might be hired for a children's party. 'Our agreement on the idea of the colour red, or any shared concept. Where does it take place? The dimension of thought.' He waved about at the Zamps. 'The Zamps are a part of the Management, occupying the same space, if you like, in that dimension. The consortium's great creation, very different parts of one machine.'

'If what you claim is true, why did the Management call me in? If he is the Zamps, he'd have known what was wrong, and he'd have surely drawn attention to them carting away half the construction materials from yard six.'

The Doctor shook his head. 'Not necessarily. As with any psychological problem, the first step is recognizing there is one. If a part of your mind starts to go wrong, you may well be the last person to notice.' He knelt down and poked gently at the nearest group of Zamps with the tip of his umbrella. 'And remember, the Management isn't a living being like you or me, but a system. A very sophisticated system, I grant you, but still only a system, designed for a particular purpose.'

'Construction?'

'Yes.' One of the smaller Zamps coiled its rear section around the umbrella, and the Doctor lifted it up to illustrate his point. 'An enormous telepathic group-mind, a particular kind of invisible intelligence, attuned to design and build battleships, while another part of the system – the part that you saw on your Inscreens – conducts the business side of things. The trouble, I think, started when nature decided to fight back.' The Zamp's feelers wiggled at the Doctor, who pulled a stupid face and wiggled his fingers back in response. 'The original behaviour pattern of these creatures started to reassert itself.'

Smith was equally tempted to pull out her hair and to trip him over. 'I know that, it's what I've spent eight years trying to figure out.'

'And not getting very far, for, I think, two reasons.' He shook the Zamp back to its fellows, chuckled, and raised his hat in farewell. 'Firstly, and you can hardly be blamed for this, there was nothing to suggest the connection between the Management and the Zamps. He didn't make things clearer because ... well, I suppose the part of him we saw had no knowledge of it. Not essential, you see. More complexity, more industrial security. So when its function was overtaken by the Zamps, it had no way of protecting itself.'

'And the second of my failings was?'

'With your equipment, you couldn't examine the change in the Zamps, because it wasn't a simple biological change.'

'It was happening in the thought dimension, I suppose?' Smith calmed herself down. She had a distressing feeling that the Doctor was right.

'Yes.' He stepped forward again, pointing to the very top of the Zamp artifact, which was obscured by a ball of white light that it hurt to look at. 'I wonder how they do that?'

Smith took his arm. 'And the upshot of this change is the building of that thing. What possible use can it be to them?'

'Somebody's found a way to trip the power circuits.' The Secunda looked over her shoulder at Mr Jottipher, who was sweating from the exertion of lugging the Chelonians' strongbox along the inert walkways of the Complex. 'Quicker than I'd hoped. Probably Taal.'

Mr Jottipher slumped against the plastic tube. 'Can't we rest here just a moment?' He lowered the strongbox. Although fitted with anti-density discs it was a prodigious weight, and his fingers ached where the grip, designed for the foot of a Chelonian, had rubbed away layers of his skin.

The Secunda strode back along the tunnel and looked down at him. From below, her face had a hard look to it he'd not noticed before. 'There's still a Chelonian wandering free in these tubeways. What will be his reaction to the sight of us, skulking away with his money?'

Mr Jottipher leapt up immediately and felt for the handle of the strongbox. Even now he wouldn't dare to ask the Secunda to help him.

He followed her upwards, thankful that the reception sphere was now in sight.

Ivzid tried to ignore Hezzka's call. He was emerging from the hatchway at the base of the warship, shaking his head. Fifty metres below was an elliptically-shaped section of gantry that ran the width of the construction yard, and tapered at the far end before passing into a gap in the wall. Ivzid estimated that there was enough room for him to crawl through, and examine what lay beyond. Powering his buffers, he counted to three and let himself drop. He landed with ease, shook the dizziness from his ears, and set off, his mind clear and his purpose fixed. He was flushed with prestige, and felt calmer and more settled than ever before. The enemy had played its hand, revealed itself. It was his task to fight back. Without the trappings and trivialities of everyday existence, life took on an epic quality. A true adventure! No more the monotonous repetition of shipboard inspections and parades and exercises.

Hezzka's voice, sounding especially fatigued, buzzed in his ears like a flying insect. Oh, he would have to shut the elderly poop up. 'Yes?'

154

'Ivzid! At last, I have been calling you for some minutes – '

'That I know,' Ivzid said priggishly. 'What, pray, is the nature of your enquiry?' It gave him great pleasure to imagine the General's spluttering face.

'Ivzid,' Hezzka's voice said, 'are you back at the shuttle?'

'No,' said Ivzid, 'I am not back at the shuttle.'

'What? My orders – '

'Are irrelevant!' Ivzid felt a flush of pietistic indignation pass hotly through his body. His voice sounded as he had always wished it to sound, strong and young, bold and heroic. 'As you are irrelevant, Hezzka of Talifar. I have no – '

'Ivzid, will you be silent for one minute!' Hezzka raged. 'Listen. The parasites have tricked us.'

'Like the large fish, you catch on slowly, Hezzka.'

'Ivzid, the Secunda has taken your footgun and opened the almonry. They have our livres and are making, I am sure, to escape in the shuttle. You must go there and stop them!'

Ivzid felt satisfied that his gravest doubts had been proved right. 'See. You should have listened. I'll tell you something else for your trouble, Hezzka. The ship we were promised, it is nothing but a hollow shell.'

'What? But we saw it – '

'It was shown to us, which is not the same thing. It is as empty as your dry old headcase.'

'Listen, you young fool – '

'No. Goodbye, you *old* fool.' Ivzid turned his communicator link off, and congratulated himself upon his brilliance. Not only was he a fine warrior, his ripostes and barbs were also worthy of record. Surely he would be known as Ivzid the wit as much as Ivzid the hero.

By Faf, he was the very incarnation of renaissance Chelonian.

It was stupid, but away from Forrester Cwej felt incomplete. They'd been together almost every moment since coming aboard the TARDIS, and striking out on his own gave him a powerful sense of wrongness. She'd got nearly everything wrong about this place, she was as much to blame as the Doctor for the trouble they were in, and still she wouldn't give ground. Her response to getting things wrong was to carry on getting them wrong. The trouble was, decided Cwej as he followed the twilit tubes, she was his only link to his old life. Bernice and the Doctor were great fun, but they couldn't share things in the same way. One of the other good things about Forrester was that, even unarmed, she radiated a ready aggression that made him, probably unwisely, feel safe.

After the lights came up, his route through the tubes became less random, his way guided by a chatter of computer activity that was carried up by the echoes. After a quarter of an hour's stumbling through the network, Cwej came upon the now familiar sight of a metal door built into a spherical metal wall at the end of one of the tubes. The door was open, and the noises came from inside. Smartening himself up a bit, he stepped through into the computer centre. It was a surprisingly small spherical area, its walls lined with flashing and ticking instruments, and lit by eggbox-shaped fittings set around the inward-curving walls. He had barely an instant to register these surroundings before a hand was clamped over his mouth, and an expertly-aimed knee jabbed into his lower back, forcing him to his knees. He tried to shake off his attacker, but she now had his head in a lock that he dared not attempt to break.

'You're an enforcer,' said his attacker. She applied pressure to his neck and he felt his consciousness rushing away. 'Yes?'

'Yes,' he managed to reply.

She relaxed her grip and he fell forward, his nose slamming on the cold metal floor. 'There's no need to get angry,' he said, rolling over. 'I'm happy to talk.' Christie stood over him, hands on hips, with a contemptuous expression quite at odds with her previous demeanour. Her hair and make-up were different, he noticed.

'I could kill you with one hand,' she said casually. 'Oh, and please don't say you weren't fooled for one instant.'

He winced as he attempted to rise. 'You've done something horrible to my neck. Er, I don't suppose you'd believe me if I said that me and my friends are only here by accident?'

'Very lame for a lie, and so probably true.' She shook her head, and returned her attentions to a screen on the wall that was flashing up schematic diagrams of Zamper ship designs. 'Nearly done.'

'You seem very proud.'

'I am. I couldn't have timed it better, really.' The unit beeped a couple of times, and she removed an inch-wide disk from its drive. 'Right, that's me done. I'll be off.'

Cwej realized that he ought to put up at least a token attempt at resistance, although his left arm dangled uselessly at his side. He stood in front of her, two feet taller but feeling utterly inept by comparison. 'You're going to use the Chelonian shuttle to get away?'

'There's no other way off. Apart from your ship, I suppose. You do have a ship?' She came closer and patted him on the shoulder. 'You're really cute, in a stupid way. Who trained you?'

'Nobody you'd know. Who trained you?'

'Self-taught.' She looked at the disk, held between her thumb and index finger. 'Worth billions, that. I'm never going to have to work again. I could buy myself out of East Galaxy, even.'

'You're going to sell it?'

'No, I'm going to put it on the mantelpiece.' For a moment, as she contemplated her future, her face took on the vacant quality that had attracted Cwej initially. 'The yards on Ryga will pay seventy billion for these designs.'

Cwej coughed. 'Er, so what are you going to do with me?'

'I'm sure I can think of something.' She took him by the hand and out into the tube. 'It'll be nice to have some company on the way back.'

'What about Taal?'

She spread her arms. 'Not my concern.' She nudged him between the shoulder blades. 'And don't think of running, baby. One hand, remember.'

Cwej's head was still thick with blood, his legs were weak. The world about him felt strangely altered, like a dream. For the moment he was content to be led by this woman. Whoever she was.

Dimly, his thoughts tumbling about his head, he registered that Forrester had finally got something right.

'I'd say that boy's got a discipline problem,' said Bernice, as much to break the silence in which Ivzid's final retort seemed to reverberate than for any other reason.

Hezzka growled. 'He is young, and none too bright. The trouble is that he has been cooped up in the fleet's ships all his years. It makes me shake to think, by Nim, that he commands our first divisi–' He broke off abruptly and a sort of anxiety came into his eyes.

'Ah,' said Bernice. 'You're talking to me as an equal.'

'You saved my life,' Hezzka said at length. 'I do not understand why.'

'I'm a compassionate sort of parasite. I don't suppose there's an Androcles-archetype in your culture?'

'A what?'

'Never mind.' She tapped her chin, going over Ivzid's revelation. 'You were being passed faulty goods, then. Naughty. The question is, what are we going to do now?'

Hezzka moved forward an inch at a time, straining his remaining limbs in his attempts to increase his pace. After a few painful moments in which Bernice observed small movements in his facial muscles that seemed to signify frustration with himself, he was almost back to his former fearsome presence. 'If I was thinking as an officer should think, parasite, my immediate desire would be to destroy this planet and all upon it.'

'But you're not? And by the way, I'm Bernice.'

'That is your rank?'

'It's my name. Chosen by my parents.'

Hezzka nodded. 'Parents. Ah yes, parasites require two to breed.' His face took on a faraway look. 'My mother named me after one of our finest saints.'

Bernice was surprised by this admission and decided to build on it. 'I was named after a character in a very old Earth film.'

Hezzka feigned disinterest and shuffled to face the exit. 'I wish only to leave this place. But I cannot return without Ivzid. My loyalty is to him. He is young and foolish, but many have been both and become neither.' He moved off stoically. 'My personal sensor array tells me that Ivzid is below the Complex. I will follow and retrieve him.'

'Hang on,' Bernice called, skipping over chunks of rubble to catch up. 'Your shuttle. If the Secunda takes off in it, you're – '

'Impossible,' snapped Hezzka. 'A parasite could not operate the shuttle. More to the point, it is protected by an anti-theft system that is beyond even my own understanding.'

'Well, if you're sure.' Bernice was torn by indecision. She thought of the TARDIS, unharmed but miles away, and the Doctor back at Smith's hut, and Cwej and Forrester somewhere else again. A powerful instinct urged her to follow Hezzka as his crippled form dragged itself off down the tubeway.

Why?

She examined her thoughts. The most logical option was to get out and find the Doctor, as planned. It wasn't in her nature to follow hunches, or even to have hunches. But now, as she stood in the doorway, the caverns seemed almost to be calling her. Strangely she took comfort in the downwardness of the Complex, the thought of the warm and moist caverns below, a place of safety, a place she needed to reach. When she thought of staying on the surface an equal but opposite force nagged her to abandon the idea.

So, without knowing why, she followed Hezzka down.

The path taken by Ivzid led him to a pool of some sticky

substance. He skirted around it, lifting his sides to avoid a fall, and came to the end of the route. The roof and the floor of the caverns almost touched, with stalactites and stalagmites barring the exit; the formation closely resembled the grinning mouth of one of the lesser beasts of Chelonia. Ivzid recalled the legend of Kalza, the young hero swallowed by a sea-marauder, of how he had lived on for thirty cycles in the beast's stomach, and floated himself out on a raft made of splintered trees in his captor's bowel. In his hatchlinghood Ivzid had taken great comfort from the stories enumerated in the Book of Time. Shunning the sports of other hatchlings – not for him the mindless games of Sub-continental whispers or leap-parasite – he had spent many hours alone in his cabin, going over the stories again and again, losing his heart to the simplicity and beauty of the prose, and wishing himself a part of the tales. He longed to run through verdant lands, to breathe non-recycled atmospheres, to taste fresh food, to hunt like heroes of yore across hill and dale, to drive out infestations and graze on fresh pastureland. The air aboard the fleetships was flat and sterile, and the artificial gravity field instilled an extra layer of deadness. Whenever General Hafril passed through the inspection centre, looking to select the most suitable hatchlings to begin training, Ivzid looked at him with wonderment, as impressed by the deference shown to him by other adults as by the man himself. One day, he had vowed, such respect would greet his own presence.

Putting aside his memories, Ivzid used his great strength to snap away the bars on the exit, and slipped through into the cavern beyond. Here, too, Zamps had passed, flowing out in what must have been a tide from the construction yard. Ivzid recalled his studies of biology, and his conjecture was that the slime-beasts had entered their swarming season, and were sloping away from their workplace in order to reproduce. A logical supposition.

Of course, being a hero, he was able to conquer his dislike of the beasts. He would discover their powers, for sure, and turn them to work of his own. An entire new fleet would be built here, and would sweep out into space, laying waste to any squabbling parasite craft that might dare to interfere. And after Chelonia had been restored to its true destiny, and the maternal standard fluttered once again over the restored palace, the great vengeance would begin. Firstly, the empire's former limits would be re-taken, then –

Ivzid froze suddenly. Something was moving nearby, he was certain. His sensors told him not, but his own senses remained positive. Something – not alone; a mass of things, moving. Wriggling. Squirming wetly. Clammy, cold and sticky, a great herd of Zamps, no, not Zamps –

Arionites.

Ivzid's mouth juddered. His sensors reminded him that he was quite alone, there was no living creature in his vicinity. He told himself that he was imagining things, that the creaks and squeaks and whistles and burbles that he heard were just the result of a far-off wind blowing around the tunnels.

'No such thing as Arionites,' he said out loud. 'No such thing as . . . Arionites . . .'

The sensation passed. Ivzid moved on. His fear still mumbled at the back of his mind, but he conquered it and was driven downward by the trail.

It had never occurred to Mr Jottipher in his twenty-two years as a dutiful and obedient employee of the Management to question the intentions or the orders of his superior. Although his devotion to the Secunda was of a considerably shorter time, his trusting character was unchanged. Although the lift wasn't working, he had not expected any difficulty in getting up to the surface, confident that she would have planned for this. Indeed she had, and with a flourish she trained the Chelonian weapon on the wall of the reception sphere beside the lift door. When the smoke cleared, Mr Jottipher saw that behind the wall was a narrow shaft, square in shape, which led upwards. 'Maintenance ducting used by the servitors,' the Secunda said. 'We must climb to the surface.'

'Climb?' Mr Jottipher looked down at the heavy strong-box clasped to his chest.

'You will go first.' She waved him forward.

Mr Jottipher examined the shaft. The ducting formed ladder-like rungs on either side, but the slit of darkening purple sky seemed to be miles above him. He looked back at the Secunda. 'There is no alternative?'

'None. It's not that far up, really.'

He clasped the strongbox under one arm and started to climb. He found as he continued upwards that the box formed an effective wedge against the opposite side of the shaft, and he was able to stop and rest several times, until the voice of the Secunda echoed from below, order-ing him to hurry up before the light faded completely. Mr Jottipher could scarcely believe what he was doing. He recalled without humour the wish he had made the morn-ing before for a more practical status.

Half an hour later he emerged onto the flat grey launch-pad. He collapsed next to the strongbox, and as his trimly-bearded cheek scraped the concrete he saw Zamper's big purple sun setting over the western rocks. A couple of hundred metres behind him sat the awkwardly-shaped Chelonian shuttle, its massive black bulk casting a long twisted twilight shadow over the launchpad. His heart pumping, Mr Jottipher stood, drawing deep lungfuls of the cold air. For the first time, he allowed himself to consider that he might outlive the day.

Christie had taught herself well. The upward journey through the tubeways took only minutes, during which Cwej's embarrassment at being taken as a hostage increased. Several times he considered making a run for it, but his left arm was completely useless, swinging like a dead weight at his side, and the way Christie stayed close left him in no doubt that her boasts were not exag-gerations.

They entered the reception sphere, and Christie swore when she saw the blasted-open service ducting. She left

Cwej's side and ran to investigate. He followed. 'What's the – '

A sizzling pink bolt dropped from above.

'Madam!' Mr Jottipher's head whipped round at the unearthly shriek made by the footgun as the Secunda pulled the trigger, aiming back down the service duct. She rolled back from the open hatch and viewed the weapon gripped in her hand with evident distaste.

'Someone's coming after us,' she said. 'It looked like that Christie girl.'

Mr Jottipher swallowed. 'You – er, have you, er, killed her?' He edged closer to the hatch. 'Shall I have a look, er, to see if she's all right?'

'The Management picked well when he picked you, Jottipher.' She slipped her hand around his shoulder, and her eyelids fluttered. 'We're escaping. We don't want anybody coming with us, do we?'

He looked sadly down at the duct, the blast still ringing in his ears. 'I suppose not. It all seems a bit cruel, though. Are we really going to leave them all here?'

'You have an objection?'

He considered. Something deep inside him, he supposed his conscience, was whispering faintly that this was an immoral business and he ought to take a stand. He couldn't understand why life had abruptly become so fraught. It was his experience that simply to follow the most authorative path shielded one from difficulties. Why were things so complicated? He was no black-hearted pirate.

'Of course not, no objection,' he heard himself reply.

The after-echo of the blast travelled around the upper tubeways. As Forrester ran in its direction, Taal panting behind her, she realized that today was shaping up so much better than yesterday. The clattering percussion of the explosion was inspirational. Thank goodness, people were trying to kill each other at last.

She loped up the ramp to the reception sphere, slightly

put out that the door was open; unconsciously she'd been looking forward to kicking it back. Inside the dimly-lit sphere Cwej was bent over the supine form of Christie.

'You don't waste any time,' Forrester said acidly.

Cwej shrugged. 'You were right. She's taken the ship designs.' He pointed to the hole blasted in the wall next to the lift. 'Somebody's up there. One of the Chelonians, I reckon. Where's Bernice?'

'Gone after the Doctor. We'll meet up at the TARDIS.' She walked over and kicked him lightly with the toe of her boot. 'Don't run off like that again. It's a damn stupid thing to do, it's against every code in the book. I ought to have left you.'

He refused to meet her eye. 'We're not governed by the book any more. And it's all right now.'

Forrester's rebuke was interrupted by Taal, who panted his way into the sphere and, at the sight of Christie, uttered a wistful cry and hurried to her side. Forrester shook her head, and wondered what she could have achieved in her life if she'd been pretty. A classical saying of the late twentieth-century, much quoted in her old neighbourhood, popped into her head. Only the plain have to work at anything.

Taal patted the unconscious girl's hand. 'Poor little dear. If anything's happened, I'll not forgive myself.'

Cwej unzipped a pocket in the girl's tunic and showed him the small disk. 'I'm afraid we were both taken in. She's a pirate.'

Taal giggled. 'Well, I know that. But she's a very pretty little pirate, isn't she?'

The Zamps' mysterious light source dazzled Smith, the luminescence bouncing off the Doctor's white suit and hurting her eyes. She wasn't certain, but it seemed to be brightening. As they approached the far side of the cavern looked over her shoulder at the rear of the artifact. Noticing something, she tugged the Doctor's sleeve. 'This side is almost perfectly smooth,' she said, and pointed to its mist-shrouded sheer face, its appearance in contrast to the crazy angles of the opposite side.

'So it is. And there are fewer Zamps here.' He tapped his chin with the handle of his umbrella. Smith risked an upward glance to the brilliant core of the light source, which the Doctor seemed to have no problem in facing directly. In the moment before she was forced to look away she glimpsed a ball of white fire, apparently suspended high on the facing rockface, at the centre of an intersection of uncannily straight fault lines. The Doctor went on, 'They must have constructed it by superheating certain metals. It's staggering, quite staggering.'

'And very strange,' said Smith. 'They don't need light.'

'No, they don't. Hmm.' The Doctor turned away from the light source and returned his attentions to the artifact. 'Smith. We're two miles down here, yes? On the same level as the construction yards?'

'Yes.'

'Tell me. How are the newly-constructed ships launched?'

'Well, there are slipways in each yard, leading to outlets on the surface. The ship powers up, under the Management's remote control, and the buyers pick it up in orbit.' She had an uncomfortable feeling that the Doctor was ahead of her again; he nodded as she spoke. 'Well. Are you going to let me in on this one?'

He raised both eyebrows. 'Sorry. I mean, haven't you realized?' He gestured back over his shoulder at the glowing split in the rocks. 'That's a slipway. Thus...' He nodded to the artifact.

'It's a ship?' Smith looked over the artifact again. 'That's impossible.'

'Why is it impossible?' He hopped back the way they had come, offering his hand for her guidance, looking for all the world like a small boy about to embark on a scrumping spree. She remained behind. 'What's the matter?'

Her shoulders slumped. 'I've worked on this problem

165

for eight years. It feels rather galling to be told I've got it totally wrong.'

'Ah.' He looked down at his shoes. He had difficulty, she noted, in expressing emotions. 'Well, failure is one of the basic freedoms. Besides, I'm sure you would have worked it out eventually. There's another thing to consider, in fact.' The enthusiasm returned to his face. 'It's all rather coincidental, isn't it? Your geological survey, leading us down here. Why did you carry it out?'

She shrugged. 'I don't know, I suppose it just . . .' She trailed off, realization dawning. 'It just came into my mind.'

'Exactly.' He offered his hand again, and this time she took it. 'Those specimens of yours, I'll wager, had something to do with it, planting the impulse in your head. The Zamps want us down here, and most importantly of all, they want us to see their product. Hence the light. All of this business has been a somewhat oblique attempt to communicate.'

'Couldn't they have been more direct?' she asked as they skirted the narrow route back through the slime.

'Ah, well, the human mind, generally speaking, hasn't much of a telepathic facility. At least not in the heavily-industrialized societies such as the one your lot come from. One of the Zamps had more success with me, but I grant you they're not very skilled at it. Not really designed for it, you see.'

'They were hardly designed to go building ships of their own,' Smith pointed out. She stretched out a leg to follow the Doctor, who had advanced on to the next dry piece of rock, and nearly fell when, without warning he straightened up and took away his hand to smote himself on the forehead.

'Of course!' he cried.

Smith lost her balance and toppled into a patch of slime, landing with an unpleasant squelch in the midst of a group of Zamps. She shrieked and tried to rise up, her hands and face covered in the tacky strands of the substance, the Zamps reacting to her presence and slithering over her. A shiver of fear passed over her as she felt their cold, clammy bodies slipping over her arms and legs, brushing wetly over her eyes.

'Grab hold of this!' she heard the Doctor cry. She managed to raise her head, although her long hair was now coated in the trail, and saw his extended umbrella. The sensation of the soft underside of a Zamp passing over her hand made her gag, and her revulsion gave her the strength to shake it off and grab the umbrella-handle. When her grip was strong enough, the Doctor pulled, displaying a surprising strength. As she emerged from the mire he flicked Zamps from her jacket and trousers, using the tips of his fingers and moving his arm back and forth in a swatting motion so as not to become struck himself. The Zamps squealed as he struck them, each landing back in its group with a revolting plopping sound. Smith pulled her heavy boots from the trail, breaking strands that clung like melted cheese. She fell into the Doctor's arms, shaking.

'That can't have been very pleasant,' he said. 'I'm sorry.' She sensed the resentment in his voice. Perhaps he'd been right about coming down here alone.

She wiped away the patches of slime on her jacket sleeve and shuddered. 'It's irrational. Why should I feel scared of them?'

The Doctor wasn't paying attention. His alert eyes were roving about the cavern, looking in every direction. He seemed to be paying particular attention to the base of the artifact, and the arrangement of holes through which Zamps were passing in and out. 'I was right,' he said at last in response to her unanswered question. 'The curious thing about this place is the eggs.'

She looked around. 'There aren't any eggs.'

'That's the curious thing.'

Ivzid stopped abruptly. His journey through the caverns had taken him to a narrow passage through which he could not pass. He checked the structural integrity of the roof, and pondered on its resistance to his strength. By pushing at lines of stress at this side, he might be able to widen the passage. He could not say why, but there was a feeling of expectation building deep in his interior. Certainly, his spiritual guide seemed to be telling him, he would find the answers to all his questions and obtain the means to his vengeance by passing ahead. He weighed the percentages. If he loosened the structure of this area, he might very well bring down a rockslide on his own head.

He motored back slightly, manoeuvering himself around the sharp corner that led to the narrow passageway. Perhaps a more circuitous, but safer, route would be best.

Before he had taken three backward steps, a wave of fear flashed through his mind. Something in his imagination shifted, something fundamental to his nature. For a second Ivzid felt his individuality stripped away. His joints froze and he found himself rearing up like an animal, all personal considerations obliterated by a terror that welled up from some walled-off corner of his being.

The moment passed.

He motored forward, shaking his head. He must not succumb to such foolishness. There was nothing to be afraid of in these caves.

The way forward, moments previously half his shell-width, was now wide, and he was able to proceed with ease. He looked back, but there was no other turning he might have taken mistakenly. Deciding not to question the irregularity he hurried on.

The Chelonian shuttle's main entrance was concealed beneath its central prow, a circular outline that was firmly closed. Mr Jottipher watched the Secunda, who stepped forward with apparently total confidence. She crouched down and felt for a hidden mechanism. The slight pressure of her palm on the concealed plate caused the interlocking sections of the hatchway to spiral open from the centre. 'Emergency entrance,' she told Mr Jottipher. He reasoned that her familiarity with the alien vessel's fixtures came from a close study of the routine scan made by the defence outposts.

Half-convinced that either of the Chelonians might spring out, he followed her through the hatch, still carrying the strongbox. The dimly-lit compartment beyond was wide but low-ceilinged, as might be expected given the stature of its crew. A further reminder of the unpleasant reptiles was the ever-present leathery odour. But there was really no need to take fright. The Secunda had everything in hand.

Something brushed across his face. Mr Jottipher squealed and fell to his knees, fearing that there might be a third Chelonian concealed inside the shuttle.

The Secunda laughed a little cruelly. 'Get up.'

He opened his eyes. 'Madam, I . . .' He examined the source of his shock, one of four flexible metallic straps ending in loops that dangled from the ceiling.

The Secunda slipped one of her hands through a loop. 'They're lowered up and down using these,' she explained. 'It's an automatic system.' She gestured for him to copy her, and he did so. Merely to touch an object that was the property of the Chelonians made him feel faint.

The strap moved, lifting him up. He hugged the strongbox to his chest and closed his eyes, terrified by this strange alien environment. Burglary and theft were not activities he would ever willingly have taken to, and stealing from the Chelonians was not the most ideal way to start. In his mind he saw Ivzid's gaping jaw and dripping fangs. To comfort himself, he took a peek at the Secunda, who was still smiling. So everything had to be all right.

The straps carried them up and into the strangest room Mr Jottipher had ever seen. A grating slid beneath their feet, allowing them to relax their grip on the straps. Both he and the Secunda were forced to bow their heads as they turned to examine their surroundings. The prevailing style was functional, but not in the same way as the gleaming white tubeways of the Complex which had so much contributed to his psychological health. No, there was something rather vulgar about the Chelonians' idea of internal design. Each element, from the flat grey sensor-pads arranged to respond to the manipulations of a Chelonian's four extremities, to the buttress that jutted across the ceiling, was pleasing in itself, but there had been no attempt made to lighten the effect. At the far end of the chamber were twin console read-outs, indicating that this was some sort of a flight station. The instrument panels were built into the floor; three screens displayed random graphic displays, casting a ghostly orange glow.

Mr Jottipher sighed. 'However are we going to be able to fly this blessed thing?' He indicated the sensor pads on the floor. 'Look at those, they're hardly suitable for us to use.'

'There's a simplification program in-built into their flight computer,' she answered smoothly. 'All we need to do is bypass the command circuit.'

'You're awfully well-informed,' he said.

'It's simple. Chelonians think like children, their technology's like building bricks.' She gestured to the left read-out. 'Go to that console.'

'Er, well, er . . .' He coughed and nodded down at the strongbox, still clasped to his chest.

'Oh, allow me.' He passed the strongbox over. She lifted it with remarkable ease and stowed it in a darkened corner. 'Why didn't you ask me to take it sooner?' she asked; rather kindly, Mr Jottipher thought. She wasn't as fierce as she sometimes appeared, despite being one of those people who raise their voices and always seem to get what they want. It was good to be on her side. Maybe people like her needed people like him.

He knelt before the read-out panel, keeping his head low. The panel was composed of a dark glassy substance, and on closer inspection he could see that beneath it were dormant oblong-shaped sensor-pads, ready for activation.

The Secunda was working at something behind him, he could hear the tips of her long finger-nails tapping an adagio over one of the foot-manipulated sensor pads. This was replaced by a series of clicks, and then a metallic rattling that sounded something like bolts being drawn back. At that moment the panel below him was illuminated, and he saw the wisdom in the Secunda's analogy of the building bricks. The oblong pads were connected by a network of simple logical routes. Basic computer technology, probably used by the Chelonians for training purposes, he supposed.

'Now, Mr Jottipher,' the Secunda called out, 'do you see the two panels marked in bright yellow on either side of the display?'

'Yes, I see them.' He felt invigorated. This far ahead, how could they be stopped? This was getting to be quite an adventure.

'Now, put your hands on those panels,' said the Secunda.

Oh, the relief, to be obeying orders again! A clear task, clear instructions, a responsible superior. He complied, with a warm heart.

'Are both your hands, palms facing downwards, on the bright yellow panels?'

'Yes, madam.'

A ticklish sensation passed over his fingertips, but he held firm, sure enough this was only an effect of the command sequence powering up. More of the oblong symbols lit themselves, and a pleasantly efficient-sounding hum came from all around. The soft orange glow of the lighting gave the interior of the Chelonian shuttle the homely air of a sitting-room bathed in the warmth of a blazing hearth.

The ticklish sensation increased. A little alarmed, Mr Jottipher tried to take his hands away from the panels.

They were stuck fast. The skin on his fingers was affixed by a strong force.

'Er, Secunda,' he said. 'Er, I'm having – '

A wave of unimaginable agony surged through Mr Jottipher's body. He saw his hands suffused by an emerald aura, felt his body twist and jerk, was aware of his legs thrashing from side to side, his head crashing against the ceiling, the flesh on his face blistering as a lethal voltage stripped the skin from his fingers, then travelled up his arms, setting fire to his clothes, blackening his neat grey

171

tunic, making every hair of his well-groomed head stand on end.

He thought of Nula, poor pretty little thing, her remains hardly more than three chunks of charcoaled gristle, ferried away on a stretcher borne by two buzzing servitors.

The force of the shock heaved him rigidly upright.

Now beyond pain, his last thoughts were of the Secunda; it was surely no fault of hers that he had failed, and he hoped that she would be able to escape.

She was, after all, so much more important than he had ever been.

Chapter 8

The chimes sounded, three high notes between which the cheers of the crowd hushed first to murmurs and then whispers. A respectful pause followed. Then the silver-shelled master-at-arms motored forward, took his place on the plinth at the foot of the memorial obelisk, and barked out harshly, '*Fa-ka-ra!*'

The invocation in narrow dialect rebounded off all points of the triumphal square, in perfect congruity with the aged but indefatigably upright aluminium spires of the ceremonial quarter. The master-at-arms turned to the imperial landau. '*Ga-ya-za!*' The escort's bearers moved back in step, their silver tabards flashing in the noonday suns. The raptors that bore the landau, trained by the finest handlers of all Chelonia, remained still, their savage eyes fixed straight ahead, immaculate in the livery of the maternal stables.

At a signal given by the master-at-arms, the cover of the imperial landau was opened, folding back on silent hydraulics in a single graceful motion. Big Mother was revealed, resplendent in a sparkling green gown. He raised his left front foot and waved regally.

The martial band played, the crowd roared. Big Mother waved on, and on.

He paused the recording as the door of the imperial chamber hissed open and his nurse shuffled in, lowered his head and set to work on changing his waste-sacks.

'The jubilee parade of '736,' Big Mother wheezed, pointing to the holoscreen. 'We suppose you are too young even to recall that.'

'I was hatched in '745,' the nurse said. 'But my line was present, in four generations.'

'Ah,' said Big Mother. 'You are of Kumzir? A fine breed, and loyal. Physicians of deserved repute and skill.' He remembered having this conversation before, and to cover the nurse's embarrassment said, 'We are an old man, our mind is crowded. Sometimes,' he confided, 'we long for the release of death. Only the demise of the usurper sustains us. Only that.'

The nurse continued his work, exchanging the filled waste-sacks for new. Big Mother closed his eyes and tried to concentrate. In his youth and middle age he had sometimes taken of alcoholic substances for social purposes, and had been particularly fond of the exotically-flavoured sherries imported from the southern flank of the empire. He recalled how his thoughts had become more jumbled the more he drank, and the pleasing merriness he had experienced. His current experience of life was similar. It was impossible to trace a thought or to reason or to extrapolate. New ideas were frustratingly ungraspable. His wandering mind became clear only when his eyes turned to the screen and to recordings of things past. It saddened him that this was so.

He spoke to the nurse again. 'How old are you now, boy?'

'Forty cycles, Highness.'

'Forty cycles,' sighed Big Mother. 'Oh, to have the body and the mind of a forty cycle-old once more. Yet I feel more pity for you than for myself. Your young life is wasted, cooped up aboard this can. Things were different when we were your age, we – ' his voice faltered ' – we could never have foreseen the fall.'

The nurse stood to attention before him. 'Highness, may I have permission to exchange the fluid tubes in your mouth?'

Big Mother opened wide in answer. He waited while the tubes were replaced, and then asked, 'Boy, tell us. When the fall came, why did you remain loyal?'

174

'My eternal loyalty is to the empire,' the nurse said hotly.

'Oh yes, that we know. But many others had sworn the same oath and were quick to renounce it.'

The nurse considered. 'I had – I have a position in life that suits me, and that position is to serve the empire.'

'I see.' Big Mother looked back at the screen and the paused image of himself, forty-nine cycles ago, rising to address his subjects. 'You do not consider the rituals irrelevant?'

'No, sir!'

'Speak truthfully.' Big Mother muted the sound and let the recording run on. His younger self rose in the landau and the image cut to a pan across the expectant faces of the massed citizens. 'You do not think that some of our ceremonials are – ' he paused ' – silly?' He extended one digit of his left front foot as far as he could without losing his grip on the support webbing. 'As your empress, I order you to answer with honesty.'

'I have never seen fit to question the rituals,' the nurse replied eventually.

'Oh, but we have,' Big Mother said pensively. 'We have examined the details of the ancient precepts in the Book of Time and wondered "Do the words of forgotten men in a forgotten world mean anything to us today? Did our beloved nation place too much of its trust in their wisdom? Were the usurper and his fawning intellectual cronies right to question the validity of the old way?"'

'I am surprised to hear you say these things, Highness,' said the nurse.

'Then do not be. It is time employed well to re-examine our strongest beliefs now and then, lest the dogma borne of repetition should blind us to their meaning.' His manner lightened. 'You see, we questioned the tenets that bound our empire together for thousands of cycles, and answered ourself.' He curled his front feet into fists. 'Yes, we were right to believe. Some of our rituals may appear silly, but any such procedure appears so to an outsider. Our ceremony requires and induces discipline, and discipline is essential.' He snarled. 'The usurper, with his doctrine of "respect for life", legislates for an impossible universe of sweet harmony between races and cultures. This is a false doctrine, and if we relax our code we soon find that no other is suitable. "The greatest happiness for the greatest number," pah! A transparent veil for the pursuit of hedonism, it can lead only to the pit of decadence!'

'Highness, please calm yourself,' said the nurse. 'It is not good to excite your passions.'

Big Mother chewed on the rubber insulation that covered one of the fluid tubes in his mouth. 'You are right, of course. Then, what news of Hafril?'

'Hafril, sir? I think you mean General Hezzka.'

'Hezzka? Oh yes.' The memory of Hafril's funeral flashed painfully through Big Mother's mind and he saw again the black-draped coffin ejected into space. He couldn't recall Hezzka, this new fellow, at all, so he couldn't have made much of an impression. 'Well?'

'The General has not reported back to the fleet as yet,' reported the nurse. 'He and the First Pilot must still be on Zamper. We expect their return shortly.'

'Ah, good.' Big Mother felt a surge of hope. 'We are confident that all will be well. Hezzka is a fine officer.'

For a while now, as he journeyed deeper into the cavern system, Ivzid had felt that he was about to make some great discovery. He was not given to such fancies, but it came into his mind that something of import was about to occur. Why else was his spiritual guardian drawing him further on, arranging for him to overcome the varied obstacles in his path?

He emerged into a small cave that seemed different from the others. Why was this? He cast about. The cave walls were matt black rather than purple, and they were leant together in a regular fashion that suggested something built by a creature of some intelligence. He moved closer and inspected the walls for markings. There were none. He turned to move back the way he had come, and his rear right foot brushed over something. It was not a piece of rock. He shuffled about, a difficult manoeuvre in the confined space, and found that the protruding object was a rusted iron bar a metre in length that was curled at each end. He thought for a moment and realized that it was most probably a handle suited for the use of a parasite's clumsy spindly upper foot. He curled a digit around the handle and pulled, exerting his full strength. The thing buried beneath creaked and he heard the tear of rending metal, but the handle remained secure. Irritated, Ivzid batted aside the large pieces of rock near the handle and blew away the thick layers of dust that covered what lay beneath. He saw now that there was another handle a couple of metres away from the first, which had rusted more thoroughly. He touched it gently and it flaked, staining his foot with brown dirt.

Between the handles was a flat metal surface. He flicked down his sensor membrane and saw that the contents of the container were shielded. Carefully he gripped the handle again, powered up his leverage capacity, and pulled, gasping with the effort. No parasite could triumph over him.

The hatch creaked loudly, causing the rock in which it was embedded to groan. It came free at last, and with all of his strength Ivzid raised it up and threw it aside. He peered into the space beneath; revealed was a container three metres in width, which was packed with clumsy parasite technology. Boards of processors connected by thin wires were positioned in a spiral, reminding him of a line of dominoes. The set-up crackled faintly and tiny forks of electricity flared at the centre. It was a very old and obviously very inefficient machine. Ivzid remained staring at it for a long while, pondering its purpose.

His attention was diverted by a faint rumbling noise that seemed to be building up behind him. A rockfall? He turned his head and listened more closely, and verified that there was no vibration. But the rumble kept on building. Whichever way he turned it was behind him. That was illogical. He upbraided himself for these unquiet imaginings.

He shivered. The rumble was inside his head. With that realization, the noise changed, slowly, the gradual roll breaking up, forming more distinct sounds. Could they be words? Words – or just one word.

Destroy.

Tormented by internal conflict, Ivzid opened his eyes wide and scanned the region, keen to assure himself that there was nothing to fear. His vision glanced over the crackling box of processor boards.

As they did the word formed again from the rumble. The thunderous voice of the Goddess. Destroy!

Ivzid saw what had to be done.

He raised his sensor-aid and brought it down on the spiral in the container, smashing at the components again and again. The rumbling decreased as he increased the ferocity of his attack. He used the pointed end of his communicator like a knife and hacked through the connections. Glass tinkled as they shattered. The centre of the spiral crackled and flared, then died, the internal glow fading to a glimmer, then away to nothing.

Silence returned. The rumble stopped. Ivzid nodded his approval. He was filled with wonderment that the Goddess had selected him as her agent. But then these were days of destiny. Whatever foul parasite trickery was contained in that box had been destroyed. He felt exalted.

The Doctor and Smith arrived back at their point of entrance to cave 74D. The area was thankfully free of Zamps, nearly all of whom were now massed at the base of their artifact. Smith took pains to avoid further contact with the sticky trails that crossed their path. She envied the Doctor's agility.

A few metres ahead of her he suddenly stopped again. 'Oh dear,' she said. 'You've not had another of your brainwaves, I hope?'

He turned, and pointed with his umbrella to a point a few metres ahead. 'I was worried this might happen.'

Smith looked. In the middle of a slime trail that meandered along the cave wall was her length of rope, neatly coiled like a dozing snake. She looked up at the rockface, intending to check the opening through which they had entered.

There was no opening. The rock wall was smooth and unbroken.

She gripped the Doctor's arm. 'They've shut us up down here. Why – '

The Doctor put a finger to his lips. He was staring intently at a small crack in the wall just a couple of metres to their left. A cascade of small rocks, not much bigger than pebbles, skittered down the slight slope. They were followed by the antennae of a Zamp. 'A latecomer,' the Doctor whispered. The creature slipped itself through the crack, plopped wetly down on the cave floor, and followed the trail left by its brothers. A moment later two more Zamps entered similarly. The strong white light from the slipway bounced off something metallic on their sides.

'They're my specimens,' she said. 'They're still wearing their tags.'

The Doctor turned to face her. 'The cell samples you took from them showed no trace of any change.'

'Correct.' She looked again at the specimens as they moved off in single file towards the artifact. Patches of tissue on their elongated necks were unhealthily discoloured. 'They're changing? It looks like a disease. But that's bad zoology, I shouldn't conclude anything from that.' She fixed the Doctor with a stare. 'Go on, tell me.'

'I think,' he replied, 'that the Zamps' cleverness stretches further than we'd thought. They could tell when they were being observed and were able to deliberately conceal the changes in their nature.' He reached inside his jacket and brought out an old-fashioned notebook and his pencil. He flipped to a particular page. 'I saw some eggs like this on my way down here.'

Smith examined his pencil sketch, which he had annotated with a key to scale. It showed three eggs markedly different from the normal Zamp type; they tapered slightly, were larger, and looked more moist. She looked up. 'And there are no eggs in this cave.' The Doctor nodded at the artifact. 'Of course. It's an egg-carrier.'

The Doctor took back his notebook and started to make a sketch of the artifact. Smith was impressed by the speed and accuracy with which he worked. 'Could well be,' he said. 'The imperative of any species is to continue itself. The Zamps have broken free, after five hundred years, and now a new life awaits them in the stars.' He smiled and waved the pencil at the three specimens, who were about to join the massed sub-herd clustered at the artifact's base. 'Nature has a way of sorting these things out.'

Smith felt dwarfed by the industry of the beasts. 'It's an incredible achievement. Oh, Doctor, if we could only get away from Zamper and tell our story to the galaxy.'

'So we shall, so we shall,' he said brightly. In the bright light his face, filled with a kind of simple wonder, looked like a child's.

It was easy to follow Ivzid's trail. Hezzka had led Bernice unerringly through the tubeways and down into construction yard six, which they navigated using a metal bridge that wobbled when it took their combined weight. She had tried to interest the General in conversation, but he replied only with mutters. Several times he stopped to get his bearings. Bernice reasoned that he was tracking Ivzid by his odour. In spite of his injury, Hezzka was able to set a good pace, his hydraulic joints giving him a definite advantage.

They moved on through the caverns. As they passed along a narrow passage that was only just wide enough to accommodate Hezzka's shell, he pointed to a line of scuffed tracks. 'Yes, Ivzid has passed this way. We must go on.'

Bernice slumped on top of a boulder and caught her breath. 'Hezzka. We need to talk.'

He grunted. 'There has been too much talk.' He shuffled on, grimacing with every movement.

'Wait.' She rapped her knuckles on his shell. 'General. Please.'

He twisted his head about and his features formed an expression that after a few seconds she guessed must be a sneer. 'Parasites tire easily.'

She decided to ignore that. 'General, the deeper we go the stranger I feel.'

'Is that all you have to say?'

She tapped the sides of her head. 'I feel as if somebody were inside my mind. An attempt at telepathic communication, possibly.'

Hezzka's expression softened. 'You speak oddly, Bernice. But I understand your meaning, and I ...' His head turned to the darkness of the deeper caves they had yet to explore. 'My mission is to retrieve that young fool Ivzid, yes; and to discover the nature of this planet's secrets, yes; these are logical. But there is something else ...' He seemed to be on the point of telling her, then shook his head. 'No, I cannot discuss these matters with you.'

Bernice knelt before him and somewhat disrespectfully rested her arm against his shell. 'Look, we're alone in a cave in the middle of nowhere. Does it matter?'

'You are a ... oh, you do not understand honour, none of your kind can.'

Bernice decided to take a risk. 'That's crap, and what's more you know it. You're scared, Hezzka.'

He reared up. 'I fear nothing.' His vivid yellow eyes met Bernice's, but she calmed herself, giving no outward sign of her discomfort. She returned his stare. His reaction was to shuffle back slightly. 'You ... you are a warrior?'

'I'm a traveller. I've seen more than any warrior could.' She rubbed the rockdust from her palms. 'Fear means something very different to me now. Because I know that I can survive, and I know the best way to survive, which is to make as many friends as you can.'

Hezzka regarded her steadily but said nothing.

'I'm not really making this very clear, am I?' said Bernice. She pointed ahead. 'Don't you feel something pulling you on?'

He replied falteringly. 'There is a sensation ... I cannot

181

find the right words . . . not fear. Something lurks in this darkness, something rather wonderful, and terrifying.' His head lowered. 'There is a legend among my people that speaks of . . . monsters, beasts defeated long ago. Arionites.'

'I see. They resemble the Zamps?'

'Who can know?' He heaved his shell in a gesture that could almost have been a shrug. 'The detail of the legend is lost, and many dispute its veracity. But since my first sight of these Zamps, I have thought of the Arionites.'

'It could be a race memory,' said Bernice. 'Or their telepathic power affecting our minds in different ways.'

Hezzka turned his head to one side. 'You would make a good scientist.'

'Thanks.' She stood. 'Let's get on.'

Blood was flowing from Forrester's nose. She felt it trickle over her mouth and down her chin. Gently she leant up on her elbows and prepared herself to open her eyes. Her ears were still ringing from the blast and she relived the last few moments of consciousness; the cries and shouts of Taal and Cwej as the shuttle roared, then being blown off her feet. The shockwave from the Secunda's escape had charged her in the gut and thrown her across the room.

Cwej looked fine. He was up and about, on his haunches over the body of Taal. 'How is it?' she called over.

'They're both alive.' He gestured to Christie.

Forrester tested her legs by bending them slowly at the knee. Satisfied that she was able to, she stood up and crossed over to the shattered service ducting. Most of the damage had been done to the lower sections, and she found that by standing on tiptoe she could reach the lowest of the remaining rungs. Most of the dust stirred up by the blast had settled; and distantly, at the very top of the shaft, was a square of purplish twilight.

She leaned back into the reception sphere. Cwej was helping Taal to sit up. 'Must have been the Chelonian ship taking off,' he was saying. 'So she got away. Must have planned it all along. I never trusted her.'

'Cwej. I'm going up to the pad to see if he's right.' Taal was looking at her strangely. She wiped the blood from her face. 'Only a nosebleed.'

'The shaft isn't safe,' Cwej pointed out.

'I've decided that it is,' she said curtly and withdrew.

She tested each rung as she ascended. Most of them were secured, and for the next few minutes she concentrated hard on keeping herself conscious. The blast had unsettled her more than she'd noticed at first, and every few seconds a wave of giddiness washed over her. To fall from the height she had reached would be fatal. She stopped, slowed her breathing, then carried on climbing. She remembered the words of an old colleague. 'If you're about to drop, think of just one thing. Can be big or small. Focus your mind on that thing and keep going.'

Forrester thought of the TARDIS.

The strategy worked. A couple of minutes later she was hauling herself out of the duct and on to the launchpad. Her shirt, sopping with sweat, was stuck to her shoulders. Her throat demanded water.

She got to her feet and stumbled forward in the dark. The purple sun had almost set. Towering before her, clearly visible despite the lack of light, was what remained of the Chelonian shuttle. Her first glance suggested that a section had been blown away. Then, as she got closer, she saw that the v-shape that now distorted the shuttle's shape like a bite taken from an enormous cheese had been cleanly formed. The entire mid-section of the shuttle had lifted off, and only a regular pattern of scorches on the indented sides of the remaining sections and the acrid tang of a fuel combination acted as evidence that it had ever existed. The Secunda had evidently activated an emergency escape procedure and detached the central pod.

She reached the side of the shuttle and walked along, taking deep breaths of the cold night air and weighing up her options. Her boot nudged something on the ground. She knelt to inspect it.

It was Mr Jottipher. When she saw the horrific burns on the corpse, Forrester was glad of the darkness. The arms and legs of the luckless clerk were now little more than vestigial twigs and there was a revolting smell of burnt flesh. Forrester almost gagged, but she'd seen a lot of death.

She turned back for the hatch that led to the ducting. The downward climb was a lot easier, and her arms and legs set to work almost automatically. During the descent she devised a plan. Cwej had been wrong. Wherever they might fetch up, they were still living by the code-book. Throw away your creed and you've not much left. She didn't like either Taal or Christie, but thirty years' experience as an enforcer made that of no consideration. She didn't like plenty of people whose lives she'd saved. Yes, it was important to remember who she was and what she did. Although she'd only known him a short while, she recognized in the Doctor a similar quality. He had principles.

She dangled from the last rung on the ducting and swung down, her boots hitting the ground with a hefty thump. 'Cwej boy,' she called through into the sphere. 'The Secunda's taken – '

The reception sphere was empty. No trace of Taal, Christie or Cwej.

She slumped against a wall and put her head in her hands.

A chirruping call-sign issued from the holo-screen in Big Mother's chamber of rest, disturbing his doze. He fumbled for his remote control and altered the setting to the fleet's internal waveband. Immediately the image of cheering crowds on the visit to Veygaphipton was replaced by the face of a young officer. Big Mother remembered this young chap. The Second Pilot. A line of scar tissue ran from the centre of his left cheek and over the lid of his disabled left eye. Thoughtful of the fellow to get himself injured, really. It made him distinctive.

'Well met, Highness,' he said. His brows were low-set, making him appear perpetually angry. Another asset in the officer class. 'This is Second Pilot Frinza reporting.'

'Thank you, we are aware of your designation,' Big Mother said loftily, lying. 'Make your report.'

'Highness, the spatial gateway to Zamper has opened.'

Big Mother nodded. 'And what about Haf – er, oh, the General?'

'That's just it, Highness. We have made a sighting of the General's shuttle's emergency pod. It is travelling somewhat erratically towards the opening, but does not respond to our signals.'

Bother. This was just the sort of knotty problem that Big Mother's old brain found difficult. What to do? 'Er, Second Pilot, er, Frinza. Why do you not report this to your immediate superior? Such matters are below the maternal interest.'

Frinza's brows shifted slightly. 'General Hezzka is my immediate superior, Highness.'

'Yes, well, of course. So make your report to him, that is our point.'

'But it is General Hezzka's shuttle that returns from Zamper, Highness.'

'Oh? Oh.' Big Mother closed his old eyes. It was so hard to keep more than three facts in his head at once. 'Hezzka, quite. Well. What do you propose, Frinza?'

'I propose, Highness, to ensnare the shuttle pod in a force beam and bring it aboard the flagship. After all, it may be that the General may be unable to answer our hailing call.'

'Very well, do it, do it.' Big Mother wheezed. In his left underside was a fluttering pain. That was all he needed, a recurrence of his old trouble. 'Do it.' He broke the link to Frinza, closed his eyes again, and called for his nurse.

The Secunda's thorough preparations for her flight from Zamper had relied upon the supposition that after the death of the Management the spatial forces holding the gateway closed would be relaxed. Less than twenty minutes after leaving the blasted planet behind her she was overjoyed to see on the escape pod's forward screen a line of coded intelligence revealing that this had indeed occurred.

'Oh, how thrilling!' She looked a little sadly at the patches of ash on the floor before the flight station. 'Such a shame, our Mr Jottipher, that you could not have lived to see this.' Her study of the shuttle's defences had proved accurate. Mr Jottipher had drained the last spark of the protective voltage through his body, giving her unlimited access to the childishly simple emergency flight system. In a ship as small as this pod she could hop through the war zone with ease in a couple of weeks; there was fortunately a plentiful supply of food concentrates in stock. Not exactly suited to her needs – she had always preferred a meaty diet – but adequate.

She let her mind wander as the inboard computer guided the pod towards the gateway. Back to East Galaxy with a million livres in guild tokens. The possibilities were limitless. In her twelve years' absence she'd kept a close eye on the Management's market reports, and had already decided to return to Gilby Co. Zamper was finished. On her return Gilby Co would be in the ideal position to expand, creaming off the excess credit lost in the collapse of Zamper and using it to swallow the smaller corporations that had leeched off it for so long. The deadlock was broken, finally. Away from Zamper, away from Smith, away from the position as Secunda. She had longed for this so many years.

The forward screen clicked and chattered. She studied the row of oddly-shaped symbols that were overlaid on the widening mouth of the gate.

And then she saw them.

Massed on the far side of the gateway, more of their appalling majesty revealed as the gate's violet maw parted, was a fleet of black starships, every one as big as a city. A fleet of Chelonian battleships arrayed in a classical horseshoe-formation. At this range their detectors were sure to pick her up.

She threw back her arms. 'No!'

Hezzka had given in to the parasite Bernice's request for another rest on their descent through the catacombs. If the truth were known, he was most probably the more tired of the pair, he reflected. The loss of his back left foot was irksome. A soothing internal chemical aided in lessening the pain, but the wound made it difficult to walk using his full weight, placing a strain on his right side. They stopped, and he regarded Bernice curiously. His experience of her kind had not prepared him for her wisdom, kindness and sincerity. There still lingered a natural series of doubts. The way she moved and her milky odour were displeasing. But Hezzka felt he was in the presence of a very special person. Given the choice between Bernice and Ivzid as his First Pilot he would not hesitate in recommending the former.

'There is a long-standing dislike between our peoples,' he said. 'My mission to Zamper was intended to lead to the eventual destruction of parasites. I now find myself conspiring with one.' He shook his head at the strangeness of life.

She frowned. 'I hear that your rivals on Chelonia believe in co-operating with humanity and the other races.' Hezzka sensed that she was choosing her words with care so as not to offend him.

He raised his right front foot for emphasis. 'The anthem of Chelonia mocks the claim of parasites to intelligence. But I fear you are intelligent.' He settled his eyes on a small pile of rocks. 'And that I have failed the empire to which I have sworn undying loyalty.'

'I know some parasite anthems about Chelonians,' she said. Hezzka recognized the slightly higher timbre of her voice, used when she was making a humorous remark.

'Oh really?' He raised the pitch of his own voice to demonstrate his friendliness. 'You will demon–' He checked himself. 'Please, sing one of these.'

187

She appeared surprised. 'Oh. Well all right.' She coughed, and then began to sing, in a most unharmonious musical progression, 'I've never met a nice Chelonian, and that's not very surprising, man, 'cause they're a bunch of arrogant reptiles that hate human beings.'

An uncomfortable silence followed.

Despite his improved opinion of this parasite Hezzka felt a surge of anger. 'You find my people amusing. This anthem is vulgar, typical of parasite thinking.'

She came closer and moved her shoulders in a nonchalant fashion. 'They aren't my sentiments. It's an old Earth rhyme. I don't have much experience of your people. It's not for me to judge you.'

'You speak wisely.' Hezzka girded his shell, indicating it was time they moved on. 'There is a similar kitchen-motto amongst my people. "Let he who is innocent of all moral taints fire the opening salvo of plasma bolts." '

The path cleared for Ivzid by the Goddess led to an area from which light streamed white and pure. He peeked his head around a piece of rock and the brightness shone directly in his face. Ivzid shuddered and recalled the sacred chapter, and the descent of the prophet Gilzza from Mount Ephyiddon carrying the 77 tablets of behaviour, his aged shell silhouetted against the glorious luminescence of the Almighty One.

The confirming moment of fate.

He powered himself forward and into the cavern beyond. Instantly he was gripped by a horror that transcended any he had known before. It was a fear he experienced not as a Chelonian but as an animal, that whitened his eyes and caused his claws to retract as a shiver passed through his frame. All about was strangeness, alienness. The cavern was dominated by an artifact of unnatural design, its facets sparkling in the whiteness that obscured its upper half in a turbid haze. The light appeared to slide down the thing in a cool mist, giving it the aspect of a monstrous living waterfall. Worst of all, huddled at its base, their greasy shapes distorted through patches of vapour, were hundreds upon hundreds of the revolting Zamp creatures. Ivzid's reasoning faculties were overwhelmed by what he could only have described as an impression of wrongness. A wave of pure unqualified evil. It was a sensation for which nothing in his experience could have prepared him.

Suddenly, something else impinged itself upon his dazzled senses. Two somethings; two shapes, parasite shapes, silhouetted against the great gleaming thing as the prophet had been. Both parasites were shorter than average, and one of them wore a crumpled circlet of some kind on its head and carried some sort of silly stick. It was talking. '. . . some kind of non-specific rite surfacing from the autonomic consciousness . . .'

Ivzid croaked, 'Parasites!'

The one wearing the circlet turned his much-wrinkled head and a curious expression that Ivzid could not make sense of dropped over his features as he stepped forward. 'Oh no,' he said acidly. 'And just when I was starting to enjoy myself.'

The other parasite, which Ivzid could now see was an aged female, huddled close to her mate. 'Ah. One of our new buyers.' She addressed Ivzid directly. 'Shouldn't you be in your quarters, sir? The Management – '

'The Management is dead!' Ivzid slouched forward, his head turning suspiciously from side to side. 'You will make account of yourselves, and this – ' he waved a foot at the artifact ' – evil object.'

'Ah,' said the circleted one. 'You seem to be rather ahead of us. The Management is dead, you say?'

Ivzid reared up. 'Explain yourself! Do not trifle with the exalted one!'

The circleted parasite spoke in an aside to his companion. 'Exalted one? Dear, dear. Even worse than usual for a Chelonian.'

'I heard that!' snarled Ivzid. 'Do not think you can hide your whispers, parasite!'

He doffed his circlet in an insulting gesture. 'I do beg

your forgiveness. We don't appear to have been introduced. I'm the Doctor. This lady is called Smith.'

Ivzid scoffed. 'Doctor? Veterinarian would be more appro–' A thought struck him. A fragment of half-forgotten legend came into his mind. 'The Doctor?' he said slowly. '*The* Doctor? Of the brotherhood of Doctors?'

He bowed his head.

'Ha!' Ivzid cackled. 'You are known to us as *Sla – Ifrok – Yalkoz – Slan!*'

'Oh really? My Chelonian's a little rusty, but I assume that means fearsome and deadly enemy or some such?'

Ivzid shook his head. 'It is narrow dialect for "interfering idiot." Now explain yourself. This device is of your making?'

The one called Smith answered. 'Of course it isn't.' She spoke with a disrespectful air. 'Now, if you've nothing constructive to contribute to this expedition, would you mind returning to the surface?'

She soon backed off when Ivzid sprang forward, baring his teeth with a growl that gave full vent to the frustration and foreboding that he had felt ever since his assignation to the Zamper mission. 'You parasites are conspiring with these Arionite beasts.' He narrowed his eyes at the Doctor. 'Your efforts to thwart the expansion of the empire are known to me. Fate and the Goddess have led me to this encounter. I sense some evil and it must be destroyed!'

The Doctor's shoulders slumped and he folded his body on top of a rock. 'Oh, for goodness sake,' he said, as if he thought Ivzid's entrance of low importance.

At first, the disappearance of Cwej and the others had been accepted by Forrester as merely another example of the sort of dim-witted error with which her life had recently become plagued. It was only a while later, as she descended the echoing and eerily empty tubeways of the Complex, that niggling doubts about the incident presented themselves. It suited her to blame Cwej for things, but she couldn't imagine what could have driven him to lead the others away. The girl Christie had been knocked flat, and Taal was hardly a threat. Of the Chelonians there was no sign.

But the really unsettling thing, the nasty implications of which sent a shiver through her aching shoulder-blades as she turned a corner without stopping to think, was that she was making her own way down through the previously baffling maze of tubeways without the slightest hesitation. She knew where she was going. The route was unfolding in her mind as if this was her neighbourhood. It was no big deal, there was no voice booming from the clouds subjecting her to an irresistible force. She just kept walking down, and down.

Weirdest of all, she wasn't worried. The doubts and fears she'd felt since stepping from the TARDIS had been lifted from her troubled brow. Her internal cynical voice, normally so strong, had been reduced to a faint murmur.

Second Pilot Frinza was waiting in the observation gangway as the drifting emergency pod of Hezzka's shuttle was manoeuvred neatly aboard the flagship. He observed as the wedge-shaped craft was lowered gently by the invisible beams of force onto the black guidemarks painted on the floor of the airless shuttle bay. Thanks to the skill of the fleet's beam-practitioners, the landing was faultless. The grand doors of the shuttle bay were winched shut, and in a matter of moments full compression was achieved.

'Very well,' said Frinza. He turned to the team waiting alongside him on the gangway, three hand-picked lads from his own division decked out in full combat gear, complete with filter-masks slung about their necks. 'We'll go in now. Prepare weapons.' He nodded over their shells at the head of medical division, who was waiting with a full sled of surgical lasers in the eventuality of either of the returning expedition needing assistance. The environments report on the pod stated that at least one living being was aboard, but could not specify further. Frinza thought it best to cover all the possibilities.

The door to the shuttle bay opened. He led his team down the ramp, the digits of his right front foot curled about his primed footgun. He resisted the urge to engage his battle-drive. Sometimes it was better to respond to a delicate situation with delicacy.

He signalled the team to halt before the pod's entry hatch. But for the accustomed rumble of the flagship's engines there was silence. Frinza felt in his equipment-belt for his all-purpose coder, personally issued only to officers of higher rank. He turned its pronged end to the concealed coder plate at the side of the entry hatch, and sent the release code.

A second later the hatch creaked open. Frinza noted the scorch marks made when the pod had been detached. The traction port beyond was apparently empty. 'General Hezzka? Sir?' He stuck his head through the opening. 'Mr Ivzid?' There was an unpleasant milky odour.

His skin crawled as a creature stumbled from the shadows. Frinza was rather ashamed of his reaction, but then again, he had never seen a parasite before except on a holo-screen. What struck him above all was how spindly and unhealthy it looked. It was wrinkled and besmirched with red marks, which he presumed to be bruises – wasn't parasite life-juice red? In the second surprised second he sensed rather than saw the soldier just to his left readying himself to open fire.

He raised a steadying foot. 'Wait, wait.'

The parasite fell before him, its bony body folding in a peculiar way. In its strange clothing, a sort of wrap that was drawn by strings about the central portion of its body leaving its pallid limbs bare, it looked like a snake that had swallowed a small animal whole, the head of the vanquished one crying out from the mouth. Frinza tried to stop himself thinking of the infections that it probably carried.

It spoke. 'Please, please, help me,' it said. 'Mercy, mercy.'

Frinza knew exactly what his men were thinking. It was as much as he could do to restrain himself. But he was a good officer and knew the value of moderating natural reactions with intelligence. He turned to the nearest man. 'Olzubad. Fumigate this parasite and have it confined.'

* * *

It was good, thought Smith, that the Chelonian was unarmed. At last she appreciated the neutrality clause of the 473 year-old standard and unalterable Zamper contract. After further insulting her and the Doctor, Ivzid had crept nearer to the base of the artifact and the slumbering mass of Zamps, shaking his head in disgust. If he'd been armed he would no doubt have caused havoc.

She whispered to the Doctor, 'Do you think he was telling the truth about the Management?'

He nodded. 'I think it likely.' He tapped the tips of his index fingers together in a nervy gesture and frowned. 'I'm a little concerned about Bernice and the others.'

'Why should they be in any trouble?'

'Why shouldn't they be?' He jerked a thumb in the direction of Ivzid. 'Chelonians never travel alone.'

Ivzid, who had made his way as close as possible to the artifact without becoming caught in the slime trails, swung his head about angrily. 'Yes, I see it now!'

The Doctor huffed. Smith was amused to see the change in him; it was as if he needed an enemy to feel truly alive. Energy flowed from him in waves. The force of his personality was almost unsettling. It was like standing next to a giant dynamo that suddenly switches itself on. 'Would you be kind enough to share your discovery?'

'This is some plot you and the Arionites have put together,' Ivzid rambled on. 'The facts fit. You thought to lure the last loyal column of the Chelonian people to this dismal cosmic cul-de-sac and entrap us using this . . . this monstrous device.'

'Oh really.' The Doctor whirled his umbrella about gaily. 'And what, in your opinion Ivzid, is the nature of this monstrous device?'

'It is devil's work of some kind, the mechanism is unimportant.' He shuddered. 'You thought to destroy us with these Zamp beasts. I sense a powerful evil.'

'That's nonsense,' the Doctor said hotly. 'Typical Chelonian paranoia. It really is past time your people grew up. What you see here is a product of a race shackled for generations, using their newly-acquired gifts to free

193

themselves. Their intent is merely to survive, to propagate their kind in the natural way of things. As a renowned twentieth-century philosopher once said, mating is better than hating.'

Ivzid looked furious. 'It is you, Doctor, who talks nonsense! I am aware of the "respect for life" philosophy you espouse. You forget that it is possible to survive only through domination. That is how the Chelonian race rose from the mudswamps of the mother world and conquered the stars!'

The Doctor gave a short, sharp laugh. 'Conquered the stars? Wiped out a few defenceless colonies, perhaps. Hardly the stuff of which empires are made. Face it, Ivzid. Don't waste years thirsting for revenge like a spoilt child. There's so much more to discover.' He patted Smith on the shoulder. 'There's absolutely no reason why we shouldn't all be friends.'

Ivzid sniffed and turned away. 'Idiot. Destiny has wrought this moment. Nothing can prevent it.'

The Doctor shook his head sadly. 'You still can't see, can – ' He broke off. 'Prevent what?'

'You think I am unarmed,' said Ivzid. He motored himself forward over the rocks and settled close to the artifact, lowering his shell regally. 'You consider me powerless. But your words mean nothing to me. It is you who are powerless. Words never changed anything.'

Smith tugged the Doctor's jacket sleeve. 'I don't like this.'

'Leave this to me.' He called to Ivzid, 'What are you planning?' Ivzid looked away primly. 'Come on, I know a Chelonian can never resist the chance to gloat.'

'How well you know us.' He twitched his upper lip in what Smith took to be a snicker. 'But not well enough. You and all the others here have evidently never heard of Strategy Z!'

'I can't say I have,' said the Doctor. 'It sounds rather ultimate.'

'It is. My internal grafting, Doctor, contains three microquintols of inert amytol. All I have to do is increase my internal temperature and the amytol will detonate. That is Strategy Z, and I will shortly implement it. Your plan will come to nought, and the nation that you consider so childish will rise again and crush the parasitic races!' He closed his eyes and lowered his head.

'Ivzid, no!' The Doctor raced over to him and rapped on his shell. His fraught gaze turned to the huddled defenceless Zamps at the artifact's base. 'If you destroy this cavern you'll be destroying an entire species!'

Without opening his eyes the Chelonian answered, 'I don't care.'

None of the medical team aboard the flagship had qualifications in parasite biology, and so Frinza had sent out a launch to pick up one of the old boys from the rear gunner craft, who had made a study of inferior life-forms in his youth. The pensioner wheezed his way into the observation lounge of the med-unit and nodded to Frinza. 'Afternoon, Second – oh dear, sorry, er – well met, Second Pilot.'

Frinza bobbed his own head curtly. The medical staff were notoriously lax on etiquette, but this was not a time to quibble. He pointed to the isolation cube and the parasite, now fumigated, who lay with her body folded, her back against the wall, and her head against her drawn-up lower limb joints. 'This is the specimen found aboard the General's escape pod, sir.'

The old doctor blinked suspiciously behind his *pince-nez*. 'Sir? You address me as sir?'

Frinza sighed. 'That is the correct form of address to a surgeon-at-arms. Sir.'

'Really? Yes, I suppose it is.' He motored his arthritic joints forward and peered through the one-way glass at the specimen. 'It takes me back cycles, does this. A real live parasite.'

Frinza felt compelled to enquire, 'What interests you about such a creature?'

The old boy tapped his chin with a blunt old claw. 'They really are a fascinating species. They're good little fighters, some of them, you know.' He pointed to the specimen. 'When they position themselves in that way they are conserving their energies. This one is a female, I think.'

'How can you tell?'

'There are ways. Some of the organs are quite different. It was the same with our own kind long ago, you know.' He rapped on the glass and the specimen raised its head. 'See, there you are,' said the old man. 'They're quite alert, ha.'

'It tried to talk to us,' said Frinza.

'Ah, and you want me to find out what it knows about the General?' The surgeon nodded. 'I'll do my best.' He looked around at the attendants and whispered to Frinza, 'Tell me, after you've finished with it, do you think I can have it?'

Frinza was suspicious. 'Why?'

'Well, there are a few tests I never got to try out in the old days,' the surgeon said nostalgically. 'The research ministry thought perhaps that parasites could make good labour, and we tried out loads of them. The trouble is they need constant supervision, so in the end machines'll always be cheaper. They keep trying to run away, you see, or else they form groups and –'

'Yes, yes.' Frinza indicated the door to the isolation unit. 'Can we just see to this one, please? It's been thoroughly cleaned.'

'Oh. Right you are.' Frinza nodded in command to the guard at the door and they passed through into the isolation unit. Although the specimen had been fumigated the rank odour of sour milk remained. Her head turned to face them.

The surgeon said, 'Hello.' He addressed the parasite as one might talk to a young hatchling. 'Do you want food? I can give you food if you talk to me.'

'I'm not a fool,' the parasite said. 'I'm perfectly prepared to talk to you. What do you want to know?'

Frinza didn't care for this at all. The specimen's high-pitched voice sounded almost mocking. The surgeon likewise appeared taken aback, but after a moment whispered, 'They sometimes like to think of themselves as cleverer than they are, but their brains are soft and small.' He spoke to the specimen again. 'You are from Zamper? What is your name? My name is Kinzaz.'

The parasite stood. 'I am the Secunda, formerly chief executive of Zamper. And if you want to know what happened to your delegation I'm more than happy to tell you.'

'Proceed,' said the surgeon.

The parasite put the digits of her upper feet together. 'Both General Hezzka and First Pilot Ivzid are dead. They died defending the honour of the Chelonian empire.'

'How did this happen?' asked Frinza.

'Zamper was invaded. A horde of stellar barbarians ... we were defenceless. They destroyed everything. I helped the General and the First Pilot to return to their shuttle ... I was injured by cross-fire, and when I woke I was here, on your ship.'

There was a long silence.

Frinza led the surgeon from the isolation room. He was glad of the guard on the door; illogically he feared the parasite specimen. 'Well?'

'Parasites are notoriously devious,' said old Kinzaz. 'Still, it is plainly terrified. I think it speaks the truth.'

'But,' spluttered Frinza, 'the General and Ivzid would not conspire with parasites!'

'Was that not the very purpose of their mission?' A cold glint came into the surgeon's bespectacled eyes. ' "The Goddess made the Chelonian race, and made the universe our garden. It was the mammal lurking in the boughs of the tree of knowledge that spawned the parasite." '

'Why do you quote sacred chapter?' said Frinza.

Kinzaz laid a hand on his shell in a familiar gesture that his great age made acceptable. He whispered, 'Frinza, I have great understanding of parasites and their ways, and I tell you, there is good reason for us to keep our distance from them.' He licked his lips. 'Hezzka and the boy Ivzid may well have fallen in with the parasites. Such a thing is possible. Look to the usurper for your example. What matters most of all is that such – ' he searched for a word ' – relationships are not encouraged.'

'Then what do you advise?'

'If you like I can question this one further. There are ways to make a parasite speak truth.' There was a savage eagerness behind his words that Frinza found distressing. He remembered lurid stories of those who took too fervent a pleasure from the torture of parasites. His own belief was that it is best to kill an enemy quickly.

'I will consider this,' he said at last. 'Zamper was our last hope. If it has fallen, I . . .' He spread his front feet wide. 'I cannot see an alternative.'

A mess of footprints had been made in the purple dust that lined the floor of the construction bay. The dim green phosphor plaques gave Forrester enough light to make out the marks deposited by Bernice's pointed boots. Close by were the tracks of a Chelonian; one of its rear limbs was missing. In the shadow of the abandoned battle cruiser Forrester stopped to consider. The urge to move on, to move down, persisted. She pressed her fingertips against her temples and concentrated, searching her mind for any sign of remote thought-control.

Something creaked, not far away.

Her eyes shot open and she backed into the shadows, where the faint greenness was cloaked in an aerodynamic fold at the base of the cruiser. It occurred to her that she had seen none of the snail-like creatures Bernice had described, the shipbuilders. The bay was empty. That noise had probably been one of the high gantries at the top of the towering structure slipping a little.

She stepped forward, her intention to follow the tracks and catch up with Bernice. A couple of metres to her left was a large piece of rock that had been split in two across its middle. She lifted one of the pieces and examined its jagged edges. The nearest she'd find to a weapon. As she walked forward her eyes scanned the ground for the tracks, which now were bisected by a dried-up slime trail. The hard substance sparkled over to where something that resembled a punctured balloon was slumped. She decided to investigate and edged forward, the rock held at arm's length. The creak, which must have been made about a minute before, resounded inside her mind.

The object was a metre and a half wide. She tapped it with the edge of the rock and established that it was an empty rubber skin about an inch thick. A long slit had been cut across its width as if with a knife; the edges of the opening were lined with hardened grey matter that put her in mind of dried blood. She insinuated the outer point of the rock under the lip of the slit and lifted it up. A foul rotted-fruit smell filled her nostrils, causing her to gag and shuffle back on her haunches. She coughed, and dabbed at her streaming eyes with an elbow. As her vision normalized she saw a dissipating string of a puffball-like emission hanging over the bladder. Swiftly she moved away.

Her boot splashed and sank in a shallow pool of slime. She cursed and unstuck herself, trying hard to keep her balance. Her hand lost its grip on the rock.

She moved backward, retracing her steps. To her side she saw a slender arch-shaped opening in the rock, and something made her move closer. Beyond was a cave about a hundred metres long, filled with row after row of unhealthy-looking orange-brown eggs.

She was distracted by a sound from the darkness ahead, from the point beyond the spill of light from the phosphor plaques. At first she mistook it for a shift in the cavern walls; it was a kind of squealing crunch coupled with a sucking sound like a plunger being pulled from a blocked plughole. The sound came again. Her breath quickened and she froze. It was undoubtably being made by a living creature.

She forced herself to wait a couple more seconds then, as steadily as she could, she walked sideways and backwards, resisting the inner voice that screamed at her to run.

The unearthly noise continued, sickening her.

Her back scraped against the metal side of the ship.

She put out an arm to steady herself, and her fingers brushed something.

Another set of fingers. Cold fingers.

This time the shock was too much. Overpowered, she yelped. Her head whipped round. She found herself staring into the lifeless eyes of Christie. The young woman's face below was white, absolutely drained of blood. Her blanched lips were frozen open in a revolting 'o' of terror. A bilious stench wafted from her in waves.

Her body was upright, and clamped to the side of the ship by the same hardened grey substance that was trailed across the cavern's rocky floor. Her arms and legs were pulled apart grotesquely. Forrester's glance passed quickly over her body. She gagged. The midriff was missing, eaten away in patches, the empty ribcage visible beneath tattered bloodied strips of her red uniform. The golden Z emblem of Zamper hung on a thread.

Forrester backed away, aware that the sucking sound of the creature was nearby. Her legs turned to jelly.

She heard a voice. Cwej's voice, calling to her, faintly. She stumbled away from Christie's body towards his call. She turned a corner of the ship's base and swore again.

Cwej and Taal were clamped upright to the side of the ship, both alive and apparently unharmed, although Taal had passed out. Cwej's young blue eyes were wide with fear. He called her name again. Too late she realized that he was attempting to warn her of something.

With a hideous squeal a thickly-muscled tentacle struck her across the back and then wrapped itself tenderly about her waist like the arm of an unwanted suitor, holding her upright. She struck at its shiny black hide, ashamed to hear herself screaming. Her legs kicked. It lifted her off the ground. Warm, sweet-smelling droplets showered her face and she closed her eyes, choking. The spray next coated her arms and legs. She was flung against the side of the ship next to Cwej, the casual flick of her attacker as it uncoiled itself both winding her and knocking her into the familiar x-shape in which it obviously preferred its prey. As she was whirled about she caught a glimpse of the monster. Her senses refused to believe the horror of its shape. The sweet-smelling substance secured her to the wall of the ship. Overwhelmed finally, she lost consciousness.

'Do you have a mate?' asked Hezzka.

Bernice was taken aback by the question. 'Eh?'

'You are a female. Where is your male?'

'Er, well it doesn't quite work like that.' Before he could go on she added, 'It's rather complicated. I'm single at the moment.'

'I see. Between hatchings.' He nodded. 'It is much the same for me, although I would like to give birth once more at least. Still, the years are passing by.'

'I know how you feel,' said Bernice. 'No, the only decent males I meet either get killed, or turn out to be gay or androids or something.'

Hezzka looked at her in complete bewilderment.

The long, straight downward channel that they had been following for some time turned suddenly and opened out into a massive, brilliantly-lit cavern. Bernice shielded her eyes from the glare. Between her fingers she saw the looming bulk of the Zamps' artifact. So this was cave 74D.

'What is that?' she heard Hezzka mutter.

'I wondered how long it would take you to get here,' said another, much more familiar voice.

'Doctor!' She opened her eyes and ran to meet him and Smith, who both wore concerned expressions and were standing close to the recumbent form of Ivzid, who oddly appeared to be sleeping. She took the Doctor's offered hand and clasped it tightly. 'Something bad?'

'I'm afraid so.' He nodded to Ivzid. 'Ever heard of a living bomb?'

Hezzka let out a cry. 'Strategy Z! No, Ivzid, I forbid it! You will bring death on us all!'

Ivzid opened one eye and said, 'Then die, Hezzka. Die with your parasite friends!'

The Doctor leapt over to Ivzid, literally hopping up and

201

down with anger. He waved his umbrella furiously in the Chelonian's face. 'Listen to me!'

'Go away,' Ivzid said obstinately.

'Over there,' the Doctor said, pointing to the artifact, 'a race of creatures that have been suppressed for centuries are starting a new life. Destroy them and you'll be committing genocide, and not for any noble motive. You are afraid, afraid of a race of harmless animals. Outside their carrier they are unprotected, you will kill them all!'

Hezzka drew himself forward, dragging his injured side with considerable effort. 'Ivzid. As your commanding officer, I order you to stop. Do you hear me?'

Ivzid closed his eye.

'Ah, he was always like this, the young fool,' Hezzka confided to Bernice.

A wisp of smoke was curling from beneath Ivzid's shell. 'Is there anything you can do to stop him?' she asked.

'Strategy Z is irreversible,' Hezzka said, shaking his head grimly. 'He'll bring this cavern down on our heads.'

Bernice took the Doctor's arm. 'Well, come on, think of something.'

He shrugged. 'Any suggestions?'

Suddenly, Smith, who had wandered closer to the artifact, shouted 'Doctor!' Her outstretched arm pointed to the base of the structure and the mass of dormant Zamps gathered there. 'Look!'

Bernice stepped forward and swallowed hard at the sight. A horrible cracking sound, like a bone breaking, was coming from the sub-herd, a series of overlapping crunches that echoed up the walls of the cavern. At the centre of the mass of inert Zamps, lying on top of each other like a shoal of dead fish, something moved. A long black slimy tentacle extended itself and flailed about with a horrendous screeching sound. She looked towards the Doctor. He was backing away, an expression of alarm writing itself rapidly over his face.

Hezzka, his voice breaking with undisguised fear, said, 'What is – '

The tentacle, about two and a half metres in length,

looped itself and sprang with nauseating ease from the herd. Bernice now saw that it ended in a bulbous, distorted knot of tissue that acted as a spring.

'Get back!' the Doctor called, pulling Smith and Bernice away hurriedly. With a fumbling spiralling motion the loop descended on Ivzid, slapping him across the shell with whip-like motions of its body. Droplets of a grey substance sprayed from the tip of the tentacle.

Hezzka cried, 'Ivzid!' Bernice glanced down quickly. The old general's face was contorted with pity and disgust.

Too late Ivzid reacted. His eyes flew open, his mouth opened wide and he screamed and screamed. The creature used its enormous strength to bat him almost playfully about. Then it elongated itself, drew itself up to its full height and screeched. Its tip split apart, revealing a hideously slavering purple, quartered jaw. Then it swooped, sinking its massive fangs into the crest of Ivzid's still-screaming head. Then it ripped at his limbs and cracked open his smoking shell. A fountain of blood spurted up. There was the sound of crunching bones.

Bernice covered her eyes. She heard the Doctor muttering, Smith cursing, Hezzka whimpering.

When she looked again, thirty seconds later, Ivzid's head had been stripped to the skull. The monstrous loop creature was feasting on his innards, its mouth jostling for space between the cracked open halves of his shell, slurping lustily as it gulped down the steaming internal organs.

Blood dripping from its malformed mouth, it turned its attentions towards them.

In the voice of the Management it said politely, 'That takes care of that little problem. Now, what are we to do with you, I wonder?'

Chapter 9

Forrester was having a bad dream. Typical nightmare, a rush of dizzy unrelated images passing her mind's eye. A pair of hands, a man's hands, were planted firmly but gently across her shoulder-blades. The man's voice, in tones that are more often heard espousing the wonders of upholstery showrooms, was saying, 'There you are, look over there.' When she looked she saw Cwej's face. His skin was pulled back over his skull and his hefty jaw drooped open. His tongue flopped out over his lip, its curled purple surface like a fat plum. Forrester thought she had never seen somebody look so terrified.

Until she saw Taal, who was next to Cwej, similarly suspended.

God. The hands on her back – weren't hands. The pressure came from a thickly muscled but flexible length of rubbery tissue that rippled itself into humps like a sea creature of legend. The loop was supporting her numbed body, rocking her gently back and forward on her heels. The sensation was almost relaxing. Damn, she couldn't feel her legs. Her arms were stiff and her skin felt tight over her temples.

And it wasn't a dream, in spite of the way her vision bobbed up and down and she couldn't follow one thought with another.

She tried to speak. Her tongue was stuck in her mouth. She managed only a gargle.

'Sorry,' said the man's voice. It couldn't be, but it seemed to be coming from the loop. A talking hosepipe.

'The soreness will pass shortly. I'm interested to hear what you have to say.'

'Who – who are – you?'

He sighed. She heard the loop slap against the floor in time to his words. 'I'm somebody terribly important. Terribly, terribly important.' His speech was too exact. It sounded modulated.

'I'm not up for a game of twenty quest– ' She broke off, coughing. Her tonsils felt as if they'd burst.

She was turned again. 'A little reminder?' On the other side of Cwej, between two of the mighty legs of the construction gantry, were the skeletal remnants of Christie. Forrester groaned. It was an involuntary sound, and not the sort of noise she could imagine herself making. The body had now been completely stripped of flesh. The male voice imitated licking its lips. 'Naughty girl. Trying to make off with all my centuries of hard work. I couldn't have that.'

'Are you going – ' Forrester's voice faltered. Her mouth was awash with a sickening acidic flavour.

'Am I going to eat you?' The top of the loop curled itself in front of her. The quartered divisions in the tip opened out like the sepals of a flower, and four rows of dripping teeth were revealed. It screeched. 'Of course I'm going to eat you.' Its mouth came level with her head and it breathed directly into her face. The rotting smell had the effect of a powerful salt. She sneezed and her head jerked back and forth. With one of its lower coils it smacked her hard across the back of her knees and she fell forward. Her arms outstretched automatically as she fell; she relished the pain as her palms slammed down on the uneven gritty ground. Sensation was returning, at least.

It spoke again over her bowed head. She curled up in a foetal position. She had never felt so powerless. 'I shall eat you, along with your friends from the TARDIS. Nothing personal, I actually think you're interesting people, but eating you is what I expect of myself. My new self.'

She looked up. The loop was leering over Cwej, breathing into his face. His eyes flickered and he tumbled forward. She caught him and nestled his face on her shoulder. Taal was freed next. His lumpen, under-exercised body thumped down hard at their side, beating up a cloud of dust.

'Aren't you going to say thank you?' asked the loop.

Taal looked up. His light blue eyes were screwed up and red-rimmed. 'Your voice. The Management.'

The loop tutted sarcastically. 'I was.' It curled into an elegant corkscrew. 'I much prefer this form. So many more possibilities.' The tip darted suddenly over to the body of Christie and ripped off one of her shinbones, then proceeded to toss it playfully between the ripples of its body.

'It's disgusting,' said Forrester.

'Am I?' It flicked the bone aside and did an obscenely jolly dance. 'Good, good. I've been so looking forward to striking terror into the hearts of all beings. To realize an ambition. How very rare and strange.'

Forrester covered her face with her hands.

'Well?' he asked. 'Go on. Ask me where I come from. I can tell you're curious.'

'Just go away,' she said in a low voice. 'Or just do it. Get it over with. Don't – '

'Prolong the agony? Well, I'm able to relax my food animals. Christie didn't feel a thing.'

'Compassion?'

'Afraid not. Expedience. But there is a choice.' It lifted her head. 'The choice is yours. Would you really prefer to be gulped down, piece by bloody piece?'

'What are you?'

'That's better. Unfortunately, you see, I'm one of those dreadful . . . people that likes to talk about himself.' It relaxed its grip. 'Well, it's a hard one to answer, really. I've been around for an awfully long time, and there are several parts of me . . .'

It occurred to Forrester, and from the startled look on Cwej's face it occurred to him at the same moment, that their captor had woken them up because it wanted a conversation.

'I can't remember when I got started up. Suddenly there I was, pop, the Management of Zamper. A product of the consortium, and goodness alone knows how long they've been about. Things went swimmingly the first two or three centuries. A bit of me designed the ships, another bit put them together, another bit did all the legwork on the markets. I suppose you could say I was happy. So far as I could understand the term. Then again, who does?'

'Oh good,' Forrester said acidly. It isn't often, she thought, that a monster decides to tell you its life story. Perhaps she should take it as an honour.

'But then it all started to go wrong. I couldn't tell why, but the shipbuilding side of me went off the rails a little. Of course now I understand.' A feral rattle issued from its tip and it shook angrily along its length, although its voice remained at the same vicarage tea party pitch. 'The shipbuilders – that is to say, we – or rather, I – oh, you know what I mean, the Zamps. They'd been adapted by my makers. Originally they'd been a peaceful little species. Lived in herds inside one of the moons of Kappa Geet Perba.' He sighed wistfully. When he next spoke it was with a more alien stiltedness that reminded Forrester of speciesist stand-up comedy routines. 'We remember home. The meeting of minds in the herd. We farmed the gas-mammals that shared our tunnels, using our herdmind to bring them floating to us. Then the aliens came. The herdmind sensed their approach. They dropped from the outer world in huge machines and killed our home, took us away and they . . .' The loop was shaking and screeching. 'They changed us. They warped the herdmind, linked us to . . . to me, the Management part of me . . . made us shipbuilders, used our imagination, working us so that they could make fire rage between the skies.' He coughed and the more polite Management side returned to prominence. 'I do apologize, the Zamp part of me tends to get a bit lyrical.'

'Don't mention it,' said Forrester.

'But the consortium, perhaps for the first time, had failed. Their genoarchitects could not chain the herdmind forever. With the new knowledge we had as part of the Management, we gradually and secretly altered our genetic structure.' It snaked down behind Forrester and then reared up with something clenched in its teeth. She identified it as the stinking bladder she'd come across shortly before she had been overpowered. 'Recognize?' It waggled the bladder and she noticed a pair of feelers dangling at one end. 'This was my previous form. Using my vast intelligence I was able to incubate my new shape within. This particular specimen – ' it bowed ' – is my rear guard. As it turned out, very necessary. Now we are almost ready to leave Zamper and swarm into the universe of the aliens. Revenge shall be ours.'

To Forrester's great relief, Cwej was sitting up and following the creature's explanation. He looked remarkably unshaken. In reply to the loop's boasts he asked, 'How are you going to manage that, then?'

'The means is at hand.' It paused. 'The Doctor and Bernice are at the egg-carrier now. Witnesses to my brilliance.'

'Egg-carrier?'

The loop swelled proudly. 'The carrier will take the race – my race, my beautiful new race – out into the universe. The crew are almost ready; they will be mature and complete as I am. It was awfully clever of me to bypass the incubation stage in that way, don't you think? We will swarm and multiply, feeding on the bodies of the aliens that thought to subdue us. Our eggs we will seed wherever we go. We will build new ships, build an empire. We can evolve at will, suit ourselves to any environment. The human race and its allies will become the lesser creatures. We will farm them as once we farmed the gas-mammals of our homeworld. The galaxy will be ours. Nothing can stop us from becoming the dominant form of life in the universe!'

Bernice winced as the great teeth of the loop-monster

gnashed proudly, and concluded the rambling and self-important explanation it had given to its fear-stricken audience. 'Nothing can stop us from becoming the dominant life-form in the universe!'

In the ensuing silence, she realized that she alone of the small group remained able to formulate any kind of reply. The Doctor, ashen-faced, was looking gravely at his shoes and twisting his umbrella around and about. Smith had taken his arm and had put a hand to her lined brow. Poor Hezzka, sickened by the demise of his young comrade, was staring fixedly at the creature with horror.

'You aim high, don't you?' she shouted defiantly up at the monster.

It chuckled. 'Professor, you possess admirable spirit.'

The Doctor was roused at last, to Bernice's relief. He stepped forward bravely and addressed the creature. 'You lured us down here.'

The loop ducked its tip graciously. 'Not you, Doctor. The others I was able to entice by planting mental impressions. As a scientist, you'll be interested to hear from someone who's had a look about both that the human and the Chelonian minds are rather similar. No trouble there. But you, you little fool, you lured yourself. You are insufferably curious.'

'The eggs I saw, the wounded Zamp progenitor?'

'For your aid, grateful thanks. A premature drop, but your assistance enabled me to get them safely delivered to the carrier.'

The Doctor's brow furrowed and he muttered a long and unpleasant-sounding Gallifreyan word.

'Now, now, be fair,' said the loop. 'If you will go looking for the good in everyone, you must expect to be disappointed now and then.'

He snarled. 'I warn you. I make a dangerous enemy.'

The loop curled down and faced him. 'Hmm, yes. I'm aware of your quite disgraceful record in these matters.'

A little of the Doctor's indomitable character appeared to return. With mock shyness he brushed a speck of dust from his lapel. 'I do my best.'

209

The loop flexed itself. 'But such pitiful opposition, all told. Dreary tin cans and potato-heads. Hardly worth the candle.' It gestured to the great mass of dormant Zamps at the base of the egg-carrier. 'In another couple of hours the full conversion will be made. The great hatching will begin. We will spawn and pilot the vessel up and away from Zamper.' A fearful screech came from its mouth, which still dripped the thick blood of the hapless Ivzid.

Hezzka spoke for the first time since Ivzid's death. 'Why do you not kill us now?'

The loop tutted. 'General, really. What do you take me for? As you can imagine I'm very hungry. It's all I can do to hold myself back. Your young friend made a disagreeable *hors d'ouevre*, far too tough and dry. Some human meat would be far preferable.'

'I think I'm going to be sick,' said Smith.

The Doctor patted her shoulder absently. 'Ivzid did us a great favour, in the end,' he said. 'His actions forced the premature hatching of the most advanced Zamp.' To the loop he said, 'But you're still very weak, and very young. The truth is you haven't the stamina to attack us. Just to stand there and gloat.'

The loop growled. 'This is your only chance. Take it! Or face the consequences. Now, I really must be getting on.' It turned and slunk back to the base of the egg-carrier. 'You will all be consumed in the end, no matter how hard you try to resist.'

Bernice turned to the Doctor. 'Well?'

He shook his head and covered his face with his hat. He groaned. 'I think I may have misjudged this situation entirely,' he said. 'But wait a moment. Something's occurred to me.' He took away his hat, and Bernice was pleased and astonished to see that some of his usual merriness had returned. 'Have you noticed?' he asked Smith.

'Noticed what?'

He stretched out an arm and scooped up a rock, then handed his umbrella to Bernice and lifted the rock up to shoulder-height. On tiptoe he hopped closer to the loop creature and took aim.

210

Hezzka lurched over. 'What are you doing? Are you an idiot? Don't provoke it!'

The Doctor threw the rock. It bounced harmlessly off the loop's thick hide. The creature looked back contemptuously. 'Oh, please. I think you can do better than that, Doctor.' It hissed. 'You're making me angry. Go!'

The Doctor doffed his hat. 'Certainly.' He scanned the opposing wall of the cavern and pointed to the aperture through which Bernice and Hezzka had entered. 'That way, I think, everybody.' She wasn't quite sure how, but the brightness behind his words gave Bernice the impression that something had changed for the better.

As they filed out she edged closer to him and whispered, 'What was all that about?'

It was Smith who answered. 'They've lost their telekinetic power, haven't they?'

The Doctor nodded eagerly. 'The price of maturity. The consortium kept them in a permanently adolescent state. Notorious for psychic ability in any species. And like most, it's been exchanged for a degree of brute force.'

Hezzka looked up glumly. 'Does it make any difference?'

'It may do,' the Doctor replied. 'Now then, we must find Roz and Christopher.'

A murmur passed between the flagship's flight crew as Frinza returned, alone, to the bridge, with his head lowered. The Environments Officer turned from his post at the sensornet panels and nodded briskly. 'The spatial gateway remains wide open, sir,' he reported. 'We are maintaining catchment formation, fixed subject to astral drift.'

Frinza waved him away. 'Continue, continue.' He made himself comfortable in the command position and slipped his feet into the grooved control pads that had been Hezzka's, and old Hafril's before that. His mind was cluttered with the business of command. It was specially galling to be clinging to the account given by the Secunda parasite. If she spoke the truth, then beyond the gateway was an invasion fleet of immeasurable power. There were,

211

however, sufficient inconsistencies in her story to stimulate his doubts.

He became aware that the bridge was unnaturally silent. The flight crew were waiting for him to make a decision. News of the apparent loss of both the General and Ivzid must have spread quickly up from the lower decks. Frinza felt cheated by the speed of events. It was unfair of life to change so quickly and for so much suddenly to be expected from him. A notion that had lingered unexpressed all his career now presented itself plainly. Big Mother was leader in name alone and his exalted status freed him from blame. Responsibility fell always on the military commander.

His gaze settled on the navigation display at his station, in which the chasm of the gateway was represented as a fluctuating ragged green line. 'Maintain constant scan,' he told the Environments Officer. 'Report the slightest activity at the gateway to me at once.'

The pronouncement seemed to calm the flight crew, and the whispering efficiency of the bridge gradually returned to its accustomed level.

Another of the regrettable aspects of her life with the Doctor, Bernice reflected, was running; usually from something very unpleasant. The Doctor and Smith set a sprightly pace back through the eerily silent caverns, but she was forced out of politeness to moderate her speed in respect to Hezzka. The old Chelonian looked wearier than ever, and she guessed that he was sustained now only by the internal power drive of his cybernetic enhancements, which were grinding and scraping, pushing his organic parts along automatically.

The brightness from the Zamps' cavern lit their way. The increase in its magnitude was accompanied by a rumble that shook the pebbles littering the passageways and coated her hair and face with purple dust. She spat the substance from her mouth. Nobody said anything. 'That'll be their egg-carrier readying itself for flight,' she said. 'I just wanted to spell it out. It's for my own benefit. Sometimes I get lost. My life gets very complicated.'

Hezzka looked up and around. 'This unholy place. We should never have come here.'

The Doctor glanced over his shoulder. 'I don't think any of us had much choice. The Zamps, as they were, lured us down using telepathic suggestion. For breakfast. If Ivzid hadn't come along . . .' He waved a hand vaguely in the air.

'You'd have been politely extolling the wonders of nature when the hatching started,' Smith said bitterly.

The Doctor looked hurt. 'Well, I . . .' he started to say.

Smith looked away. 'Failure is one of the basic freedoms.'

Twenty minutes later, they reached the construction yard where the hollow battle-cruiser had been constructed. In the faint glow of the green phosphor plaques Bernice saw the movement of another loop monster. It was arranged in a macabre spiral surrounding Cwej, Forrester and Taal. As the Doctor approached, leading their small party, the loop broke the formation and slithered aside. There was a distinct clumsiness to its motion. It was like an old spring.

'I love a reunion,' the Management voice said as the three captives, who looked bloodied and exhausted, stumbled forward.

'Doctor,' said Forrester. 'This thing is out to –'

He smiled. 'I know, I know.' He made a swatting gesture with the back of his hand and addressed the loop. 'Thank you. You can get back to your egg-carrier now.'

'Don't tell me what to do,' said the voice as the loop hissed and swooped menacingly down. Bernice again noted the weakness and confusion of its movements, a direct contrast to the smooth assurance of its voice. It was like watching a toddler straining to reach a biscuit-tin on a high shelf. She found she was smiling, and the Doctor must have noticed that because he leant closer to her and whispered, 'In a few hours it'll be as deadly as anything we've ever encountered.'

'I've noticed,' said the loop, curling itself around a spar of rock as it slid away, 'from my scans of some of your exploits, Doctor, that it's customary for your opponent at this point to warn you against "trying anything".' The sucking sound it made as it slipped off the rock made Bernice turn away and take Cwej's hand. 'Well, this time, you can try anything you like. Because this time you don't stand a chance.'

When she looked back the loop had gone.

'I need to change my underwear,' said Taal.

The Doctor was pacing up and down now, craning his head and looking up at the empty construction yard and the huge empty ship. He turned to Smith. It was the first time he'd spoken to her since their abrupt exchange during their flight from the tunnels, and Bernice sensed the contrition underlying his words. 'To think that this was going to end up in the hands of the . . .' He stopped short as he caught sight of Hezzka pushing himself into view.

Hezzka seemed amused by the fearful way they must have been looking at him. 'The Chelonian race as I knew it is finished. Poor Ivzid was right about one thing. This is a moment of destiny. We are all doomed.'

Taal spoke. 'You lot have got a ship somewhere, though, haven't you?'

In response Forrester drew out the crumpled test flight report from the back pocket of her jeans. It was wet and covered in dirt. 'How long would it take us to get there, though?'

'Even if we do get away, the Zamps are free to do what they like,' Cwej said glumly. He clasped Bernice's hand more tightly, and for the 53rd time she wondered why she just didn't fancy him. 'Perhaps we ought to forget this one, eh?'

The Doctor stared at him. 'I never forget.' He took the report from Forrester and a look passed between them. Bernice felt a pang of envy and insecurity. Forrester was the only person she'd seen that the Doctor wasn't putting on an act for. He hadn't dropped his facade for the Master or Tanith and Gabriel or President Flavia, for anybody really important in the universal scheme. Only Forrester. His eyes dropped to the report. 'Smith. Those air-buggies of yours . . .'

'They've got independent fuel cells,' she said. 'If we find one, we could get to the crash site in, say, four to five hours.'

'Very well.' He chewed on a thumb-nail. Everybody, including Hezzka, was waiting for him to pull the rabbit from the hat, thought Bernice. Even Taal, who'd met him only moments before, was taking comfort from the air of showmanship he was even now affecting. 'But we have to deal with this monster, there has to be a way.'

Bernice slumped to her knees and rested her forehead on one of Cwej's legs. 'Let's do the show right here in the barn,' she muttered.

The Doctor lifted a professorial finger. 'Wait, wait. Hezzka. You and Ivzid. Were you alone?'

'Yes, of course.'

'No, no, I mean, there must be some others of your people hanging about.'

Hezzka shrugged his shell and wiped dust from his eye. 'The entire maternal fleet awaits our return.'

'A fleet?' Forrester smacked her fist into her palm. 'Beautiful!'

The Doctor shook his head. 'The Management must be aware of that. The egg-carrier would be able to withstand massive bombardment.'

' "The force aura on a Zamper ship can pass through a minor-mag sun and emerge without a scratch",' said Taal ruefully. 'Catalogue page 17.'

Smith said, 'He's right. You'd need a blast-intensity upwards of 61 blarks even to mark it.'

The Doctor's face fell. 'Then we may have to forget it,' he said. 'And clear off back to the TARDIS.' And it was at this point that Bernice's security in relation to the Doctor was strengthened again. She alone of the small group that followed him out of the construction yard recognized that he was lying.

* * *

The Management sensed the return of its advance guard. Weakly the loop creature emerged into the bright light of cavern 74D, its head section drooping. Its brother lurched forward to greet it.

'Hello,' it said tentatively.

'Hello,' an identical voice replied. 'Hmm. We are two, not one. It is an interesting feeling.'

'Yes,' said the other. 'Oh, I've – we've – been held back for so many years. Now we have them. At last!'

'Yes. The flesh of the Chelonian was hard and too chewy for our taste.'

'The girl Christie was more suitable.' Its jaw snapped. 'I can still taste the blood on my tongue.'

The loops slapped their bodies together enthusiastically. Already the rumble of the egg-carrier was increasing, and the base was starting to shudder slightly. From the mass of dormant Zamps came an occasional click or squeak or whistle as the conversion process neared completion. The Management sensed the awakening of many new minds, great regions of ability unfolding before him. Every mind was his, each new Zamploop infused with his unalterable purpose. A purpose that would expand exponentially, filling all eras and all places. There could be no limit to his power. He would become the universe. Each Zamp, however they might evolve, would be a sensory organ, the input by which he observed himself and his doings. It came to him suddenly. He would become more than the universe. His power to change his nature at will and dominate the furthest reaches of all time and space would make him God!

The loops sat before the egg-carrier in two neat coils, conserving their energy, waiting patiently for the birth of the Almighty.

It was hard to believe, thought Forrester, that beneath the Complex lurked a threat to the universal order. Up top the ghostly white tubeways were unchanged, silent and convoluted. They ascended swiftly. Bernice stopped every couple of minutes to let Hezzka catch up, and the unlikely pair slowly fell behind. Cwej was helping Taal to walk, and Taal was explaining the Secunda's absence to Smith.

The Doctor made a minute movement of his head, summoning her to his side. 'The Chelonian shuttle,' he whispered. 'The Secunda took off in it?'

'She took the escape pod, yes.'

'Ah.' He nodded, and stared directly into her eyes. Her legs wobbled momentarily. 'I can rely on you to get the others safely back to the TARDIS.' He phrased the words as a statement rather than a question. 'Don't let Chris or Bernice follow me. When you get in, go to the console and press the yellow and green-spotted button.'

'What will that do?'

He looked at her as if it was obvious. 'Widen the door. For Hezzka. Shut the doors and don't let anybody except me inside.'

She nodded. 'And what are you – '

He shook his head. 'It's better you don't know. It's a matter of time. If there was another way I'd come with you. My way is quicker. Now.' He raised an eyebrow. 'A diversion, please.'

Immediately Forrester sank to her knees, clasping her chest and groaning. She thought she was quite convincing until Cwej asked, 'What are you doing?'

'I'm – I'm – ' She gasped for breath, counting off the seconds in her mind. Ten, fifteen, twenty. That should have given him enough time. 'I'm feeling better now.' She stood up. 'Let's get on.'

Smith was the first to notice. 'Where's the Doctor?'

Cwej shot Forrester an accusatory glare. 'Don't look at me like that, will you?' Over Cwej's shoulder she saw Bernice and Hezzka coming up the tubeway. 'He's given me a job. We're going back to the TARDIS, as planned.'

Bernice's face took on a resentful expression. 'What's he up to?'

'I don't know.' She spread her arms wide. 'Honest.'

'I know what he is planning,' Hezzka said slowly. 'It is something I had considered myself.' He rested a foot on Bernice's side. 'The Doctor is not as our histories depict him. He is a brave para– ' He nodded. 'He is a brave man.'

Bernice frowned. 'Explain.'

'The shuttle contains a detachable one-operative flight unit, which can make short journeys in space, although it was designed for expeditions in planetary atmospheres. He means to contact the fleet, I am sure.'

'What's the point of that?' asked Taal. 'What – oh.' His fingers fluttered nervously and hope and trepidation chased each other across his face. 'The Deimlisch manoeuvre.'

Smith swore. 'Of course. The little . . . genius.'

'This is a multi-cultural expedition, lady,' said Forrester. 'What's this manoeuvre?'

Taal rubbed his sweaty palms together. 'In the punitive campaigns of the third Wobesq-Majjina war, mad old Major Deimlisch had orders to destroy a wave of Wobesqan vacuum-to-vacuum missiles.' He shivered. 'Nasty little things, those, they can slip between sensor beams four seconds out of every five.'

'Get on with it,' said Forrester.

'Ah, right. Well, Deimlisch knew that his fleet had no chance of stopping all of the missiles. The best that could happen was that three-quarters of his ships would be lost stopping a quarter of the missiles. So . . .'

'So?'

Taal looked at his shoes. 'The Doctor's a very clever man, but I can't see – '

Forrester grabbed him by the shoulders and shook him, hard. 'So?'

He shrugged. 'Diemlisch gave orders for each ship in his fleet to self-destruct. The chain reaction destroyed the fleet, the missiles, and half of the star sector.'

Hezzka grunted. 'Each ship in the maternal fleet is powered by a stabilized core of time-cooled anti-matter. It is a simple matter to remove the temporal baffles.'

Bernice stamped her foot. She looked dangerously close to tears. 'Why does the Doctor always have to be so crukking clever?'

Cwej leant against the side of the tubeway. 'He's going to sacrifice his own life for the sake of the universe.'

Hezzka chortled. Forrester pointed a finger between his eyes. 'What's funny?'

'He cannot succeed,' said Hezzka bitterly. 'An unarmed parasite, asking Big Mother, godhead of the empire, to destroy his own fleet? It is impossible. Yes, he is a brave man, the Doctor. But stupid.'

Guided by infallible instincts, the Doctor raced up through the tubeways. When he reached the reception sphere he paused for a moment before hurrying over to the hole in the wall next to the lift shaft. Without hesitation he climbed up through the service duct, his hands, legs and umbrella working in unison to propel him with ease.

He was unobserved as he left the Complex. Nobody saw the expression that settled over his rubbery features as he hopped out on to the launchpad and padded silently towards the remains of the Chelonian shuttle, an expression that combined rage, humiliation and deep concern.

With the furthest extrusion of his senses, the Management felt the minds of living creatures. Although the power of the herdmind over objects was all but lost, he had made sure to retain the part that could direct him to food. How he craved food. The stomachs and throats of the Zamps about to hatch were aching for food.

Thanks to the stupid Ivzid, the food had escaped.

But no! He must have nourishment, he must be satisfied. God could not be denied his dinner! He licked the rows of teeth that had eaten Christie. Human flesh was delicious. The savage animal part of him, what remained of the farming instinct of the long-dead world of Kappa Geet Perba, had longed to consume the Secunda, Mr Jottipher, Taal and Smith. Watching them on Inscreens all day, day after day, observing the swell of their limbs against the fabric of their clothing, desiring to leap out and gnaw at their ample human frames.

He must feed. He must feed.

Another of him burst free. He savoured its first leap, a quicksilver dash through the air and into the open. An impetuous young one, this, its jaws snapping. Then more, more, and still more of his progeny, splitting open their useless, blind, snail-shapes and vaulting over and over. Filling the stale air of the cavern with their screeching cries, sliding the lengths of their bodies around and against each other. Young, dumb and full of life. And so, so hungry.

They must feed, and soon.

The nearest settlements, the line of independent medical outposts at the fringe of the war zone, were a day and a half away. He pictured the descent from space, the futile efforts of the humans to destroy the carrier, the emergence of his offspring.

Patience, my children, he told himself. Think of the feasts to come.

No! We demand food! the young screamed.

The Management calmed them. There was a feast to be had, here on Zamper. The Doctor and company. Their deaths would satisfy at least some of the herd, reduce the desperate need slightly.

One for each, then. Six of the young, taking strength from the awakened minds of those around them, split away from the mass and made their way leaping and coiling out of the cavern. The others cheered them onward.

The Management concentrated. The eldest of the new Zamps uncoiled themselves and made their way through the crowd of their fellows to the base of the egg-carrier. Their long necks curved up elegantly and applied pressure to concealed mechanisms. A hidden entrance whirred open.

The crew of the carrier began to board.

Frinza had now waited an hour for developments and his crew were getting edgy again. A study of the escape pod had been fruitless, neither proving nor disproving the

Secunda's account. He was being pushed by events to authorize Kinzaz's interrogation of the parasite. As yet he had not conquered the mechanism of his mind that referred difficult decisions to a superior. He, the daughter of a blackberry farmer from Falzot, was now the leader of the fifteenth column. He hated it.

'Sir.' The Environments Officer looked up from his position. 'Sir, there's some small activity, gridmark fifteen by four.'

Frinza felt a rush of adrenalin. 'Enlarge, forward screen,' he heard himself saying.

A blip was revealed as the grid zoomed and one square filled the screen. 'It's very small. A meteor?' said Frinza.

The Environments Officer choked. 'Sir, it's the shuttle's domestic flyer!' The aspect of the object became clearer and Frinza saw the truth of the statement. Starlight glittered faintly over the transparent dome that topped the tiny vehicle, although the occupant of the pilot's position was not visible. The flyer buzzed about the square like a puzzled flea.

The Environments Officer said a word. Frinza missed it, and waited for it to be repeated. 'Orders? Sir?'

'Guide it in. I shall inspect it at once.' Grateful for the chance to absent himself from the bridge, he made for the door. He remembered how Hezzka, and old Hafril before him, had always given further commands as they left a room. It made them look busy and authoritative. 'Inform Big Mother of this incident. And tell Kinzaz to begin his further study of the Secunda at once,' he said as the partitions of the bridge door swished shut in his face.

The bubble on top of the domestic flyer clicked open, its release system activated from inside. A second later a strangely-shaped stick emerged; knotted to its end was a square of stained white fabric. The stick was waved about.

Frinza, because he was in charge and nobody else was going to, stepped forward. 'Who is there?'

221

The voice of a parasite said, 'This is a flag of truce. I must speak to somebody in authority.'

Frinza sighed. Another one. 'Identify yourself!'

The new arrival popped up. He was very different from the Secunda, and appeared dirty and mad. He wore white coverings bespattered with purple dust and mud. Oddly, he appeared perfectly at home; he hopped nimbly down from the flyer and looked about genially. 'I have news of your expedition to Zamper. And I respectfully request an audience with your Big Mother.'

Frinza swelled up. 'What are you to make such requests?'

The little parasite swung his stick over his shoulder. 'You can tell him it's the interfering idiot,' he said without humour.

The hungry young loops followed the scent of the humans up through the caverns of Zamper, their bodies slapping against each other, overwhelmed by the rush of new sensations tingling between their synapses. To hunt again, after so long! It was difficult to orientate with all of these new senses buzzing about the brain. But the Management had designed them well, and they were adapting readily. Hunger was a good motivator.

And hunger would lead them to satisfaction.

The rumble of the egg-carrier was increasing steadily, and could now be felt rattling through the floors of the Complex. Forrester brought up the rear of the party now, her head turning every few seconds to look back down the tubeways for any sign of pursuit. Smith and Taal had good local knowledge and led them unerringly up to the garage terminal. Bernice and Cwej weren't looking her in the eye. Amateurs. She and the Doctor understood what it means to take on responsibility in the name of fairness, and that was all. Envy is a stupid reaction, and wasteful when there are a bunch of flesh-eating monsters at your back.

They came to an open doorway and Smith turned

back to address the others. Her long grey hair was dishevelled and her face dripped with sweat. In her eye was a dangerous look that Forrester had seen before in civilians. In a bad situation, inspired by cheap holo-cable shows, they started to see things like they were part of a story, complete with winners, losers and martyrs. It took years of street exercise to loosen that way of thinking. 'Through here,' said Smith, slipping off her thick woollen jacket. She stood aside to let them pass. Bernice helped Hezzka through the door. Cwej helped Taal through the door. They looked like attendants in an old peoples' home.

Something overturned, way down below. The tubes, in that irritating way they had, muffled and twisted the clangor, making it impossible to trace. 'Probably just something falling over,' she said without the slightest conviction. Cwej caught her eye and smirked. She was forgiven, then.

Another crash. Forrester swore and waved at Bernice to hurry up with Hezzka. 'Get him through, get him through!' She looked back down again, slapping her fists against her sides in frustration. Not one gun in this place.

Hezzka slipped through the door, grunting and mumbling like the old man he resembled. Taal and Cwej hopped down, and Forrester followed as another series of crashes reverberated and a ghostly ululation was carried up to their ears.

It was only when she hit the concrete floor of the small garage, and heard the servos on the door activate, that she realized Smith was still outside. A quick glance about the garage revealed only that it was clean, crowded with small vehicles, and that the main exit was closed.

'What's Smith ruddy playing at?' said Taal, who was already showing signs of recovery as he staggered over to the nearest air-buggy. 'We've got to get out!' He threw open the back door of the buggy. 'Well, come on!'

The others were frozen. Before Cwej or Bernice could do anything dumb, and both looked as if they might, Forrester raised a hand. 'We're getting out.' She pointed to Bernice. 'Get Hezzka aboard that thing, both of you. Then get the door open. Move!'

'I don't have to follow your orders,' Bernice started to say, but she and Cwej were already bending down to lift the floundering Hezzka, who had closed his eyes to shield himself from the indignity.

Without stopping to think Forrester leapt up the entrance platform of the garage and hammered on the door. Her trembling fingers hovered over the locking panel. 'Smith! I'm going to open this door for three seconds. You are going to get in here!'

There was no answer.

Forrester kicked the door. 'Listen! Forget it. Nobody's a hero!'

'Leave – go now!' Smith shouted back. 'I am not stupid!'

The screech of the approaching loops cut through the air. Forrester's hand settled over the door control, her long fingers fitting between the moulded ridges of its edges. She rested her forehead against the cool concrete of the door and cursed again and again. She didn't actively register the noise of the garage's exit door as it was winched up.

'We're ready!' she heard Cwej cry.

The cry of the loops got nearer.

Forrester removed her hand from the door control. 'Nothing we can do,' she shouted to them as she leapt over the sides of the buggy and jolted into the passenger position. Cwej powered up the motor, they were lifted up on a cushion of air, and they sped out of the Complex. Hezzka's weight tilted the buggy back and Cwej compensated, wrenching the steering stick forward and angling the nose section upward.

Nobody said anything.

Forrester let her aching head fall back on the padded rest and watched the stringy, violet-edged morning clouds pass by.

There were tears in Smith's eyes as the loops slithered into view, dragging the lumps of raw stubby tissue at their bases behind them and screeching wildly. She prepared herself, flattened herself against the garage door. Her lips were twitching.

'Ah, Smith,' said the voice of the Management as the creatures coiled to strike. 'Curious to the last. I remember how we suffered at your hands, your foul experiments on our brothers.'

She managed to speak. 'You ordered me to experiment!'

'I was a confused young boy,' he said defensively. 'We all make mistakes in our youth. Not to worry. I've sorted myself out now. Nicely, I think.'

'Oh well that's all right, then!' She closed her eyes and her body slumped as one of the loops swooped down and almost tenderly showered her with droplets of a foul-smelling substance. She fell. It thwacked her across the back, then propped her prone body up against the wall.

She couldn't move her legs.

Her senses faded out. The screeches disappeared along with the voice.

'It's such a relief. I've finally got what I intended to do. No compromises. I'm talented, I'm an achiever, and nothing's going to stop me . . .'

Each crew member had found its way to its station aboard the egg-carrier, guided by the superbly efficient mind of the Management along the curving white arteries of the upper levels. The Zamp herdmind had not created a better design. Even the smallest of the control mechanisms had been crafted with utmost forethought. The tenacious loops squealed gleefully as they curled sections of their bodies around the spoke and hook-shaped instruments that bristled from the walls. In the lower levels nestled ranks of eggs, safely incubated. From each, soon, would sprout a fully adult loop.

Time for the off.

Power was diverted to the carrier's concealed thrusters; the acutely sensitive scanner array confirmed that the slipway was free of obstruction; the defence auras were shifted up to full capability.

The carrier shook, bellowed, glowed, and lifted, its irregular sides sliding effortlessly through the cavern. It angled forward slightly and its enormous bulk entered the slipway.

Two minutes later it burst from a wide gouge many miles from the Complex, engaged its secondary thrusters and soared up through the atmosphere.

'There it goes.' Cwej pointed to the thick white vapour trail left by the curving carrier as it shrieked upward, its sonic boom pressing down on his forehead. Momentarily he lost control of the buggy; Forrester slapped him hard against the wrists.

The shadow of the carrier passed over them, accompanied by a wave of displaced air that howled across the empty purple plain of Zamper and blew stinging particles of grit in their eyes.

Hezzka spoke falteringly. 'Bernice . . . this TARDIS of yours . . . without the Doctor . . . can it be flown?'

'He'll be back,' she said.

'I hope so.' His shell creaked as he shuffled to make himself more comfortable. 'It can go anywhere?'

'Theoretically.'

'Good.' He nodded. In the daylight the dent in his brow looked more serious. 'I will request to be dropped off back at Chelonia. I would like to see my grandhatchlings. You see . . . I don't care anymore. About the usurper or the cultural reformation. Let history take us where it will.'

'I'm sure the Doctor will be happy to take you there,' she said.

The newly-arrived parasite had identified himself more formally as the Doctor only after Frinza had menaced him at the point of a gun. With a lack of concern that seemed almost ill-mannered he had covered the end of the weapon with the fingers of one hand and pushed it aside, muttering all the while of 'pointless distractions'. He also displayed a most singular familiarity with minor points of daily etiquette, nodding his head slightly to the guards at the door of the shuttle bay as he swept out in the manner of a touring dignitary. He claimed that he was in possession of facts vital to the security of the fleet but refused to specify until audience with the supreme authority was granted. Frinza had flatly refused; the Doctor had then nonchalantly swiped a communicator from a wall-point, patched himself through to Big Mother's personal input with ease, and uttered a string of words in narrow dialect. He was restrained instantly, but a matter of moments later Big Mother's hollow whisper came into Frinza's personal link ordering him to grant the request.

And so the Doctor was led at gunpoint into the imperial chambers in the rear of the flagship. Frinza had attended this quarter of the vessel only three times before, keeping to the background, as his temperament dictated, at official functions and cheese and leaf-extract parties. The chambers were grand, almost a separate estate in themselves. He was too young to recall the time before the fall, but as he escorted the Doctor along the bejewelled and velvet-draped corridors that connected the outer aft companion-ways to the maternal sanctum Frinza could well imagine the majesty of the old court in Chelon City. No matter what hardships the crews of the fleets had endured over the past thirty cycles, Big Mother had always done conspicuously well for himself. Frinza checked his thoughts. To think along such lines was to invite downfall. The maternal family were exemplars of civility and a symbol of the past's importance. That made the granting of the Doctor's request appear ever more bizarre.

As the great doors of the inner chamber slid apart a nurse adorned in pale green surgeon's apron and cap motored forward with the unhurried and disdainful air of the maternal retinue. The nurse's glance passed quickly over the Doctor. 'Has this creature been properly fumigated?'

The Doctor himself answered. 'I am an enthusiastic washer, I assure you. Now please let me pass.'

The nurse addressed Frinza. 'It is not good for His Majesty to be placed under stress. He has become most agitated upon learning of this . . . beast's presence on the ship.'

The Doctor pushed past the retainer rudely. 'Out of the way.'

Frinza followed him into the large inner chamber, where the shockingly decrepit form of Big Mother hung like an overgrown hatchling in his reinforced webbing, his limbs drooping, drool caking his chin in a dry grey crust. His almost-white eyes flicked alertly over them as they were presented. Frinza had to step up his senses to see clearly in the dim light, but the Doctor seemed to have no trouble. The little parasite raised the circlet of white cloth on his head and said distinctly, *'Ka' shar-rath erd kallpok eyja gralk.'*

Big Mother grunted. 'However your appearance changes, we would recognize your presumptuous character and want of manners, Doctor.' Frinza drew himself up, startled. Big Mother addressed the parasite like a noble. 'Tell us. What became of the fellow in the apron of colours?'

The Doctor sighed and shook his head. 'Cut off in his prime, poor chap.' He patted his mid-section. 'At least I learnt never to exercise on a full breakfast.' He folded his body on the platform below Big Mother's webbing and swung his stick back and forth sadly. It occurred to Frinza that this unlikely camaraderie might be explained in part by an examination of the Doctor's physical processes. His sensor membrane confirmed the suspicion. The innards of the Doctor were substantially at variance with the organs of the Secunda. For a start, this one had two hearts. It seemed a most useful addition. The cell structure also was quite perplexing. Frinza had heard tales of freakishly advanced parasite species; it seemed the Doctor was a member of such a race. Even so, the informality exchanged between him and Big Mother was unsightly.

'What is the nature of your urgent mission, Doctor?' Big Mother asked in a more suitably curt tone. 'We have lost our General Hafril.'

'Hezzka.'

'Yes, yes, and our First Pilot, er – yes, our First Pilot. Is this your work?' His eyes narrowed. 'Whatever favour you may have done us in the past can be easily forgotten if you mean once more to oppose us.'

A strange animal noise came from the back of the Doctor's throat. 'You know that I have opposed your activities as a matter of principle and would do so again.'

Big Mother gnashed his gums. 'Speak, Doctor. What is your interest in Zamper? Where is our brave General?'

Before the parasite could reply the wall-point chirruped. 'Answer that, Hezzka,' said Big Mother.

'I'm Second Pilot Frinza, Highness.'

Big Mother rolled his eyes. 'Can nobody stay in a job longer than a quarter-cycle these days?'

Frinza toed the wall-point. The call was for his attention. 'Sir,' said the Environments Officer. 'There's a massive energy trace flaring on all wavebands of the sensornet. Its source appears to be a large object approaching from the Zamper gateway. We cannot identify or make a full analysis, the flaring is too strong.'

'What is its approach speed?'

'Estimate it will reach range of our close-range cannon in thirty-two minutes, sir.'

'Ah, yes,' said the Doctor. Frinza could not read the faces of parasites, but there was a gravity to the Doctor's bearing that sent shivers along his shell. 'It's that I want to have a word about. In private, if possible.'

Frinza turned his head. 'Highness?'

'Dismissed, He– Haf– boy.'

Bernice was able to sleep for a while, resting her head against Hezzka's big warm shell in the back of the air-buggy and trying to blot out Smith's fate from her mind. The longer she stayed with the Doctor, the easier it became to forget the nasty things. When she woke she was certain that a good couple of hours had passed, but Taal told her it was closer to forty minutes.

The roar of the rushing wind prevented her from talking to Cwej or Forrester, and she was too tired to shout. She let her head fall back on Hezzka again, and angled her face towards his head. 'You'll like the TARDIS,' she told him. She smiled when she saw that his eyes were also closed. He looked dignified even in sleep, and she was reminded of Ice Lord Savaar. She looked over at Taal, who was crumpled, ungainly and lascivious. 'Ah, why can't a man be more like a reptile?' she mused.

And it was then she realised, with a little jolt of the head, that Hezzka was dead. Exhaustion had claimed him. She shivered and wiped away a small tear, straightened up and shouted, 'Chris, Roz. The General's dead.'

Forrester looked back. Bernice new her well enough by now to realize that holding a grudge against her would be pointless. If it had been her own hand on that door control . . . well, that was the whole point, really. She wouldn't have got herself in a corner like that. It was only people like Forrester, like the Doctor, like Ace, who put themselves in such situations. Most people, herself included, just froze. 'We'll stop and lift him off,' Forrester said matter-of-factly. 'Without the weight we can pick up speed.'

Taal suddenly stood up, his head twisted over his shoulder. 'Oh my God. Oh no. No!'

Bernice followed his gaze.

Another buggy was pursuing them. Its seating was occupied by six of the loop creatures.

As the Doctor explained the situation, Big Mother's head slumped further in his webbing. All of the worry and perplexity in which his aged brain had been immersed for however long was lifted and he saw the enormity of his plight with clarity. It was the seriousness of the news that had perked up his faculties, he realized. The monotonous snippets which he was more commonly plagued with by his underlings were so much of a blur that they barely registered, but the Doctor's grave pronouncements had struck a heavy chord in his heart. It was certainly true that a continuity of character was present in whatever form this ancient enemy inhabited. The unfortunate turn of events that had brought them face-to-face many cycles ago – Big Mother's yacht had been trapped for months at the centre of an agglomeration of frozen stellar matter and the Doctor had succeeded in digging them all out – had forged a bond that, while it could not be considered a friendship, took the form of a grudging mutual realization that for one to kill the other would be appallingly vulgar. Big Mother could not be merciful or thankful to the Doctor, such lowly and platitudinous expressions were the reserve of commoners, but he could at least refrain from ordering his death during their meetings, no matter how irritating or obstructive the freakish parasite became.

At the Doctor's entreaty, the bridge had patched through the visual scan of the fast-approaching egg-carrier. They watched as the strange grey shape slipped through the yawning purple gateway, its energy trace coating it in a repeated fall of crackling white waves. It was hard to be certain, but from the agitated way in which the Doctor twisted and rattled his cloth-covered stick, Big Mother assumed his visitor was in a state of great agitation. 'There's no alternative,' he concluded. 'Believe me when I say that I truly wish there were.'

The implications of his words hung in the air like a wind that blows from fallow pastures. At length Big Mother said, 'You are asking us to destroy ourselves?'

The Doctor gnawed his knuckles. 'If only there'd been more time. But if those creatures reach populated space the consequences would be horrific.'

'Why us, why now?' asked Big Mother. 'There are parasites destroying themselves throughout this star-sector. Can they not sacrifice themselves for a nobler purpose?'

The Doctor shook his head firmly. 'By the time such a deterrent could be set up the creatures might already have multiplied a thousandfold. They could be unstoppable.' He came disrespectfully close to Big Mother. 'In time they would reach the empire. Then on to Chelonia itself. Your race would be obliterated or condemned to a miserable life of drudgery, as little more than cattle.'

Big Mother spat. 'Impossible. The empire would triumph.'

'I'm not one of your courtiers,' the Doctor snapped. 'Listen. I may not agree with your viewpoint, but I can at least understand it. You know as well as I do that the empire is finished.'

'Heresy!' Big Mother shook with fury. 'You can only go so far, Doctor.' He indicated a small space between his front feet. 'At present you are that far, that far from death!'

'We all are!' yelled the Doctor. 'And believe me, if you don't stop these creatures, all our deaths will be pointless and prolonged. The Management has no mercy.' He paused and took a deep breath. 'Do you really want your race to be conquered?'

Big Mother thought aloud. 'The destruction of the fifteenth column . . . we die, and you and your kind continue to flourish. And our own sister, the usurper, would lead the people further into treachery and complicity. Unopposed.' He hissed. 'We . . . I cannot bear that thought.'

The Doctor threw up his hands angrily. 'We all have to live with disappointment.'

Big Mother's fury increased. 'But that is not the case, is it, Doctor? We die, we sacrifice ourselves. You live. It is . . . unfair.'

He pointed at the screen. 'I'm sorry. But you must see that there is no other way.'

Big Mother was silent for a long while. He had often found that a simmering silence served to assert his station whenever it was challenged, but this time the technique failed him. 'Well?' the Doctor snapped.

Big Mother looked between the Doctor and the egg-carrier depicted on his screen. He thought of the long years of his exile, the letters from his sister that arrived now and then and always remained sealed, the news broadcasts from Chelonia that he picked up on his personal relay and concealed from all others, that spoke of the success of the cultural reformation, the relaxation of trade barriers and the great wealth of the people. In

232

his mind he saw again the sacking of the court by the militant scum of the Respect for Life brigade, watched the towers toppling as the rabble swarmed like ants through his belongings, scoffing at his surfeit of ceremonial shoes and carrying away the gold fittings of his exalted washroom. 'What kind of a Chelonian,' the newscaster had said, the digits of his foot straining against the grips of his microphone, 'lives in a house like this?'

They could not understand. They could never understand. Even when the empire lay ruined and they were reduced to mere lackeys of the parasites, even then they would babble of equality and fair representation.

And he admitted to himself, finally, that this would have been the outcome even if the mission to Zamper had been successful. Their crusade relied heavily on inspiring the citizens to join them; one ship alone, no matter how strong, could not win a war. The strategic council and the ranks had not seen what he had seen in the bulletins.

The people. Damn them, damn them all, the treacherous mutinous overfed scum. They were happy.

His heart flipped over and a great calmness settled on him.

'Doctor,' he said evenly. 'Your plea has reached our ears and been noted. In the absence of the strategic council, it falls to us to answer you.'

'Yes?' the little parasite said exasperatedly.

'We comply.' Before the Doctor could react, Big Mother put a restraining foot on his shoulder. 'With this proviso.'

'What proviso?'

'We're afraid that for us to die and for you to live is an unfairness that it is within our ambit to correct. Particularly in view of your past interference in our business.' He fixed the Doctor with his most menacing stare. 'It would feel just a bit too much like you had won. You will grant us a small piece of satisfaction, we are sure.'

'What do you mean?'

'You stay, Doctor!' bawled Big Mother. 'In the true spirit of your liberal philosophy of co-operation between species, you must sacrifice yourself alongside us!'

Chapter 10

The Secunda remained slumped in one corner of the isolation unit. She raked her long finger-nails over her bare knees, drawing blood. 'I was so near,' she said to herself. 'So near.'

The door slid open and the grizzled old Chelonian entered. He now wore a green gown and was sliding a pair of rubber gloves over his front feet.

She stood and backed hurriedly away. 'No. Keep away from me!'

He pulled out an instrument from a pouch in his apron and pressed a button on the handle. A blade shot out and started to whir. He advanced.

'Come here, you silly little thing, you silly little thing . . .'

When the bell tolled, every Chelonian at work or resting in the ships of the fifteenth column stopped what he was at, exchanged a disturbed glance with his neighbour, and hurried to the nearest vision screen. The clang had been simulated after the fallen bell in the high tower above the old court; its sounding signalled an address of the utmost import from Big Mother.

'Loyal warriors,' the piping voice said from between frazzled lips, 'comrades at arms. You will be aware of the approach of a powerful hostile spacecraft. The urgency of the matter has forced us to decide on our response swiftly, without ample time for reflection. That alters nothing; the following order, to the Pilots of all divisions, is to be obeyed without question.'

He paused. The Chelonians were taken aback by the

lucidity of the speech. Most believed secretly that Big Mother was simply a figurehead, and not a terribly useful one, so his sudden return to form increased the air of apprehension.

'Pilots. You are to order the removal of the anti-matter containment snares from your engines.'

There was an immediate rumble of distress.

'Let there be no dissent. There is no time.' The ranks were embarrassed to see a wetness forming in Big Mother's eye. 'We give our lives so that our poor lost hatchlings, and their own hatchlings, may live. Somewhere, sometime – not too far away, we are sure – Chelonians will come to see the error in the path of appeasement. And then the names of all those who so gallantly offer up their lives this day shall become a call of angels.'

One of his feet, outside the frame, fumbled for a control. Seconds later a stentorian bass-drum roll surged out from all speakers. The crews rose on their back legs, and a guttural chorus rang out.

'*Chelonia, Chel – o – nia!*'

Although he had switched off the central processing unit of his computer self, with the unwitting help of Ivzid, in order to open up the gateway, the Management retained much of his ability to interface with external systems. It was most odd; he was floating about in the dimension of thought, he supposed, but didn't want to get carried away with introspection. He'd never been a one for navel-gazing. Besides, there were more pressing matters in hand.

Reading the computers of the fleet was a tortuous business. Chelonian technology was spiky and awkward. Often a simple solution to a technical problem acknowledged by the rest of inhabited space seemed to have passed them by. In other ways their systems were frighteningly advanced; such developments he filed away in the memory part of his disembodied intelligence.

The order to self-destruct came as something of a surprise. Suicide was against the Chelonian character and he suspected the Doctor's hand. Never mind, it was easily dealt with.

He blocked the security clamps on the warp-snares. Try it now, then, he thought with a contented burble that sent a continuous ripple of pleasure through the crew of the carrier.

Frinza had listened to Big Mother's address along with the bridge team. When the anthem's last bars had faded – thankfully, his Highness had curtailed the sing-along to three verses – the flight crew all turned to face him. They gawped at him as young hatchlings gawp at zoo-beasts. He wanted to scream. They relied on him to react. He was sure that if he shrugged his shell and laughed they would do the same, and that if he said that Big Mother was clearly insane the crack-brained old fool would be thrown overboard in the next half hour.

The weight of the centuries being what it was, however, he could do neither of those things. 'Engineer,' he said, not quite believing it was himself talking. 'Follow Big Mother's orders.'

The engineer moved swiftly to obey. His front feet moved gracefully over the pads at his station. A yellow light flashed and a bleeper sounded. 'Sir, the safety over-rides on the warp-snares have been tripped by an external source. To comply is impossible.'

The next second, a hidden strength of Frinza's character emerged like a new mountain after continental quaking. Its tongue was such that it tipped the scales, and the weight of the centuries was forgotten. 'Countermand previous order,' said Frinza. 'Give me tertiary vision linkage to all Pilots at once, and block His Highness's outlet. Now!'

The commands were obeyed with a tangible sense of relief. When the blue transmission light came on, Frinza drew himself up and addressed the camera. 'Pilots. Fellow Chelonians. We cannot allow the unsupported word of a parasite to destroy us all! I say to you, join me in standing against this insanity!'

* * *

236

The screen in the imperial chamber fizzed and then displayed a white board with a black line running down the middle. Big Mother almost fell from his support. 'No! They have blocked our outlet! How dare they do this!' An alarm began to warble shrilly.

'I remember Marie Antoinette saying much the same thing,' said the Doctor. He was edging slowly towards the door of the imperial chamber. There would be time for him to debate the morality of his escape later. The fact remained that in the universal scheme of things he was important, and owed it to others as well as to himself to stay alive. Even a Time Lord would have difficulty surviving a warp reaction of this magnitude.

'Treacherous fools!' Big Mother spluttered, his eyes rolling. One of his back feet slipped from its support and he tipped forward dangerously with an alarming creaking sound. He sought his communications unit and punched at a line of controls without looking up. 'It is unthinkable for them to disobey an order!'

'I never thought I'd say it,' said the Doctor, stretching out an arm for the door control, 'but I happen to agree with you on this occasion.'

Big Mother saw what he was up to and instantly threw the communicator box aside. The next instant, and the Doctor couldn't be sure how, there was a huge yellow rifle in one of his feet. 'Stay right where you are, Doctor. Whatever happens you are not leaving.' He chuckled. 'People may think we are a senile toothless old trout, but they forget the active service we saw in defence of our realm.'

'I haven't forgotten,' said the Doctor. 'I suppose you want me to put my hands up.'

Big Mother never got to reply. At that moment the door against which the Doctor was leaning whirred open and a grotesque figure entered. A grizzled Chelonian wearing a brocaded garment and lorgnettes shuffled in. In one foot he was carrying a severed human head. He was wearing surgical gloves that were spattered with human blood.

237

'Where's that Frinza?' asked the new arrival. 'I was told he was in here. Sorry, Highness. What's all this singing?' He squinted resentfully at the Doctor. 'Another one, eh? Thinking of starting a collection?' He jiggled the woman's head at Big Mother. 'She was lying, incidentally. Wretched fraud.'

At this grisly sight whatever objections to flight the Doctor might have harboured evaporated. He leapt past the surgeon, pushing him to one side to spoil Big Mother's aim. A salvo of pink energy-bolts rattled off the roof, dislodging great chunks of the ceiling.

The Doctor dodged them and ran.

Silence had fallen over the bridge once more. Frinza's plea to the other Pilots elicited no response. He spoke again. 'At least let us examine this hostile craft before we make a decision. It is small. A concentrated burst of fire would surely disable it.'

The engineer looked up from his post. 'Sir,' he said urgently. 'Our weapons systems have been knocked off-line!'

A chorus of sighs went up.

Frinza slammed a fist on his control panel and cursed. 'Then we are powerless.'

The alarm was deafening. The Doctor scurried through the outer companionways of the flagship, thankful for his infallible sense of direction. The Chelonians on duty were startled as he ripped by, but the trauma of Big Mother's order overtook what would have been their normal reaction. For most the presence of a fleeing parasite running crazily across decks acted as confirmation of their predicament.

The shuttle bay was unguarded; the security staff left on duty were milling about confusedly, their shells bumping together hollowly as they fought for space around the vision inlet. The Doctor raced down the ramp leading to the bay and made for the escape pod of Hezzka's shuttle. Also available was the tiny domestic flyer he had travelled in previously, but he did not place much faith in its ability to navigate spatial hazards. His understanding of Chelonian technology was rudimentary, but he could see from the open hatchway and the warm glow coming from inside that the pod's anti-theft devices had not been reset. He clambered in and without waiting for the traction port to lift him up climbed on to the cramped cockpit. The flight systems were active, and a row of winking coloured pads were arranged in a pattern that was familiar and simple.

He closed the hatches, blew the locking clamps, and keyed in the signal to open up the bay. Automatically the escape pod's forward screen illuminated. It showed him that already the bay doors were opening; beyond he saw the far distant stars of East Galaxy, stretching in a random series of softly flaring blue. 'I'm doing this for you,' he whispered as the pod shot out into space.

The last he saw of the flagship was a blur of green through the glass of the shuttle bay's observation gallery, as some of the terrified Chelonians arrived in the vain hope of an evacuation flight.

Panic reigned aboard the bridge. Frinza was surrounded on all sides by frantic cries, groans and screams. The lighting flickered down to emergency levels. He turned his head from the sight of the engineer and the Environments Officer fighting for a place in the cramped bridge escape pod.

All the while the hostile craft was coming closer.

A parasite voice boomed from all around, as the Goddess had spoken to the prophets on the day of the last Arionite's death.

'All this rushing about isn't going to do you the slightest good. Your paltry sensornet has let you down, so I'd better bring you up to the mark. I am armed with an extendable neutrino-tickler attachment. Very clean, but then you'd know that. In fact I'm extending it right now. You're in my way, and I'm going to pick you off safely, one by one. Goodbye, you presumptuous nincompoops. You thought to destroy me, eh? I shall make a special point of enslaving every Chelonian in your pathetic little empire. They will be employed to spread manure.'

Frinza seethed with rage. Almost without thinking he engaged his battle-drive and let the waves of alertness wash over him. The adrenal-amyl combination made his heart hammer like a steam-pump. The options chattered between his brain and his reasoning graft, and he realized why he was such a good officer, why crafty old Hafril had promoted him.

He wasn't much of a thinker but he had a good imagination. Coupled with the reasoning graft it made a fine weapon.

From whatever corner of the dimension of thought his mental processes were taking place in sprung the idea. No, not the idea –

The certainty.

He saw how it could be done.

The Doctor wrestled with the navigation of the escape pod. He stretched himself out like a Chelonian, shucking off his shoes and then nestling his toes in the moulded grooves of the rear control pads. He experimented, ducking and weaving the craft until he felt more confident.

A dazzling tracery of light passed over his face. It came from the sides of the egg-carrier as it passed by, dwarfing the tiny escape pod, and filling him with some of the awe he had felt on his first sight of it, when he had believed it to be the triumph of nature over slavery and mortal interference.

Perhaps it was that, whatever its ambitions. But there were limits, and it was his role to enforce them.

Unfolding from the sheer side of the carrier was a long studded prong. Electricity crackled between the bristles on its surface.

'I could crush you now, Doctor,' the voice of the Management said suddenly. 'But I want you to see the corpses of your friends before you die.'

'No! If they're dead –'

'Oh, shut up.' The voice appeared to sniff. 'Not much

240

of a riposte, I know, but I have got other fish to fry. Toodle-oo for now, Doc.'

Frinza motored through the crowded companionways that led from the bridge, trying to ignore the cries for help that came when he was recognized. His passage was aided by the prevailing air of terror, precisely because he was trying to reach the centre of the ship whereas the crew were making for the escape pods on the outer lining.

He turned off down an empty sub-tunnel, his battle-drive carrying him on unchallenged to the nearest engineering sub-station. The large room was deserted. On the diagnostic panels were the remains of a meal and a hatchling's toy. The alarm stopped sounding.

Frinza breathed in the sudden quiet. This was how he had always imagined the ancient sepulchres of the fallen saints.

He gripped the edges of the widest diagnostic panel and ripped off the protective covering. The food cartons clattered to the floor. Beneath the covering was a mix of components interlinked by bunched strands of raw circuitry.

The vessel shook, and Frinza held on tightly to the sides of the panel. The attacker had destroyed his first target. The battle-drive reacted; Frinza sensed the death-agonies of his lost comrades and wept.

He put out a foot and tweaked at an exposed section of metal, pressing hard on the plate for a full ten seconds. His body shook and he lurched upright. A wave of scorching agony boiled him from his middle outwards. He felt several of his innermost organs split open and screamed.

What did it matter?

The flagship's engineering computer linkage had been blocked for a third of a second by his interference. In that third of a second the containment fields on the warp-snares were lifted.

He fell heavily, his head smashing against the sparking circuitry. One of the components, a savagely sharp spike, entered his brain just behind the ear.

Before he died he saw something and he heard something. He heard the wail of the flagship's internal systems warning for the first time since his days of emergency training. He saw Big Mother, rifle in hand, staggering in through the opposite door, his wizened head bobbing up and down.

The instruments in the escape pod warned the Doctor of an enormous release of energy only seconds after the first wave of neutrinos had blasted away the ship on the fleet's furthermost left flank. He examined the profile of the energy build-up provided by the sensornet and nodded.

Big Mother cradled the ruptured body of the young officer and raised his head. 'We are not idiots, nor cowards,' he said proudly. 'You are an enemy – and we defeated you!'

Not the enemy he had thirsted to defeat, he admitted to himself. But compromise was perhaps an important part of growing up.

The Doctor curled himself into a crash position. He shut down the forward screen and watched the reaction begin on the sensornet panel. First the flagship crackled and disappeared, as if beginning a jump into hyperspace. But it did not totally vanish. A moment later its warp-snares slipped and the mass of time-cooled anti-matter at the ship's heart burst forth with all the furious power of nature unleashed. A hole was punched in the fabric of time and space, distorting the shapes of the nearest ships on either side. It strained, wobbled, and gulped horribly, wrenching them apart and setting off the series. The distortion expanded, tugging at the Doctor's senses. Before he was overcome he checked the navigation status of the pod.

He was beyond the range of the warp snare.

He collapsed.

The still-smoking crash wreckage covered a mountainous region two miles wide. Bernice looked over the side of the stuttering air-buggy, looking for the tiniest patch of blue amongst the torn heaps of grey. Taal was looking behind them at the pursuing loops, whose nightmarish screeching and howling had kept at a steady distance after the initial sighting. Cwej had pushed the buggy to its limits, but after so much strain it was now showing signs of weakness.

'If it stops now . . .' Bernice heard Forrester say.

'It's not going to stop!' Cwej barked. 'Keep looking for the TARDIS!'

For a moment Bernice wasn't sure if she'd jumped at the sound of the word. Then she saw it, tall, blue and beautiful, leaning at forty-five degrees in an area clear of rubble to their right. 'There!' She pointed.

Forrester stood up, craning her neck to see. Cwej banked the buggy to one side and the police box came into view again, emerging from the shadow of the buggy in all its unlikeliness.

'That can't be your ship,' said Taal, who stared at Bernice as if she was mad.

'I'm afraid it is. Now how the hell are we going to reach it, without . . .?' She jerked her thumb over her shoulder.

'Whatever happens,' Forrester shouted, taking command. 'We stick together, right?'

Cwej swung them round again, veering at an acute angle to put the loops off the trail and then zig-zagging backwards to bring them closer to the TARDIS. 'If we stop, they'll have us,' he said.

'I know!' Forrester shouted.

The door of the TARDIS was only feet away from them as they passed by it a third time, but Bernice didn't have to point out that to attempt to leap across would be pointless. The loops were gaining, and somehow had converted Cwej's manoeuvre to their advantage. They were closer to the TARDIS than its crew members.

Cwej turned the buggy almost sideways and zoomed away, stoking up the vehicle to full power, the muscles in his back straining with the effort of keeping them away from their pursuers.

The buggy's concealed motor sighed, spluttered and

fell silent. In the second before they dropped and were scattered, toppling over and over onto the soft sandy ground, Bernice heard Forrester's cry of pure rage and frustration.

Her face was buried in the sand. The jolt of the crash had numbed her shoulders and midriff, but she forced herself, with the extra reserve of energy she had come to depend upon, to stand up.

Of course, the other three had all been knocked out.

She bit on her knuckles.

The loops giggled with the voice of the Management, a macabre chitter that resounded about the purple dustbowl. Overcome by glee they leapt from their buggy, flying metres through the air to land with hard thumps just before her. Abandoned, their buggy dived into the side of the TARDIS. In a less fraught moment it might have amused Bernice to see the way the nose-section crumpled on contact with the outwardly frail wooden exterior of the time-space craft.

She backed away from the loops, which were between herself and the TARDIS. Instinctively she scampered to one side, thinking perhaps she could outrun them, at least lead them away from the others. But there were six of the buggers, and three were already slithering over to the bodies of Cwej, Forrester and Taal.

Two of the loops struck at once, the first knocking her to her knees with one cracking lash. The other wrapped itself around her and lowered its foul glistening jaw.

She closed her eyes.

The loops spat.

The Management had no time to trace the source of the disturbance. His crew flexed their looped bodies in agitation as the carrier shuddered and began to elongate, its front dragged into the reaction that consumed one of the Chelonian ships after another. They shrieked as the pain pressed against their compacted brains and shredded their monstrous bodies to ghoulishly wriggling fibres.

A part of him was dying.

He tried to withdraw. The herdmind. It was separate, it was his link. The source of his great power. Half of his soul. He needed it!

It screamed and died with its spawn.

The carrier, flattened impossibly, was crushed along with the Chelonian ships, torn asunder, torn to fragments, pulverized and swallowed by the huge invisible rip in space.

And he was alone, finally.

Alone, but alive.

Chapter 11

Taal focused on the man. The little man in the white hat carrying the umbrella. Silhouetted against a perfect purple sky. The Doctor fellow.

'You saved us.' He laughed. Something felt wrong, but he'd worry about that later. 'You went and bloody saved us, you little marvel.'

The Doctor smiled, although he still looked troubled. He put the back of his hand against Taal's brow as if checking for a fever. Taal's eyes wouldn't focus, but then that was nothing unusual. 'Taal. I can take you somewhere. Anywhere. Where would you like to go?'

He tried to sit up, but there was something wrong and he couldn't. 'Careful now, Doctor. We're not supposed to talk about the old life. Management doesn't like it.'

'Please.'

'He is gone, isn't he? Dead and gone?'

'He's gone, yes.'

'Ha ha.' He raised two fingers and stuck them up in the general direction of the rest of the universe. 'Got you at last.'

'Taal, it's important. Your choice of destination.'

'Can't it wait? I need to think.'

'No.'

Taal closed his eyes. 'Bikkornal terminus. That's on Aristarchus, a housing cube.'

'You have family there?'

'Maybe. Well, it's been fourteen years ... apartment 1235. My sister.' He smiled. 'Can't believe I'm going back. You're a marvel, a ...' He tried to lift his head and his

246

mouth fell wide open. The Doctor blurred again, the wind brushed a stinging cloud of grit against his cheeks, and the afternoon sunlight grew dimmer and dimmer as life left him.

Holding back her tears, Bernice fetched the medical kit from the TARDIS. The Doctor took the slender grey box, nodded his thanks and started to fuss over Cwej and Forrester. He had propped both of them up against the side of the crashed buggy in the recovery position. Taal's shattered body lay in a shapeless bundle next to them.

After several years of eventful travel she was beginning to learn about perspective and the difference it made to your emotions. That was where people got the Doctor wrong. He wasn't heartless. He was efficient. She'd woken to find him unwrapping the lifeless loops from her body and wiping the fluid from her face.

'Your plan worked, then?' she'd asked.

'Not quite how I'd expected, but in all the general details. The Management's link to the physical world is gone. And just in time by the look of things.'

At the news of Smith's death he had only winced and closed his eyes for a moment.

Now, he dabbed at Forrester's brow with a piece of cotton wool dipped in iodine. 'Superficial injuries. Doesn't she look sweet when she's asleep?' He rattled inside the kit and drew out a probe which he used to examine her eyes for concussion.

'I'm not ready yet, Doctor,' said Bernice. He looked blank. 'For cracking jokes over dead bodies.'

'Oh. Sorry.' He squinted up at the sun, and she noticed that he was wearing a very strange pair of spectacles. 'A rest called for, I think. Earth? Allen Road?'

'Whatever.'

She kicked at one of the rubbery coils with the toe of her boot. 'Only an hour ago you were very frightening,' she told it. 'But in the end you were all mouth and no knickers, like the rest.' She started to laugh.

'What's the matter?'

'I really am beginning to sound like you.'

When Forrester eventually woke some hours later it was to find herself in a particularly weird room, which was decorated in gold-striped wallpaper. She was tucked up under a woollen bedspread. On the wall facing her was a framed photograph of a woman eating candyfloss.

Sat at a table by a grimy window was Bernice, who was doing a jigsaw. She wore a fluffy jumper that made her look very much younger. She smiled when Forrester sat up. 'This is our retreat,' she said. 'We all need a rest.'

'Where's Chris?'

'Safe and well and out shopping with the Doctor. We need light bulbs.' She slotted another piece into the puzzle. 'Do you want feeding?'

'What happened? On Zamper?'

Bernice told her. 'The Doctor got the TARDIS repaired and we cleared out,' she concluded. 'Last night he went out for a word with Taal's family.'

'Did he find them?'

'Yes, but he won't elaborate.' She stood up. 'Do you want feeding?' she asked again.

Autumnal light came through the four squares of the dirty window, framing Bernice's lithe fluffy-edged form. Forrester felt for the first time some of the culture shock the Doctor had warned her time travel could bring. Her head fell back on the pillow.

Zamper. Thousands of years in the future, on the other side of the galaxy. The Management, thwarted in its scheme to break out and dominate the universe. The Chelonians, at this moment probably still living in the mire of their homeworld, unaware of their rise and fall.

Unsought, a memory flashed up. She saw herself in the construction yard, retracing her steps in her search for Cwej, Taal and Christie. She squeezed her head through a gap in the rock. Beyond was a small arched cavity, about a hundred metres long. Packed with row upon row of slime-coated orange-brown eggs.

'Bernice,' she said. 'On Zamper, I saw – ' She stopped herself.

Bernice raised an enquiring eyebrow. 'Roz?'

'It's not important.'

Not now, perhaps. In forty thousand years, when those eggs hatched, the Management would have its link restored. And it was her responsibility. She was the only person in the whole of time and space that knew. She would have to tell the Doctor, and one day he could go back, or forward, or whatever, and sort it out. Save the universe again.

Because it wasn't her job.

A couple of days later, when she had grown to feel a bit more happy with the notion of having slipped nearly a thousand years back from her own time, Forrester allowed the Doctor to take her on an exploratory walk around the nearest town. He assured her that she was absolutely safe from most of the period's common infections, and after a while she got a kick out of listening to the conversations in the street.

'It's like an old photo come to life,' she told the Doctor.

His nose was stuck in a mould-encrusted annual he'd picked up from a stall outside a bookshop. *Schoolboy's Companion.* On the flyleaf was written in watery fountain pen *To Douglas, from Aunt Eve, Christmas 1919.* 'Pardon?'

'I said it's like an old photo come to life.'

'Eh?' His eyes flicked back down to the open book. 'Old, new, yesterday, tomorrow.' He shrugged. 'Lost their meaning to me many . . .' He trailed off and smiled broadly. 'Many years ago.'

Encouraged, she revealed what she knew of the eggs.

He listened in silence, then scribbled a note on the flyleaf of his book, under the dedication. 'Thank you,' he said finally, and strode off purposefully down the high street. Big drops of rain started to fall and he put up his umbrella. There was a mean set to his features.

Forrester groaned inwardly. 'We're going back there?'

'Oh no. Not yet, anyway. I've a thousand and one things

to do. Yesterday and tomorrow. Whenever.' He chuckled and pointed out a cafe. 'How about breakfast?'

'It's nearly four o'clock in the afternoon.'

'Not when we're going it isn't.'

Recently published

FIRST FRONTIER
David A. McIntee
When Bernice asks to see the dawn of the space age, the Doctor takes the TARDIS to Cold War America, which is facing a threat far more deadly than Communist Russia. The militaristic Tzun Confederacy have made Earth their next target for conquest – and the aliens have already landed.

ISBN 0 426 20421 2

ST ANTHONY'S FIRE
Mark Gatiss
The TARDIS crew visit Betrushia, a planet in terrible turmoil. A vicious, genocidal war is raging between the lizard-like natives. With time running out, the Doctor must save the people of Betrushia from their own legacy before St Anthony's fire consumes them all.

ISBN 0 426 20423 9

FALLS THE SHADOW
Daniel O'Mahony
The TARDIS is imprisoned in a house called Shadowfell, where a man is ready to commence the next phase of an experiment that will remake the world. But deep within the house, something evil lingers, observing and influencing events, waiting to take on flesh and emerge.

ISBN 0 426 20427 1

PARASITE
Jim Mortimore
The TARDIS has arrived in the Elysium system, lost colony of distant Earth and site of the Artifact: a world turned inside out, home to a bizarre ecosystem. But now the Artifact appears to be decaying, transforming the humans trapped within into something new and strange.

ISBN 0 426 20425 5

WARLOCK
Andrew Cartmel
On the streets of near-future Earth, a strange new drug is having a devastating impact. It's called warlock, and some call it the creation of the devil. While Benny and Ace try to track down its source, the Doctor begins to uncover the truth about the drug.

ISBN 0 426 20433 6

SET PIECE
Kate Orman

There's a rip in the fabric of space and time. Passenger ships are disappearing from the interstellar traffic lanes. An attempt to investigate goes dangerously wrong, and the TARDIS crew are scattered throughout history – perhaps never to be reunited.

ISBN 0 426 20436 0

INFINITE REQUIEM
Daniel Blythe

Kelzen, Jirenal and Shanstra are Sensopaths, hugely powerful telepaths whose minds are tuned to the collective unconscious. Separated in time, they wreak havoc and destruction. United, they threaten every sentient being in the universe.

ISBN 0 426 20437 9

SANCTUARY
David A. McIntee

The Doctor and Bernice are stranded in medieval France, a brutal time of crusades and wars of succession. While the Doctor investigates a murder in a besieged fortress, Bernice joins forces with an embittered mercenary to save a band of heretics from the might of the Inquisition.

ISBN 0 426 20439 5

HUMAN NATURE
Paul Cornell

April, 1914. In the town of Farringham, a teacher called Dr John Smith has just begun work. Struggling to fit in, he finds himself haunted by memories of a place called Gallifrey – somewhere he knows he's never been. Can it be true that, as his niece Bernice claims, creatures from another planet are invading the town?

ISBN 0 426 20443 3

ORIGINAL SIN
Andy Lane

The last words of a dying alien send the Doctor and Bernice to 30th-century Earth in an attempt to avert an unspecified disaster. There, Adjudicators Roz Forrester and Chris Cwej are investigating a series of apparently motiveless murders. And their chief suspects are the Doctor and Bernice.

ISBN 0 426 20444 1